Insatiable Nix

J.J. Reichenbach

Insatiable Nix

Nix Trilogy: Book Three

By J.J. Reichenbach

Buried Crown Publishing

Production Credits
Cover Image: © iStock Photo LP / neoblues
Published by: Buried Crown Publishing | Alberta, Canada

Dedication

Patricia and Rick Richardson.

Chapter 1

Nix could trace the downfall of their plans to the moment she ate the pizza guy. It wasn't as if everything was all rainbows and puppies before this. Nix had been curating a mental list of complaints leading up to the matter. But ultimately, the cannibalism took them over the top.

The hunters she'd been traveling with found her squatting over a dead body in the foyer of their rental cabin.

Flesh had lodged between her teeth as she slurped and crunched. Her arms were elbow-deep in the guy's warm entrails. Three steaming pepperoni pizzas were smooshed into the welcome mat and scattered down the front steps, adding a rich cheese-and-meat smell to the sharp, iron tang of the blood.

Her host body twitched, shivered, and jerked with adrenaline. She couldn't calm the tremors, couldn't be bothered to care. It was so hot, and she was *so hungry.*

On a normal day, the hunters would have pulled her off, attacked her, taken her down without a second thought. This day, not so much.

It must have been the sight of a partially eaten corpse when they'd expected Italian thin-crust that threw them. Or maybe it was the fact that their beloved kin, Elliot—Nix's willing human doll—was the one chewing on a dead man's dripping organs.

Daniel Whipsaw, a veteran who'd seen some shit and never once batted an eye, doubled over next to the staircase and puked. His adopted daughter, Rachel, stared with wide eyes. Nix-in-Elliot kept on chewing.

Not her best moment, she could admit that. Thing is, it wasn't her fault. Okay…it's not as though the guy's throat accidentally fell into her mouth and she had an uncontrollable jaw spasm. But big-picture-wise, the whole situation had little to do with Nix and she was just sort of…*there*. Incidental. Unlucky. Blameless. Some individuals, who'd remain nameless, might have argued otherwise, but they weren't sharing a ravenous body with her—they didn't *get* it.

This was, in fairness, the kind of thing Nix had often *threatened* to do to people who pissed her off—usually in graphic detail to get the point across. But it was all showmanship.

She would threaten, idiotic humans would back off or give her what she wanted, and they'd all go their separate ways. Some of them died violent and entertaining deaths at her hands, but she'd never actually *eaten* any of them raw like this. What was she, an animal? If it wasn't paired with a nice Chianti and prepared by a qualified chef, long pig was not on the menu. She did not sign up for this.

It wasn't *her* nature that was responsible for this mess—it was Elliot's, Lunatic Hunter Number 2, in order of age. Rachel was the youngest at a fresh-faced twenty, making her Number 3. She was the one Nix made the grave error of underestimating while riding around in her body until Rachel turned out to be a disturbingly powerful witch. Number 1— Danny, the burly old father figure of the group with vomit clinging to his beard—he was just an asshole, nothing special. But Number 2, harmless big-brother soldier boy, turning into a cannibal?

Nix hadn't seen that one coming.

Unfortunately, since she was currently sharing his body, she was also sharing his meal.

The hunger had started slowly. Barely noticeable. So easy to overlook and underplay. It was nothing...until it was *everything*.

Chapter 2

33 Hours Earlier

The phone shrieked like a screaming baby. They all continued to ignore it. Unlike a screaming baby, it would not die from continued neglect as Nix hoped. There was a missing girl—that was the story of Nix's non-life. There was always a missing girl at some point. And with every missing girl, there was a phone that never stopped ringing.

This particular missing girl was their teen psychic, Violet, who'd been whisked away by an archdemon wearing her uncle. Another day without an answer and Violet's mother might come looking for her at good ol' Uncle Blaine's house—the paranormal investigator was still missing, too, but no one cared about him, least of all Nix. Maybe the cops would get here first with the mother so far away. Hard to predict, but it wouldn't be long, so Danny insisted they couldn't stay.

Nix was pulling out stacks of prime rib from the garage freezer when she heard Danny call out to her.

His gruff voice pierced through the closed door of Blaine's mansion as he hollered, "Demon!"

Her silver-gray eyes flicked to the door. She scoffed and returned to her task, Elliot's stomach growling. Young men were known for their appetites, but this host body never

4

seemed satisfied. She swore she spent more time eating than anything else over the last two weeks to get Elliot to shut up. Nix arranged the prime rib in her arms and knocked the freezer closed as an afterthought. She was starting to get the hang of this annoying having-roommates thing, though she much preferred servants to these whiny hunters.

"De—I mean…Nix," came Danny's voice.

She grinned, Elliot's lips stretching over his white teeth. The hunters were adjusting, too. It was like training dogs—consistency was the key. Pleased with this progress, Nix stomped inside, shouting back, "The hell do you want, old man?"

"We're leaving in the morning, and you still haven't dealt with your—" Danny intercepted her, interrupting himself. "Why are you lugging meat around? I'm not putting all that in the van." He spat the word *van* out like it had a foul aftertaste, clearly still pouting about losing his ugly Ford truck.

Nix shrugged as she pushed past the hulking old man. Elliot's body was taller but lithe, so Danny took up more space. "I'll eat it before we leave."

Danny ran his fingers through his graying beard. "All of it?"

"I'm hungry."

His bushy eyebrow rose as he followed her into Blaine's huge kitchen. The morning sunlight sparkled off the white granite countertops. "You mean Elliot is hungry?"

Nix dropped the frozen meat packages on the counter, watching them skid and slide. Only seven left in the whole house. She'd eaten everything else. Shoving as many as she could into the microwave to defrost, Nix wondered if it was even worth the time it would take to cook the damn things. "Yeah, whatever. Same difference."

As soon as she turned around, Danny was in her face, giving her whiplash with his subject changes. "You need to deal with your boyfriend."

"Cirrik's not my boyfriend," Nix said automatically. "And what do you expect me to do with him?"

Danny huffed. "Well, ya can't leave him chained up in the attic."

Within the confines of their shared mind, Elliot mumbled about prime rib and steak and how amazing fried chicken would be right now. "Where else would I put him?" Saliva welled up beneath Nix's tongue at Elliot's imagery, driving her to distraction. It was grossly unfair that she should be responsible for Danny's insatiable son *and* the asshat cuffed to a pipe two stories above them.

"Ya tie up all your gentleman friends and hold 'em prisoner?" Danny asked.

"Don't you?" Nix frowned in a mocking display of sympathy. "Oh, right...your boyfriend's *dead*."

Danny slammed one meaty fist on the granite countertop. "Now, if you think for one goddamned second I'm gonna—"

"Pops?" Rachel strode into the room, her tone sharp. She planted her hands on her hips. Her vivid green eyes glared at both of them.

Danny sobered, growled under his breath like an old dog disturbed from his nap, then backed toward the door. "I ain't dealing with this. I'll be on guard in the attic. You two figure it out."

Nix and Rachel watched him walk out of the bright kitchen. A door slammed behind him. The phone rang again and this time they heard Danny wrench it from the wall. Finally, reprieve. Nix endured the silence for a second then switched on the TV built into Blaine's fancy refrigerator.

"So much for his whole strategic-message-listening-whatever," Nix said. For the past two weeks, Danny had insisted on leaving the last wailing phone plugged in and turned on at all times so they'd have a heads-up in case Violet's mother or the cops were on their way over. Apparently, the rule only applied when he said it did. Humans.

"We're leaving in the morning anyway. Are you watching the cooking channel again?"

"Yeah. So?"

"It's weird." Rachel tightened her ponytail. Dark curls slipped free anyway, framing her face.

"It isn't."

"I made coffee." Rachel motioned to the coffee pot as she strode over. Nix didn't say anything, but Rachel poured her a cup, making it the way Elliot preferred. She slid it beside Nix before grabbing one for herself. Looking to Nix, like everyone always seemed to in this warped little dollhouse psychodrama, Rachel said, "What *do* you want to do with Cirrik?"

Nix leaned against the counter, stretching out Elliot's tall, lanky form. She picked up the cup and took a sip—one sugar, no cream. Bittersweet. "About that…"

"You want to leave him here." Rachel mirrored her posture from across the room, her arms crossing over her black leather jacket. Nix didn't know how the other two hunters could wear jackets and heavy jeans nearing the end of May in California; she always felt like she was sweltering in Elliot's skin, even in a light cotton t-shirt.

Nix held one hand up. "All I'm saying is it's probably going to be the least obnoxious option. He's useless on the best of days, but if he can't give us any information on the Order's endgame and whereabouts, then why bother hauling him around? I am not riding in the same vehicle as Cirrik—I'll kill us all, I swear."

Rachel didn't blink, but she didn't argue either. "Even if he could get out of the salt circle up there eventually, with those gold bands on him, he can't escape his host."

Nix considered this. Danny's stupid magic bracelets were not a fond memory of hers. Those suckers did not come off unless they were intentionally removed by whoever put them on—in Cirrik's case, Nix herself. She knew from experience there was no way a demon could body-hop with those restraints. But so what if he was stuck in his host? The sigils freshly carved into his ribs prevented any other demons from summoning him away, body and all, or even searching for him—but given enough time, they'd heal.

"He could still escape *with* his host," Nix said. "I'm sure it would only take him a couple unmonitored days. The only thing keeping him up there, besides Danny's paranoid vigil, is his lack of imagination. If not, in a couple weeks, the sigils will heal on their own and his little entourage will at least be able to locate him. Probably."

Although, given how well-protected the paranormal investigator, Blaine, had made his home, maybe not. The reason they'd stayed here this long was because it was protected from any supernatural entities. If you didn't already know how to find this place, it was basically off-the-grid energetically, tucked deep into the woods at the edge of Yosemite National Park. If Cirrik didn't get out of the circle himself, he couldn't be summoned out of it. Was he stupid enough that he wouldn't be able to escape? Crap. She already knew the answer.

Rachel said, "Even if he did get out in the same body, the body would already be degrading, right? What if it didn't last long enough for the sigils to heal? How long could he survive in the corpse? If we don't take the restraints off, he could die up there...or, I guess, *extinguish*?"

Nix pursed her lips. She'd made corpses last a couple weeks, when she got to them fresh and the spark was still there, but the expiration date was highly variable. "Wouldn't that be poetic fucking justice." A normal demon *would* chew his host's arms off to lose the gold band restraints and figure a way out of a simple salt circle, but knowing Cirrik, he'd probably sit there like an asshole and write a melodramatic soliloquy about his suffering until he snuffed out of existence.

"So you're fine with it?" Rachel asked, gaze locked on the chef flaying a fish on the tiny TV.

"That's not what I said." In most ways, yes, Nix wanted the bastard dead. But she also *didn't*. She hated her own indecisiveness on the matter. Sure, he'd left her to die at the hands of a mad exorcist a long time ago, and he'd annoyed the hell out of her since, but it was also sort of their *thing*.

"I think it's the best option." Rachel sipped her coffee. Nix remembered when she met Rachel, how sweet she took her coffee. It was black now. "Leave him up there, let him rot. If he did make it out somehow, it's not like he knows anything besides the obvious fact we're searching for the Order. And if he doesn't escape and dies up there, it's not our problem."

Nix bristled. It was just like Rachel to go around making decisions for everyone else. "He dies, so does his host. That would be, what? Negligent homicide? Aren't you some bleeding-heart, anti-homicide crusader?"

"We can't leave the man to die," Elliot said in their shared headspace.

"Your brother vetoes it, too," Nix relayed. The microwave beeped, and Elliot's attention promptly returned to his own growling stomach.

Nix collected her meat packs, found a pan, and grabbed a bottle of oil off the counter. She glanced at the label—extra-virgin olive oil. Whatever happened to the dirty little whores of the olive family? The world seemed to be all shades of gray this century and lacking in vibrancy. Nix sighed, setting the bottle down and grabbing some canola. She set the meat on the stove to cook and returned to her coffee.

"Besides, if we left him up there...oh." A thought occurred to Nix in a flash, and with it the imaginings of a massacre so bloody she almost wanted to keep it to herself, but a grin spread across her face before she could pull it back.

Rachel's eyebrow rose and she took a step back. "If we left him there, *what?*"

Nah, Nix wouldn't be able to participate, so it wouldn't be fun. She might as well share with the class. "Danny said we

9

have to leave because the cops and Violet's mother are going to show up soon, looking for Violet, since she's been out of touch so long. If we leave Cirrik and they find a guy chained to a pipe in the attic, they'd let him go thinking they were saving him." She couldn't suppress the chuckle.

"And he'd definitely butcher all of them," Rachel said, not sharing in Nix's joke. "Probably take one of their bodies and ditch his old one, too, if he could get the bands off. Good point. Well, we could do an exorcism."

"*The* exorcism? Still kills both Cirrik and his host body."

"Not *the* exorcism," Rachel clarified. "Just, you know, a regular exorcism. Let the host go, bounce Cirrik off to who-knows-where, be long gone from this place by the time he gets his bearings."

Nix considered her offer, but it still didn't hold up. "There doesn't seem to be anyone else around for miles in every direction. If he can't get to a new host in time, he'll still extinguish."

"And that would be bad…why, exactly?"

Sputtering, Nix straightened. "Well, he…I mean…okay, fair point. But if he *does* know something—maybe something he doesn't even know he knows—we lose that information, permanently. And if he does survive the bounce, finds his way back to the Order, even if we don't think he's got much on us, it doesn't mean he won't still be a threat standing against us."

"Then he has to come with us."

Nix groaned. The TV chef slammed his knife down on the chopping block. A fish head tumbled away. "Damn it. You played me, didn't you?"

Rachel's head tilted. "You see another option?"

"Fine. But he rides in the trailer. And stays tied up."

Rachel smirked. "At least he's used to it by now. You really hate him, don't you?"

Nix shrugged, hands around her coffee cup. The hunters didn't get it. "I don't *hate* him. I like him like I like my coffee, submissive and in chains." Her brow furrowed. "Wait. That comparison fell apart somewhere."

Rachel moved to turn away but stopped. "You know, it would help if you'd talk to him. Maybe with you, he'd let something slip."

Nix refused to pout or sulk, but the inclination gnawed at her. Instead, she held her head high. "You've said yourself, he doesn't have anything left to give."

"That's what Danny thinks."

"And you don't?"

"I think torture and threats can only persuade someone to share what they know, not what they don't know they know, like you said. Could be he doesn't realize he has any more information to give. But you know him. Maybe you could find something we couldn't."

Nix looked away. "He doesn't want to see me." He'd made that very clear, going so far as to refuse to speak in her presence even under threat of holy water. Rachel and Danny had accomplished more in the last two weeks without her than with her.

Rachel shrugged away her argument. "He's chained up, trapped in a salt circle, and confined to his host body. He's a prisoner. He doesn't get choices."

Danny lumbered back in. Nix ignored him, returning to the meat she'd been preparing. She sliced open another package and dumped it in the pan, licking the bloody juices off Elliot's fingers as she did so.

"Who doesn't get choices?" Danny was asking.

"Her boyfriend," Rachel said.

Nix cringed but didn't bite. She stabbed another package of ribs and tore it open. A twinge of melancholy hit her as she remembered the last time she'd stabbed anyone in the ribs and how *long* it had been since she'd had any fun at all.

"We're talking about bringing him with us."

Danny made a huffing noise. "We'll see. Can talk more about it tonight. Need supplies."

"Sure." Rachel ducked her head. "Need any help?"

He grunted in a way that seemed to indicate he *didn't*, judging by Rachel's lack of reaction and strained smile as he all but stomped back out of the room. The tension was so thick between Danny and Rachel that Nix could slice it with a knife and *eat it*—she was *starving*.

"I'll keep an eye on our guest for you while you're out," Rachel called after him.

When Nix turned back around to find another package, Rachel was right beside her. The hairs on Elliot's arms stood on end.

"Before we leave," Rachel said, "there's one last interrogation tactic I want to try."

Chapter 3

Nix and Rachel stood around Cirrik. He glared. Nix avoided eye contact. She already regretted agreeing to this. "This is the stupidest idea you've had so far," Nix told Rachel.

In their shared mind, Elliot prodded, *"We need the information—all of us. You're being avoidant."*

He wasn't wrong. Nix hadn't been up to the attic in more than a week. She and Cirrik had nothing to say to each other. Cirrik wouldn't give her any information, not after what he considered her betrayal of her kind. He'd called her a traitor. She wasn't sure why it bothered her. It didn't, really. Nothing he could say would bother her. He'd certainly called her worse.

The smell up here was getting ranker by the day. The large space stood like an insult to the rest of the house, the bare bones of the wooden beams and the plain wood-plank floors a stark contrast to the opulence and dripping wealth of the rest of the place.

Rachel set her supplies down and arranged them on a small table beneath one of the attic's thin lancet windows. After several minutes of observation to ensure Cirrik's restraints weren't tampered with, Rachel risked stepping into the salt circle with him and checked that the gold bands were still firmly in place. Doubly trapped, doubly damned. But it could be worse—they could have exorcised him. They would have, without Nix's intervention. But did Nix get credit for her little demonitarian aid mission? No.

Cirrik sat with his long legs artfully sprawled in a manner she knew had to be intentional, leaning against a pipe jutting out a few feet from the wall. His dark-brown hair was mussed and stringy, his face unshaved since he'd been here. Blood and grime gave his black Armani suit a warzone-chic edge. Fitted as the suit was to Cirrik's current host, whom he'd probably stolen off a catwalk somewhere, Nix was confident this style would soon be gracing the cover of the GQ Magazines Elliot secretly read. If Cirrik made it out of this.

Host aside, there was something about the way he held himself that was all Cirrik, and he retained the same inky darkness behind his host's chocolate-brown gaze that always pulled her in. The gag and chains were a good look, too, come to think of it.

"Jesus Christ, can you not ogle the guy?" Elliot said within their mind.

Nix pursed their lips and swallowed, looking away. *"With the nonsense I put up with between you and Rachel, you have no room to talk. And I was doing no such thing."* Damn, the air in this attic was stale and stifling. She was sweating through Elliot's white t-shirt. Nix walked over to the small attic window, pulling the moth-eaten lace curtain back and cranking open the glass as far as it would go, which wasn't far.

She rubbed the back of her neck and reminded herself Cirrik was the enemy. She wasn't the traitor, he was.

Rachel stepped away to retrieve supplies, returned to the circle, and tugged the gag out of Cirrik's mouth. She held up a glass of reddish-gray liquid to the bound man's lips. Cirrik looked at it with squinted eyes, staring up at her like a kicked dog.

Nix knew Danny would have played a decent bad-cop, but she didn't doubt Rachel was the one packing the real cruelty and malice during their Q&A sessions. Danny probably had to keep her tightly reined so she didn't lose control and accidentally burn the whole house down around them—again.

"Uh, uh, uh," Rachel intoned at Cirrik's reluctance, "no holy water this time. This won't hurt. Drink up, and this can be easy-street all the way." She smirked. "You like easy-street, don't you?"

He nodded, dark hair falling into his wary eyes. Nix's attraction to him dropped back to contempt, but an interesting little spike occurred at seeing Rachel working the dominatrix thing in her tight leather jacket. Probably Elliot's body acting up again.

Cirrik accepted the drink, because he was weak. Weak in body now, yes—his host sported a ripe bruise along one side of his chiseled jaw that looked like a map of Portugal—but weaker still in character. Not long ago, Nix would sooner have guzzled a bucket of holy water, done keg-stands tapping that, rather than cooperate with a hunter. Yet here she was, on the other side of the salt circle, working with…the enemy? Allies? She couldn't keep it straight in her head. Whose side *was* she on? Oh, right: *hers*. Always hers. Nix fought for Nix, and for now that meant these hunters would continue to be her brothers and sister in arms.

"Keg-stands?" Nix thought belatedly. Elliot's subconscious must be leaking again.

Rachel jumped up from her crouched position and brushed her hands off. She turned back to Nix, stepping out of the circle with the empty cup and setting it on the window ledge. A cool breeze swept in from outside, but it wasn't enough to combat the smell of sweat and filth up here.

Rachel picked up another glass, this one full. "You say it's stupid, but I'm not hearing it's impossible. We try everything."

Cirrik's gaze flicked between the two of them but he didn't ask questions.

15

Nix sighed as Rachel handed her the cup. Rachel didn't look up while dragging one foot through the salt line to break it and flipping through the pages of one of Blaine's old books—one of many she'd been perusing during their stay here. A Book of Shadows.

There was a reason they waited until Danny was out to test this—witchcraft was something he considered nearly as dangerous as the monsters they hunted. The fact that his adopted daughter was a skilled witch herself still set him on edge, but it wasn't as though he could stop her. They all knew he knew this by the way he'd stare at her too long sometimes and keep her away from the more dangerous weapons. Made for awkward family dinners, which Nix got a kick out of.

"It's open. Wait till you're in the circle to drink it," Rachel told her. "You should be touching him."

Nix's jaw tightened. She set the drink on the window ledge. "No one said anything about *me* getting in the circle. No way. No salt circles. Not happening. We're done."

Rachel intercepted her before she could take a step to leave the attic. "Hold up. It's fine. We can work around that. No salt circles. Jeez, I get it. Take this." Rachel handed Nix the book. "I'll find a broom. Not like he's going anywhere anyway."

Nix let out a breath.

"Any other excuses?" Elliot asked.

She ignored him, reading over the spell as Rachel swept the offending salt away. It glittered like shards of glass in the morning sunlight. If the spell worked—and with Rachel's volatile abilities, it was a big *if*—it might allow her to get a glimpse into Cirrik's mind without his permission, bypassing the need for his cooperation.

Nix frowned. Even if she could enter his mind with her own and peruse the thoughts of Cirrik and his host, what if she didn't like what she saw?

"Your book makes this sound like a mental convergence more than anything like Violet's mindreading. What about the gold bands? Won't those keep me out?"

Rachel shrugged, panning the salt into a dust bin. "Only supposed to keep things in, far as I know. Guess we'll find out. Not like you're trying to fill the same body or anything, just…sinking some psychic fingers into his brain. It'll be fine."

Nix glanced at Cirrik, then looked away when she met his eyes. "Why don't you do it, and I'll handle the incantation?"

Rachel brought the drink back over to Nix. "Because I'm the one with witch's blood. And even if we did swap, and I peeked inside your boyfriend's skull, I probably wouldn't know what to look for—or if something was significant. Now, kneel next to him, make some skin-to-skin contact, and drink this. Danny will be back soon."

Nix sighed again, cursing herself and Cirrik and the whole situation that had brought her to this point. She took a breath and sat beside him. Nix looked up to find him staring at her again. Maybe he'd never stopped.

His voice was rougher than a gravel road as he said, "You want to know my thoughts, my dear, it will cost you more than a penny." He coughed and his host body rattled.

Nix downed the bitter potion. Time to get this experiment over with.

Cirrik shifted toward her, tucking his legs under him so he was facing her. His chains scraped against the metal pipe. "Get to it, then," he mumbled, forcing her to meet his eyes. "For you, the first is free. I think you will find it familiar."

Rachel chanted nearby.

In spite of herself, Nix reached out and laid a palm against his stubbled cheek. As Cirrik leaned into her, eyes falling closed, a *zap* snapped Nix's head back and whited out her vision. She felt a pull away from Elliot's body and thoughts until she couldn't sense him at all.

A familiar presence brushed by her with a feather-light touch. With it, the lingering scent of petrichor and rusted metal. She shivered.

When the light dimmed, she could see a dirt road beneath her, wet with rain and blood. Euphoria rushed through her veins. Other sensations flooded her: the chill of the early-morning air on her host's skin, the heavy smell of a leather overcoat and scattered mugs of ale, the rain soft on her face and the blood slick between her fingers.

She remembered this.

They'd stolen horses on the way to the Spanish village of Rincón de Soto. They'd made a detour at a mine and butchered all the miners, laid them on the road after, posed. When she glanced up, she was surprised to see herself, arms outstretched and head back, spinning and laughing along the ruts in the road. She hardly recalled that host body, but she'd loved this day.

She felt herself move forward as if in a film reel, motions beyond her control as she replayed this memory through Cirrik's eyes, scooping her host body up and earning a squeal and laughter. They fell to the ground, tripping over a body, and the hysterics began again but they didn't try to get back up.

Nix pulled away from the memory. She saw the flash of a new one and went to pursue it full force only to slam so hard into a wall that she felt herself get knocked right back out of Cirrik's sphere, away from Elliot, away from Blaine's manor—so far, she couldn't catch her bearings or sense anything around her.

Cirrik had bounced her out of her host body. This was freefall, and there was nowhere to land. Nix tried to rein back the spiral, bracing herself for impact.

Chapter 4

Nix was spinning when she came to. She opened someone else's blurry eyes, blinking at a yellowed popcorn ceiling. Weird smells permeated the air. Everything hurt. Her back ached all along the spine and into the hips. One knee felt like it was on fire. She sat up with a groan.

Something fell into her lap. Grasping around, her fingers latched on to a pair of tortoiseshell glasses. She put them on. The world became clear.

Nix looked down to see wrinkled, liver-spotted skin on the backs of her hands. She pinched a lock of long, gray hair between her fingers. A hideous flower-print muumuu covered her from throat to ankles. A pair of fluffy pink slippers poked out from the bottom of the frock. An old lady. Great. Because her day wasn't bad enough to start with. This obviously wasn't Blaine's place.

Something moved from the corners of her eyes. Nix jolted backward, prepared to fight, only to find a fat, fluffy little creature crawling up her chest to sniff at her nose. A long *meow* followed.

She started to push the cat away but lingered to card her fingers through its soft fur, so sue her. It had been one hell of a day, and she was not expecting to crash land in a geriatric ward.

She glanced around. Maybe not a ward, after all. Just an old house—but that wasn't much better.

The cat purred at her touch, pushing its head into her hand. Nix didn't want any problems, so she scratched its chin until it seemed satisfied before dragging her aching sack of bones off the hard floor and leaving the bedroom.

She sniffed the air again, cringing at the strange scents. Pulling at the sleeve of her muumuu, she inhaled, choking a bit as she did so. "Sage?" she muttered. "Why's it always sage?"

Her eyes watered. She didn't see any obvious anti-demon paraphernalia around, so maybe it was perfume, or she did a lot of cooking. Peering around the small house, Nix found another cat sitting on the kitchen counter. Another on the back of the sofa in the attached living room. Two under a TV stand. And another. And another. And wow, a box of kittens, too? How did this woman have so many cats? *Wonderful, now I'm a crazy cat lady.*

"Litterbox," she realized, placing the other weird smell, the one not coming *from* her.

She did a quick sweep of the house—as quick as the lady's joints would allow, as Nix adjusted to her. A million cats, but otherwise it seemed she was alone here. Wherever she'd bounced to, she'd bounced *hard*. She must have bounced so hard she skipped right over Rachel and Elliot, the two available hosts she could've landed in nearby, and been thrown like she was caught in a gale.

A chill ran through her for no apparent reason. Nix huffed, reaching for a cardigan off the end of the woman's sofa. *Maria,* Nix determined as snippets of thought resettled themselves in Nix's borrowed brain.

She knocked into a waist-high stack of Reader's Digests beside the door and grabbed for it before it tipped over. She couldn't make out a single word on the covers. Maria needed some new glasses, damn. But it didn't matter. It was fine. Nix wasn't extinguished from existence, so that was great. Just needed to get out of this place.

"Breakfast, breakfast, desayuno," Maria sing-songed in her mind, then transitioned into a Sinatra tune. She didn't seem bothered by Nix controlling her body. If she noticed at all.

Cats wailed at her as she passed, working around piles and piles of junk. It seemed like they were following her around. Did they sense the change in Maria? They looked pissed and demanding. Most animals could tell when Nix had replaced their masters, but cats had no masters, and they rarely cared as long as they were fed. *Wait.*

Nix looked toward a wall clock decorated with painted birds. She chuckled and sifted around under the sink and through the cupboards until she found a treasure trove of cat food. The cats lost their minds as she opened a bunch of cans and set them out. In moments, the house was silent but for the tiny, punctuated slurps.

In their shared mind, Maria asked Nix if she was hungry and offered to fry up some empanadas. Nix pursed her lips and snooped around for some keys in all the regular places, finding about six dozen in one drawer alone, but none were car keys.

"Where'd you put your keys, Maria?" Nix muttered aloud.

Maria informed her there were two kinds of cookies in the pantry if she wanted them and a special tin of fig newtons in the china cabinet, which *"You're quite welcome to, cariño."*

It occurred to Nix that, for the first time in *ages*, she actually wasn't hungry. Nix swirled through a rush of memory, skipping the autobiographical crap and focusing on the habitual.

"Keys, keys, keys," she chanted as Maria serenaded her with a Peggy Lee song. Frustration rocked through her when nothing came up. Not a single thing, not about *any* keys—wait, what were keys again?

Nix's new eyes snapped open. Well, shit. Maria couldn't remember. Nix wavered for a moment, perfectly still, trying to recall what it was she was *trying* to remember. Didn't she have somewhere to be?

Several seconds later the realization snapped through her like lightning, and she found herself shouting "Keys!" at the startled cats, as though this were a great epiphany. She needed to get out of here *now*.

"Oh, but cariño, at least have a little pudding before you go. I'll whip it up real fast—it's no trouble at all."

Nix took a deep breath, thinking that Maria was possibly the most welcoming host she'd ever had and how strange it was to feel like a welcomed guest for once and maybe some pudding would be nice, actually, thanks—no, wait, she was looking for something. She shook herself out of the derailing train of thought and tried to focus.

This is fine, she reassured herself. *It'll all be fine.* She'd skip the key part altogether. She could call Rachel and have Rachel retrieve her. Nix grabbed Maria's phone, holding it to her ear and listening to the dial tone as one knobbed finger hovered over the buttons.

A moment passed. Nix slammed the phone down with a huff. She couldn't recall a single phone number having ever passed through Elliot's or Rachel's minds, let alone their own cell numbers. Damned millennials. Even if she'd known the number for Blaine's house, the phone was torn out.

Nix located the front door and stepped out of the house, climbing over meowing cats. No garage. No vehicle. "How do you not have a car, Maria? Are you kidding me with this?"

Growling, Nix swung around to examine her surroundings. No neighbors. A mailbox at the end of the driveway. No traffic on the road. Just a sprawling garden and a million cats. The cloying scent of rose bushes floated on the warm air.

How did an old lady survive in the middle of nowhere with no vehicle and what felt like two barely functional hips? She wasn't jogging anywhere, that was for sure.

Her hands dropped to her sides. She couldn't have landed more than about six miles from where she'd been without extinguishing, she knew that much—unless Rachel's spell had done something screwy. The trees had to be obscuring her vision. It would be too risky to abandon her host without knowing where she was going; if the closest available host ended up being too far away, she might not survive another trip. All she really needed was a direction and she could…very slowly shuffle there. Maria probably had a cane somewhere.

Another black cat emerged from a thicket of red rose bushes and rubbed against her legs. All the cats were black, it occurred to Nix. She took another look at Maria's garden, realizing a structure she'd initially dismissed as a decorative arch appeared to, in fact, be an altar.

Moving through the massive rose garden, she could see handmade sculptures, some small and others life-sized, scattered throughout the garden and far out into the woods. They looked like imps, and some were fairies. All made of twisted branches and flowers. The little altar contained a dish full of coins, bowls of fruits, and a bronze cup of wine. Drunken fruit flies circled. A pagan?

Bruja flittered proudly through Maria's mind.

Huh. What were the chances? Well, this was California. "Aren't you a treat, Maria?" She took a sip of the wine for fortification.

Leaving the garden for now, she tried to focus. She had a strange craving for a cup of hibiscus tea with exactly two sugar cubes, but she shook it off. Grabbing the mail from the box, Nix examined the letters to get an address, but all she could see were blurs of ink.

Thinking Maria must surely have a separate pair of glasses for reading, Nix stomped back inside and put the kettle on the stove. Searching the living room for glasses, she discovered some next to a glass bowl of candies. Nix plopped one on her tongue and flipped through the mail. Maria was pleased.

From her best estimate, lacking a map, Nix figured she'd landed somewhere north-west of Blaine's place. Fair enough—she could work with that.

The sound of an approaching vehicle snapped her out of her thoughts. Maybe Rachel had tracked her here. Or…someone less friendly, now that she was off Blaine's protected land and without the concealing sigils on Elliot's body.

If she were unlucky, some enemy could take advantage of this vulnerable moment to summon her. She needed to fix this situation faster than she thought. Quietly, she grabbed a cane from an entire rack of canes tucked into a half-open closet. She waited for the car to stop, the engine to silence, the door to slam shut. Footsteps moved toward the front door.

She peeked out, glimpsing a guy in a baseball cap, thirty to thirty-five. Someone she'd never seen before, but that didn't mean they weren't here to attack her. His eyes gave her no indication he was one of her kind. Maria stirred with recognition. That's when Nix smelled the smoke.

She rushed into the kitchen at the same moment the man from outside flew in through the door, scattering groceries all over. He shouted some obscenities, dashing past Nix to swat at the fire on the stove with a dish cloth. The silver kettle there was burned black and steaming.

A kettle…had she set that on the stove? When had she turned the stove on? For the life of her, she couldn't remember doing so.

"What the hell is going on in here?" the guy demanded once the fire was out. "How many times do I have to tell you not to leave the damn stove on?" He stormed through the house, slamming the burned kettle into the sink. "*Stupid old bat,*" he muttered under his breath. "If you turn *on* the stove, you have to turn it *off* after. Can you figure that out? *Off?*" He pointed accusingly at the appropriate knob.

Tears welled in Maria's throat and she felt so small she could barely stand herself. As soon as Maria's shame and hurt washed up onto Nix's shore, it curdled into a hot, blinding rage.

"Don't you *dare* speak to h—*me* like a child, you ungrateful little shit," Nix shouted, too mad to be startled by her own outburst. Images of the boy in front of her as an infant and a young child flipped through her mind like a photo album. "She—I mean, *I* wiped your ass for *five* years and had to teach you how not to piss on yourself. So what if I forget things now and then? You should thank me for not drowning your colicky ass back then." She shook Maria's knobbed finger in his petrified face. "You ever speak to me disrespectfully again and I will *gut* you. You're going to help your sweet *abuela* and you're going to goddamn like it. Now, apologize and clean up this mess."

Maria's chest filled with a pleasant, tingling confidence. Nix would cut this little bastard out of the will before she left, or at least leave Maria with the distinct inclination to do so.

The man's mouth opened and closed in a gaping motion, his skin ashen and his ego popped. "S-sorry, abuela, I-I didn't... Sorry." When he didn't immediately get moving, Nix raised an eyebrow and tilted her head toward the front door.

He scuttled over to the strewn groceries and started gathering them up. "Stupid little brat," Nix muttered just to see his cheeks flush with embarrassment. A delayed thought struck her and she added, "Oh, keys!"

Every time she remembered a word, she felt like she'd won a gameshow prize. Pleased with herself, she grinned. Nix looked the boy over but discarded the idea of jumping his body for a ride. Assholes were out of season.

"Give me your keys. Abuela's going out. And I want the cat litter cleaned before I get back."

His brow furrowed. "But, um, you don't have a license...I can't let you..."

Fed up, Nix beamed him with the wooden cane, knocking him out long enough to pick his pockets and take what she wanted. It was the standing back up after leaning down part that proved most difficult. Bracing one hand against her lower back, Nix left the groaning man on the floor with cats meowing around him and climbed into his red convertible.

She started it up. A standard. *Hmm.* Maria temporarily blanked. The grandson came running out, ranting.

Nix threw the car into drive and floored it, only to be jerked backward several feet and feel a distinct speed bump wobble the car. Maria gasped internally, concerned for her cats.

Nix braked. The ranting had stopped. She adjusted the stick, this time finding the right gear and not reverse. The car wobbled over the same speed bump and Nix noticed the crumpled man lying bloody and mangled in the rearview mirror.

"Ah shit, sorry about that, Maria. I'm sure he's fine." Jerking through the gears, Nix and Maria found their way to the open road.

Chapter 5

Nix dropped Maria off at the service desk of a fancy dress shop and jumped the clerk. When someone walked out of the backroom, she shoved a piece of Maria's mail into her hands along with the grandson's credit card and keys.

"Help her buy anything she wants, then take her home so she doesn't get lost." Nix motioned to Maria's slowly recovering form on a settee. "Also, someone may or may not have been hit by a car at her place—definitely not by Maria—so…deal with that, I guess? And make the woman some tea." To Maria, Nix whispered, "If your asshole grandson survives and gives you any grief, kick him in the balls for me."

Twenty minutes later, she was pulling up in front of Blaine's mansion on a Harley.

Danny opened the door before she even reached the steps.

Shit. They were already caught. Well, Rachel was. Nix wasn't impressed with Rachel either right now. For a moment, she thought about turning back around, returning to her non-life of no commitments, no strings. But here she was. Working with these hunters was her best chance at getting her revenge against the Order. She had to see this through.

"I guess you know what happened." Nix shuffled her newest host body's feet.

Danny glared.

"And that it didn't work," Nix finished.

He stared at her. "You can't keep him." He motioned to her new store clerk, whose nametag cheerfully announced *Hello, My Name is Gerry G. Ask Me Anything!* "Elliot's waiting for you. You better not have exposed us with this."

She looked down at herself. Gerry was okay. Gerry was chill. "It's fine—the guy's asleep. He won't remember anything about this place." She wasn't exactly looking forward to returning to Elliot, but she supposed there weren't many options. And she sure as shit didn't appreciate Danny's tone—it wasn't her fault any of this happened. Not like he was a saint.

"I'll get the kid back to wherever you stole him from." Danny stepped into Nix's personal space and gave her a pat-down before she could back up. He jerked Gerry G.'s jacket open and pulled out a wallet Nix hadn't noticed, flipping it open to the driver's license. He plucked the keys from her hand and was already walking toward the bike, leaving Nix standing there feeling violated, when he added, "I'll hitch the trailer and load this up. Make the switch, and be quick about it. They're barbequing in the back."

Nix sighed. "Great."

By the time Danny returned sans store clerk, Nix-in-Elliot had filled Rachel in on her misadventure and they'd concluded that although the spell had been executed to the letter, the added variable of demons must have messed it up somehow. Nix was of the opinion that shit happens and the whole thing was kind of funny to her at this point.

"Bet you five bucks those cats started eating the guy as soon as I ran him over." Nix stuck a forkful of cooked sausage in Elliot's mouth, much to his approval.

"You don't even know if he was dead," Rachel said.

"Like that's ever stopped a cat before."

A door slammed and Danny's heavy footsteps followed. Rachel straightened in her chair, setting her glass down.

He was arguing even as he walked out onto the patio, saying, "—cleaning up messes. I hope you're all comfortable out here."

"Welcome to Round 3001," Elliot grumbled within their shared headspace.

A wave of mental exhaustion swept through him. As far as hosts went, he was holding up surprisingly well, even a little too warm for Nix's liking. Usually, her host bodies started to chill and stiffen after the first week or two, sometimes even faster—though hosts that fit better lasted longer. They'd start to rot, parts would crumble away, and not only fingers or toes. The essence of them would start to crumble, too, fade into nothing. She could never stick around long in one body before she wore it out. But Elliot was warm to the touch and wired with energy, even though he wasn't a very good fit. He pinched and chafed in all the wrong places against her. She couldn't quite figure out why he was holding up like this, but she wasn't complaining.

"Can you do the thing where you let me sleep?" he asked her. *"I can't take this argument anymore."*

Nix propped Elliot's feet up on the table and leaned back in her chair. *"Sweet dreams, puppet,"* Nix said, whisking Elliot's consciousness off into his dreamland with a mental shrug. Seemed like he was missing some quality entertainment, but who was she to judge? Poor boy was so sensitive when it came to conflict—made his stomach all rumbly. Nix noticed a beer near her foot and grabbed for it.

Rachel was saying something as Nix tuned back in, "—like a child, as if we haven't beaten this horse dead already. I won't stop practicing spells or anything else I want to practice, and you can't make me. It was out of pure courtesy I waited until you were out of the house to try it—"

"And look how well that turned out! The demon could've escaped, and then where would we be—you'd be dead! But no, it was *courtesy*," Danny spat.

"More like I knew what an ass you'd be because you can't handle not being in control!"

Nix chugged the beer contentedly. Leaning further back on the chair proved hazardous, however, when the thing slid out from under her and left her flat on the ground in a cacophony of noise. Rachel and Danny stared at her. Nix stared back at them.

Cracking his neck, Danny ran a hand down his grizzled face. "The whole time I was gone, no one's been watching the demon in the attic? Goddamn it."

Rachel pursed her lips. "He doesn't need watching constantly. He's secure up there. I made sure—"

Danny pointed at Nix. "Go. Guard duty; you're on it."

Askance, Nix muttered, "But I—"

They both tilted their heads in opposite directions, mirrored scowls twisting their mouths.

Whatever. This scene was boring anyway. Nix gathered up Elliot's unwieldy limbs, stole the remaining tray of sausages, and stomped back into the house. *Guard duty. Pfft.*

Nix planted herself at the base of the attic steps next to the closed door and chewed on a sausage. This was as close as she was willing to go. Cirrik could be gone, for all she knew. The attic could be empty. That would be their fault, not hers. She'd been otherwise occupied, and Cirrik was not her responsibility. If he *were* gone, though, it would still be her *problem*.

She glanced up at the door. It was probably fine, like Rachel said. Damn, hunter paranoia really was contagious. She shook her head.

For you, the first is free, Cirrik had said in the attic. *I think you will find it familiar.*

Rachel's spell had worked for a moment—or rather, for a memory. Cirrik's words seemed to indicate he'd known they'd only get that one glimpse into their shared past. Maybe the wall she'd hit wasn't a problem on their end, but something intentional on his. Perhaps he'd learned a few psychic tricks during their time apart. He'd always loved that sort of thing—magic tricks, sleight of hand, any form of mental manipulation. She'd been the practical one, the pickpocket, the lockpicker, the one who got her hands dirty without flinching.

Cirrik would always be so busy playing his little games, trying to weasel his way in to get what he wanted. Nix would slit some throats and take it. That's why he was chained up right now and she wasn't, or at least that's what she'd been telling herself. His bullshit had landed him here, but he never went anywhere without it.

There must have been a reason he chose to show her that memory. Something he thought he could gain from it—her favor? Did he think he could sway her by appealing to their shared history and nostalgia? She hoped she hadn't done anything stupid like let him see her smile when she was watching that first memory unspool. How mortifying.

The light carding through the crack under the attic door was already the blood-orange of sunset.

They'd painted so many towns red in their time, though, hadn't they? The streets had been awash with blood. She did miss that. Her non-life had been more fun back then. How had they gotten here?

Nix set the empty tray beside her and tugged on Elliot's collar, begrudging the heat in this house. Even from here, she could hear Danny and Rachel's muffled ranting.

In her head, Elliot dreamed, the occasional spike of adrenaline picking up his heartrate. She glanced inward. Ah yes, hunting in the woods, a favorite of his—no, not the woods this time. A graveyard. How sweet.

The attic above was silent. Possibly vacant.

She could peek in, make sure he was still there. If she was quiet about it, he might not notice her. She knew she was going to regret this.

With a huff, Nix eased the door open and slipped inside.

31

Chapter 6

Nix paused on the first step up to the attic, listening for signs of Cirrik's presence. Nothing. Tiptoeing as carefully as she could in Elliot's gangly, oversized body, Nix kept to the edges of the stairs to make the least noise possible. At the top, back pressed flat against the wall, she peeked around the corner.

Cirrik's dark eyes met hers. Nix shrank back, scrunching Elliot's silver-gray eyes shut, but she knew she'd been caught.

"Nix," Cirrik called. Had he heard her creeping up the steps, or had he been waiting for her? She moved to go back down the stairs but paused.

He'd *called her name*. Either Danny or Rachel had forgotten to put the gag back on during their shouting match, or they'd done it loosely enough he'd managed to get it off. He could be halfway through gnawing his own arms off right now in order to escape the chains and the enchanted bands trapping him in his host. If he got through those, there'd only be a salt circle between them. Glancing back at the door at the bottom of the steps, Nix steeled herself and walked into the attic.

When she came close enough to see clearly, there was blood trailing down the corner of his mouth and staining one shirt cuff. Nix swallowed. At least he hadn't gotten too far. Must have worked the gag off himself then, to be only a couple bites through one wrist. In his position, Nix would have made short work of both—five minutes, tops.

Cirrik looked up at her, curiously unreadable.

Staring down at him like this, with Cirrik in chains and as helpless as a spider trapped in an airtight jar, she should have felt powerful. It should have been heady and euphoric, having him laid out at her mercy like this.

Nix frowned. He wasn't playing the game right. Sure, her typical victims would quiver with fear, and that role dynamic was always enjoyable. But she wouldn't expect it of Cirrik. She knew him too well.

He was supposed to sit there all prim and proper with his smug lips pulled up on one side in an infuriating smirk, a confidence in his eyes making it clear he believed he held all the cards. And then she'd have to prove him wrong and wipe the smirk off his face. They'd play their game, dance their dance. Only now, she kept expecting him to play the part and he kept confusing her. She'd just caught him trying to chew his wrists off to escape—where was the shit-eating grin? The look in his eyes was neither fear nor confidence. She didn't recognize it at all. What game was he playing here?

She kept staring at him, trying to figure out his angle, until he huffed and rattled the chains. Teeth stained pink with red spiderwebbing up the spaces between them, he said, "Can't blame me for trying, love." Only he didn't sound so sure.

He was speaking to her again, with the casual tone he'd had this morning during their botched spell. That was something. More than she expected. Maybe the days up here had softened him. She worked Elliot's bottom lip between her teeth but relented and pulled over a chair from the corner of the skeletal room. Turning it backward, Nix straddled it and leaned into the backrest.

The sun finally dipped below the horizon, leaving the room dark enough she could almost pretend this wasn't happening.

Everything took on a slight glow through Elliot's eyes in the darkness as his night vision adjusted.

When she didn't say anything, Cirrik shifted, chains clinking.

"He doesn't suit you," Cirrik said, looking her up and down in the light of the moon coming through the still open window.

"He's what's on offer at the moment."

The hunters had agreed to trade off as voluntary hosts once one of them couldn't hold her anymore and started deteriorating, and Elliot had insisted on taking his turn first. Rachel and Nix were sick of each other after their previous quality time. Danny loathed her for the whole butchering-a-bunch-of-his-hunter-friends thing. Elliot was the most neutral party.

At first, Nix had wanted to pick up some stranger and perma-sleep them until they started to fade or croaked, repeating the cycle as necessary. Apparently, this was unethical, so she was vetoed. But staying in one of the hunters was a safety to her, as well, compared to some stranger, and she was well aware of that fact every time Danny glared in her direction. With their demon-killing exorcism always hanging over her head like a guillotine, at least this way she had the comfort of knowing they'd never use it on her so long as she was in one of them, or else they'd kill her host—their kin—along with her.

"Is he...?"

"He's asleep. It's just you and me." Nix touched her temple. "The mindreading thing. You bounced me out on purpose, didn't you?"

"I thought you might find that entertaining." He smirked, at last. His gaze wandered to the window. "I could show you my technique sometime, should you find yourself interested."

"You didn't have to throw me so far. I landed miles from here."

"Did you." Cirrik looked at her strangely, then shook his head. He chuckled mirthlessly. "Well, I hardly expected you to pry so forcefully. That's why you *bounced*, as you say, such a distance. I merely placed a wall in your path. You're the one who propelled yourself into it at full speed." His brow furrowed. "Very well, I suppose I *should* have anticipated that from you."

Nix restrained a grin, pursing her lips instead. "And the old cat lady I landed in after the bounce, pure coincidence?"

"Cat lady?" Cirrik squinted at her. "Can't say I know anything about that."

"Costa Rican. Tons of cats. Asshole grandson. Impressive garden. No bells ringing?"

His eyes widened and he shrugged, lightly rattling his chains.

Nix shook her head, dropped the subject. She wouldn't bring up the *bruja* aspect and hadn't with Rachel or Danny, either—she couldn't completely predict their reactions to learning about another witch living nearby, but she knew they'd be polar opposites and didn't need the added trouble right now. Of course, it was a coincidence—he couldn't have predicted where she'd land. But in case it wasn't, she'd keep it to herself and see how this played out.

"They do a number on you?" Nix's eyes trailed along the outline of Portugal painting his jaw a muddy brown. There would be many more countries mapped beneath his clothes, she knew. The real damage would be internal, the rivers carved into his host's trachea and guts from that hot new holy water cleanse all the hunters were promoting these days.

"They are amateurs." He coughed but smiled. His earlier display of fear was at least partly an act then, as she'd hoped. "Under your tutelage, they may have promise. The witch, though. She has a certain...malicious streak."

Nix leaned in. "Unexpected, right?"

"Quite. You know," Cirrik said, looking back to the window, "if you'd taken me up on *my* offer, you could have had your pick of host bodies."

Nix bristled, thinking back on the lackluster host bodies she'd had lately and adding the little old lady and the store clerk to the list. "I can have anyone I want. The circumstances—"

Cirrik shook his head. "No, no. Not like these. Your hunters, in one of their many failed interrogations, they attempted to suppress me and bring out the consciousness of my host to glean information from someone more receptive. They couldn't."

"So they're incompetent. So what?"

"They couldn't, because there is no host consciousness. This body is mine alone. I am not bound to it—usually." He motioned to his wrists. "But without me, it is empty. And there are others like it. Empty vessels. I've had this one for a while now, and if not for the torture it would be in better condition and last longer. And they do last. Not forever, but we're getting there."

Nix perked up at the prospect. She wondered why he would share this with her but didn't want to risk asking outright. "Long-term hosts. I'd wondered how you were holding up so well. But...I've never been one for empty vessels."

"No," Cirrik said, a warm smile gracing his battered features, "you always did cultivate a fondness for the voices in your head. Ever the odd one, they called you. I found it endearing."

Nix couldn't help but ask, "How'd they do it? How'd they figure it out? Was it the Order?"

"So many questions." He tsked. "So many questions you would have had answers to if you had joined us." His eyes locked on the window again. "Too late."

Nix stilled. She looked at the bait he'd rolled out between them, cheese set in a trap and she the mouse. For once in her non-life, she didn't take it. Instead, she donned a mask of indifference and watched it sit there, let the history between them and the string of betrayals linger, fester, and rot, like they always had.

Silence stretched and yawned between them. Cirrik was the one to finally break it.

"Go on. Ask what you truly want to ask," he said.

Nix narrowed her eyes. "Why tell me any of this at all? Why risk me telling the hunters your host is empty?"

"What risk? I'm dead tomorrow. Time's up no matter how this works out between us. You should know what you've missed out on. What could have been." His eyes flicked to hers. "What still could be, if we left right now. Together."

Nix ignored his hollow, desperate proposition. "You aren't dead tomorrow. Why would you think that?"

"They speak of leaving come morning. They will perform their exorcism on me before you leave this place. It is logical."

"You're wrong. We're taking you with us. On the road."

He laughed. "Road trip with those Neanderthals? A fate worse than death. Our time is limited, love. How do you think this will end? They have the power to eradicate a demon permanently with their exorcism. They *will* utilize that power on me—they've demonstrated that once already. And when you no longer prove useful to them, when the opportunity presents itself, they will use it on you."

Nix sucked in a breath. She couldn't deny he was right, no matter the hunters' reassurances otherwise. She could see it in Danny's eyes, his hatred and lust for vengeance. Once their common goal of taking down the Order was completed, they would come for her. Still, she said, "You're wrong about them."

"It is their nature. We cannot help our natures." He looked away from her, as if he couldn't bear the sight of her naivety any longer.

Nix followed Cirrik's gaze back to the window. "You won't escape, if that's what you're thinking. You couldn't even fit through that window."

"The moon is nearly full. It no longer matters."

Chapter 7

In the darkness of the attic, Nix watched Cirrik closely. "What's that supposed to mean? Why does the moon matter?"

"The witch," he said, reverting their train back to an earlier track, "why not take her as host again? Take advantage of her power?"

Nix rolled her eyes. "More trouble than she's worth. I was stuck with her for *ages*. I mean, I helped her out after she got impaled on some glass, but she's got this crazy thing where if she doesn't want to be possessed she can kick you *out*. Never seen it before. Right now, I've got the brother on a voluntary basis and we've agreed to switch off as necessary if he starts to fade. But I've had him for weeks and the boy's like a furnace, just have to keep feeding it—" Nix trailed off as she noticed the confused look Cirrik was giving her. "Oh, it's the eyes, right? He lost his, so we got him some replacements—ghoul-sourced. They're pretty good. They come with night vision. The irises are a little grayer than normal but it's not that noticeable they aren't human, right?"

"You are possessing your host only because he *volunteers*? You helped the injured witch. You replaced a human's eyes for...for what? Simply to recover his lost sight? Out of the goodness of your *heart?* Are you working *with* them, or *for* them?"

Nix straightened, the air in the room shriveling up like the corpse of a long-dead rat. She didn't know what she had expected, why she had for one moment thought this could go any differently. *"With* them," she ground out. "You knew that already."

He hung his head, face cast in shadows. "I didn't want to believe you'd fallen so far."

"Don't feed me bullshit lines, Cirrik. We're demons. We *are* the fallen. I owe you nothing."

"It may have been foolish of me, but I have held out hope for you, Nix. Hope you had a plan in all of this madness. That you were playing *them,* not sitting here blindly while they played you. They are *hunters."*

"Hope?" Nix scoffed, shaking her head. "You always were weak. That's how you got caught up with the Order and their lies in the first place. They made you promises of wealth and greatness, and you were an eager little puppy following behind them without ever questioning your masters. I'm not the one who's blind. At least I had the balls to make a stand. Even if that stand put me here with a bunch of hunters, it's on my terms, not the Order's."

He leaned his head down conspiratorially. "You could release me from these manacles. We'll slay these dreadful hunters together and return triumphant. The Order was grateful to you for releasing them from their glass prison; they would surely forgive this lapse."

Nix sighed. "Don't you get it? There's nothing left for you. If we let you go, you couldn't return to them and neither could I. If you'd have brought me back to them to be your *queen,* they would have stamped me out of existence knowing I'd spent time with these hunters and their exorcism. And they'd never trust you didn't give us information—never take the risk. They'd think we turned you into a double agent, kill you just in case. They made us. They can unmake us. Wasn't that always the company line? You can't tell me you think things have changed."

His shoulders fell.

"That's what I thought," Nix said. "You called me a traitor yourself. We both know what they do to traitors, suspected traitors, anyone who even looks at them the wrong way. They aren't the forgiving types, let alone capable of gratitude. If I thought otherwise, we'd have planted a tracking device on you, released you, and followed you back to them to locate the Order—of course, you'd probably chew your way out of those bands real quick and prove that task pointless." Nix waved to his bloodied wrists. "We still considered it. And tracking you by spell once you body-hopped. But you'd eventually conceal your presence with sigils and we'd lose track anyway. We considered a lot of options, but none of the catch-and-release ones panned out because even if we did release you, you've got nowhere to go. They'd take you out as soon as they got a bead on you. You wouldn't get near them."

"You ruined *everything*." Anger. Finally, something she could work with.

"No," Nix told him honestly, "they did that. I already had *everything* before I met them, and they took it from me, deliberately. I told you about my little sister, about how she died."

He shifted in place, shrugged. "Ignorant villagers, sacrificing her to some ancient god for fertile crops. I know the story. A devotee of the Order came to you when she died and offered you the chance to avenge her death in exchange for your soul. The deal that made you what you are. They saved you, gave you a new family, eternal life, and now you've turned on them."

"That's not the whole story, Cirrik. She wasn't dead when I got to her. She was poisoned by the villagers, and…maybe she would have died either way, I'll never know. But he came to me and convinced me the only way to save her soul was to make a sacrifice, to destroy the thing I loved most in the world—to kill her myself. And I did. I thought she would die anyway, and I had to save her immortal soul, and that was the only way to do it. I sold mine in the process. But it was a trick, Cirrik. Don't you see? Her soul was never in danger—they could never have taken something not willingly given. They set the whole thing up, beginning to end. They made me kill her."

He was quiet for a long moment and Nix felt even more foolish for having shared this with him. She slumped into the chair, her forehead on the backrest. It didn't matter what they'd shared in the past. He was their puppet. He'd never understand.

"Perhaps you've misinterpreted something," Cirrik said. "Maybe your sister *did* willingly relinquish her soul?"

Nix sputtered. "She was an innocent child. Even if she had, they couldn't have taken it from her unless she sacrificed the thing she loved most in the world, and she certainly didn't kill anyone. It was a scam, Cirrik. Plain and simple. She was only ever placed in danger because a shepherd from the Order convinced the villagers they had to sacrifice a child to secure their harvest. They're con artists."

Nix pushed away from the chair, paced the perimeter of the new salt circle. He may be an idiot, but she would make him see. Her village had been sent a shepherd, one of the three archetypes the Order used. They took immense pride in perverting human symbology. They had taught her to do so, as well. Cirrik would have been approached by one of them directly, too. They trapped him somehow. A traveling shepherd, a wise preacher, a shaman healer. Any era, any culture, any body, they always donned the same basic personas.

"What about you? You had to kill the king, your grandfather. You loved him more than anything else in the world. You sacrificed him to save your people. Why were they in danger?"

"A plague," he said eventually.

41

"And where do you suppose the plague came from? Did it show up around the same time a mystical stranger started hanging around, granting wishes?"

Cicadas chirped in the trees beyond the window. The muffled argument from below continued.

Cirrik opened his mouth, closed it again. He scratched his bloodied wrist against the pipe. "She was a healer, traveling with missionaries."

"Some coincidence. Have you ever even met the top tier of the Order?"

"They're…very private."

"Because they're busy sitting around laughing at us, at what idiots we all are. And they should be. They've played us all."

"So many were dying. The plague—I saw it myself. Without the Order, my kingdom would've fallen. Grandfather's sacrifice…it was the only way."

Nix lifted her hands. "By design."

"I was a hero!" he snarled, lifting his head.

"You were a fool," Nix spat back.

He stared at her.

"You see it now, don't you?" she asked.

Cirrik's head dropped to his chest and he went limp like a snipped marionette. He sat completely still. He wouldn't meet her eyes.

That wasn't a good enough answer. "Don't you?" Her voice echoed through the barren room.

He stared at the wall. In a small voice, he breathed, "A fool?"

Nix wiped her hands down her face and dropped back into the chair. They were quiet for several minutes. Nix was about to leave but stopped. "Cirrik. Why does the moon matter? What did you mean? Please, tell me."

Cirrik started to laugh. "You released them. The Order had been trapped for centuries in that silly bauble. No one knew where they had gone, and you freed them while attempting to save the world from some other mad archdemon. You saved me, too. They were grateful, yes—that was why they allowed me to pursue you and attempt your extraction from the hunters. But they do not care about lesser demons or even hunters. You are correct that we are expendable. However, you have never once asked who forced them into that bauble in the first place."

"Some long-dead hunters? Rival archdemons?"

"At the time, the Pope."

Nix leaned back. "Uh, so they want revenge on the Pope?"

"Humans imprisoned them. It's humanity itself that will suffer retribution. They already have everything they need. Long-term hosts for all their keen new recruits. A growing army. Their compromised power will be recharged completely by the time the moon is full."

Nix swallowed. A chill crept through her. "What will happen then?"

"They'll be unstoppable. Not even your pedestrian exorcism could touch them. They have taken measures to ensure it."

"Shit. I imagine they're planning on destroying the world, too?"

"Why destroy something when you can control it. Recruitment will be so high, eventually there will be more of us than the humans. We'll grow new hosts in factories. Streamlined manufacturing. The humans will serve us in ultimate utopia."

Nix gripped the chair. "Are you lying to me? Why tell me this?"

Cirrik laughed louder. "There is nothing you can do. It's over for both of us, love. You are right. It is over." He jerked at his chains, moving to stand in a clatter. "It's *too late!*"

The thump of footsteps sounded on the stairs.

Chapter 8

Danny's voice shot up the attic stairs before he could, shrill and out of place in this private moment as he demanded, "The hell's goin' on up here?" Panting, he stopped beside Nix. "Is that...? Did you take his gag off?"

Rachel appeared at the top of the steps. "How could she have taken it off? There's a salt circle, Pops," she argued, since apparently that hadn't ended.

Danny sputtered. "Well, I put the damn thing on myself, how else did it get off?"

Rachel crossed her arms. "You didn't tie it tightly enough, obviously."

"Only because you were distracting me. Now look, the demon's gone and gnawed on the poor fella's hand." Danny's fingers brushed over the anti-possession amulet around his neck as he gingerly stepped over the salt line to rectify the gag issue. Cirrik didn't acknowledge any of them.

"And that's my fault? Unbelievable!" Rachel stomped back down the stairs.

Easing the gag into a suspiciously compliant demon's mouth and tightening it securely in place, Danny glanced at Nix. "What's with him?"

Cirrik stared at the wall.

Nix shrugged. "Does this mean I'm off guard duty?"

"Pass me the med-kit. I need to clean this wrist before it gets infected." Looking down at Cirrik and receiving no reaction, Danny squinted and said, "No funny business."

Nix set the first-aid kit at the edge of the salt line. "What do you care?"

"I care about the man," Danny said, "not the demon. There's someone suffering inside there. Don't gotta make it worse than necessary."

Nix stilled as it finally occurred to her the gravity of what Cirrik had confessed. She thought about telling Danny about Cirrik's host body being empty. Assuming he was telling the truth, it would remove a significant ethical hurdle for the hunters. They'd agreed with Nix's argument weeks ago that they couldn't use their demon-killing exorcism on Cirrik since it would kill his host, too. Not that she cared about either of them, but at the time, she felt compelled to keep him alive *while* wanting to kill him all the same—story of her non-life. Without the host in play, there was nothing stopping them from using it now.

She hadn't been lying to Cirrik when she said the Order would take him out if the hunters released him, but there was also the possibility they'd use him for information first to get one up on them—not that he knew anything worth knowing about the hunters, since at this point if what he'd shared was true, he'd divulged enough to her tonight to initiate him into the traitor club. If they exorcised him with a regular exorcism, that would be equivalent to releasing him and saving the host. It could come back to bite them, and so could he. They were either stuck with him as a prisoner, or they could take him out permanently—which was suddenly an option without the ethical ramifications of a host. Danny would be all over that.

Cirrik had to have known. Why else would he show his cards? He couldn't think he'd actually entice her into joining him. And the risk of sharing the information was far too high if he believed even for a moment she was, indeed, a traitor. Did he want an easy out? Nix couldn't be sure. This was some sort of trick. Had to be. Even if he was lying, there was no way they'd know about it until both the host and Cirrik were extinguished, so what the hell kind of play was this?

And if he'd been truthful about the Order's endgame, they'd all wasted a good two weeks aimlessly.

She looked out the window. Four nights, including this one, until the moon was full. Maybe it really was too late.

"There, that's better." Danny stepped out of the circle. Sighing, he said, "I hope we can figure a way to deal with all of this soon so we can get this demon outta his host. I wouldn't wish that on anybody." He glanced at Nix a little awkwardly and looked away with a forced cough. "So, you get any information while you were up here? Anything we can use?"

It was a test. Cirrik had put a loaded gun in her hand and held it against his own head just to see if her finger would flirt with the trigger.

She already knew she wouldn't mention his empty host. That was one trigger she couldn't quite bring herself to pull.

"We need to talk," Nix said.

Chapter 9

Downstairs, Nix shared enough of what Cirrik told her to turn the hunters quiet. She told them about the human-factory plan, the ramped-up recruitments, the full moon deadline only four nights away, and that soon their big-guns exorcism might not matter.

She left out the fact that the Order had somehow figured out how to make their upgraded long-term hosts consciousness-free. Neither Rachel nor Danny seemed to pick up on the omission, though to Nix it felt like there was a flashing neon sign over her head.

Both the hunters had finally gone to bed heavy with the knowledge that their species would soon be enslaved as hosts to the Order's army if they declined recruiting efforts—though hunters probably weren't on the enlistment. And Nix, as a known traitor, could only expect a grim personal outlook.

The stress of impending doom didn't sit right with Nix, left her on edge, made her want to work off the fluctuating energy.

Nix had been quietly stealing items of interest from the house over the last two weeks, waiting for one of the two hunters to notice. They didn't. It was disappointing, but she was optimistic and chose to take their ignorance as a personal challenge. Games weren't fun unless they were challenging, after all. And sure, all she had these days for companionship was Elliot, and he was boring, but Nix would make do.

Their current situation had left her in a peculiar position. Nix wasn't used to remaining in a host body long enough to entertain the idea of collecting physical objects. Usually, she'd slip in, slip out, and ditch any baggage as soon as she did so. Couldn't exactly carry a backpack around in non-corporeal form. Sometimes, sure, she'd stick around for a while, months even, but as soon as she got bored, she was on her way. This time, she was stuck in a host body *and* restless, but she didn't intend to leave until her mission was completed. Hence the petty larceny.

Danny intended this to be their last night in the house, and Nix was going to make the most of it. He was camped out in the attic, snoring loudly. Nix couldn't go up there and yell at Cirrik, ask him what the hell game he was playing, or shake him. Rachel occupied a room down the hall, also presumably asleep—Nix neither knew nor cared, though it was basically the only thing Elliot thought about besides hamburgers. Cirrik, like Nix, would be awake, but that wasn't relevant, so she tried not to dwell on the thought.

Nix slipped down to the bottom of the stairs, toward Blaine's office. For all she complained about Elliot, one thing she did like was his impeccable night vision—thanks to the ghoul eyes Nix had so kindly used to restore his sight after an archdemon burned his eyes out. It may as well have been daytime, if not for the slight glow the world acquired through Elliot's gaze when night fell.

She dug into the pocket of Elliot's pants and pulled out a slim skeleton key, one she'd found while snooping around Blaine's room when they'd first gotten back here. Quietly, she slid the key into the lock and eased open the door, which demanded in a red-lettered sign *Do Not Enter.* Slipping in, she closed the door behind her and left the lights off.

The air quivered inside Blaine's office. She cleared her throat, coughing. The rancid scent of ceremonial sage still permeated the walls, making her eyes sting. So many objects in the room called to her. Ancient medallions, dusty grimoires, clay effigies, wooden figurines of unknown origin. A suit of armor stood watch in one corner. Some items were clearly fakes, like their curator had been. Others were quite legit and rippled with power.

Nix wondered if Blaine was truly aware of the powder keg he'd been sitting on. He must have been, to some extent, or he wouldn't have gone through the trouble of protecting his home from prying eyes—human, demon, or otherwise.

Nix sat cross-legged on Blaine's desk and played with the wooden figurines, posing them in inappropriate positions in case the cops really did come here, so they'd have something entertaining to photograph and speculate upon.

From Elliot's back pocket, she slid out the last three Slim Jims from Danny's earlier supply run and peeled one open, taking a bite and trying to savor it. Unfortunately for Danny, he would soon wake up to find the worthwhile products from today's supply run no longer in supply. His use of a combination lock as an attempt to keep her out of his storage container was adorable on so many levels.

Searching around in the drawers, she found a permanent marker. Grinning, Nix scrawled *Helter Skelter* across Blaine's desk and proceeded to defile other flat surfaces.

"I'm not condoning this," Elliot said appreciatively as Nix demonstrated her artistic abilities, *"but I'm not condemning it, either."*

"I always knew you could be fun if you wanted to be."

"At least it's a non-violent outlet for your emotions."

"Everything's about feelings with you. How boring. Can't you enjoy the moment sometimes? Oh, hats!" Nix pulled open a previously undiscovered cupboard containing a variety of hats and... *"A*

toupee. *What do you think?"* She placed it atop the suit of armor's helm.

"I'll deny any participation if they see this," Elliot said, *"but I think the top hat would be a better choice."*

"Fair." Nix set the hat in place and had to admit it did look dashing—until the suit proved suddenly unstable and she found herself with a mass of metal falling into her arms.

The suit crashed to the ground, breaking off into pieces. The head rolled into the doorframe as Rachel and Danny came bursting into the pitch-black room with rifles, flicking on the overhead light and temporarily blinding Elliot.

"What in tarnation?" Danny said.

Nix watched the hunters look around the room at her handiwork. "It was Elliot's idea."

"You're cleaning this up," Danny said, as if he could make such demands.

Neither of them looked surprised at what they were seeing. Rachel bent down and scooped up the helm, tugging a paper bag free from the inside.

"Maryjane?" Nix asked, interest piqued. Elliot's stomach rumbled.

Tearing the bag open, Rachel pulled out a silver cord with a heavy pendant attached to the end of it. "A scrying crystal. Why would he have kept this hidden?"

Nix reached out to touch it but pulled back as her fingertips brushed against the crystal. "Damn. It's blessed. Powerful."

Rachel's eyes flashed. "Maybe we could use it to find Violet or Blaine?"

Danny didn't even protest, his guilt at having lost their teen psychic was so strong he probably would have attempted a spell himself to get her back. "How?"

"I'll find something of hers in her room. You get a map. I can't sleep tonight anyway."

They both turned to Nix, glanced at the room, shook their heads, and left her there.

Chapter 10

As they stepped out the door the next morning, Nix lugging a bulging bag over one shoulder, she pulled out Danny's prized lighter and flicked it on. "Who's got the accelerant?"

Rachel didn't bat an eye. "Put it away. We're not burning the house down."

Frowning and muttering under his breath, Danny snatched the lighter from her hands.

Nix understood their rejection. As both humans and hunters, the two often found such things as murder, maiming, and arson to be actions contrary to their self-image as do-gooders—though Rachel was quite the firebug herself. Cognitive dissonance was hard for humans. Lucky for them, Nix didn't have such concerns. They could go about acting like white knights all they wanted. Nix was the one who made sure things got done around here, and often those things required she get her hands dirty.

In a way, it was a healthy, balanced relationship they had formed together. Where one faltered, the others picked up the slack. Nix pulled Danny's second-most-prized lighter out of Elliot's jeans and lit it. "Gotcha." She winked. "We *aren't* burning anything down."

Rachel stopped hauling luggage and stared at her. "No. No winking. I'm serious. Arson is off the table. You'll burn the whole damn state down."

"Right. Of course." She winked again in Rachel's direction.

Rachel sighed, storming up the steps. She reclaimed the lighter and grabbed Nix's hand, dragging her down the driveway. "Why is it you always want to burn things?"

"*Me?* Don't pretend like you don't."

Rachel blushed. Rachel had burned far more property in their time together than Nix had…probably. Well, it mostly evened out. It was nice to have things in common, though. As they got closer to the vehicle and farther from the house, Nix wondered if they actually were going to leave it standing. What a wasted opportunity.

After they'd caught her defacing Blaine's office—then failed to clean up the mess—she'd assumed they were planning to burn the whole place down. Evidence, and all that. But who was Nix to deny anyone a fun surprise if they dropped by? She shrugged and let it go.

The bags under Rachel's and Danny's eyes were heavier than the ones in their hands. Their late night had been unexpected but successful on the scrying front, and Rachel in particular had an extra skip in her step this morning despite the depressing news from Cirrik.

Even though they'd been planning to leave today anyway, they'd only had vague plans about where they'd go. Away, mostly. Now they had to figure out a legitimate plan and execute it before the full moon to have any hope of stopping the Order. The task seemed impossible at square zero, with only three more nights to go. How could they? The hunters could barely travel as it was, let alone find the Order and take them down on a deadline.

After the Winterspoon farmhouse had burned down— Rachel's fault—they'd lost their old piece-of-shit Ford on the property and the authorities had shown up to find a bunch of dead host bodies scattered all over, which was a Very Bad Thing according to Danny. Between the seats of Danny's Ford, Nix had forgotten a set of keys belonging to Callie's mother, which *might* have tied them to the little girl's *happily resolved* kidnapping and also the bloody murder of a creepy clown…and Fuckles the Clown's blood *may* have still been on those keys, according to the news reports. Danny found all of this problematic from a human legal perspective.

"All of that was your fault," Elliot said.

"Um, no. Your sister burned the house down. I was busy saving her life, if you'll recall. And it was your Pops' fault a bunch of demons and all your hunter buddies were pissed off at all of you. I had nothing to do with it. You threatened demons with a demon-killing exorcism. You made enemies. You worked with an archdemon and burned bridges with other hunters."

"Well…I was there, and your demon friends said they were there to rescue you, not kill us."

Nix considered this. *"Still. Never would've had the problem in the first place without your Pops making a big mess of everything."*

"The kidnapping and clown-murder connection was definitely your fault."

Nix scoffed out loud. Rachel gave her an odd look. *"It's my fault a creepy clown deserved to die? Now you're being ridiculous. And Callie was with me willingly. If you idiots hadn't summoned me away from her mother and kept me hostage, it wouldn't have been a kidnapping."*

Elliot was silent. Nix kept him that way. The hunters were responsible for their own messes. Not to mention, their vehicle and therefore their family was also being connected to the unfortunate death of a motel attendant in Modesto. The man's arm had been recovered in the parking lot in front of their motel room along with a massive amount of forensic evidence. Oh, and then there were the deaths of their extended family of hunters in La Grange, for which Rachel was a wanted suspect. And another arson in relation to it, but that was basically inconsequential at this point. Nix may have played a role, sure, but was any of it her *fault* in the grand scheme of things? It would be absurd to think so.

Internally, Elliot huffed. Externally, his stomach rumbled and growled since they hadn't had breakfast yet and Nix had polished off the last of the Slim Jims last night.

The whole lot of them were hotly sought after by the human police, which was funny if you really thought about it—though they never laughed when Nix pointed this out.

Bright side: Nix was kind enough to steal them a van after they ditched the Audi they'd abducted Cirrik in. She was thoughtful like that. Danny hated it—partly because it was a van and mostly because Nix gave it to him.

Still, the prospect of cops showing up at Blaine's house to search for a missing teen psychic whose mother was worried about her was concerning enough for the hunters that they were willing to leave an otherwise excellent supernaturally protected safehouse. And now there was the added pressure of finding the Order, which they were having no success with from Blaine's house.

After finding what they hoped was a location for Violet last night, they had renewed purpose.

"At least we have a destination," Rachel was saying to Danny, "even if it doesn't pan out. We owe it to Violet and Blaine to try. Maybe it'll give us direction to deal with the Order."

Danny zipped up his old brown-leather jacket against the chill of the morning air while Nix felt beads of sweat trailing down the back of her neck. "That's right, darlin'."

Rachel even lit up at the term of endearment, so apparently their argument from yesterday was resolved. "What do we do if we run into the archdemon who took them?"

Releasing a reality-bending archdemon bound to the bones of a dead hunter, which then inhabited Blaine and whisked him and Violet off to who-knows-where? Also not Nix's fault—entirely Rachel's.

"Maybe he's discarded them by now and they're confused, or in hiding, or trapped," Danny answered.

"Or they're dead," Nix said.

The two of them turned to glare at her as they walked down the long driveway. "But the crystal gave us a location," Rachel said.

"It's probably where their bodies are," Nix said. "Besides, you don't want to run into an archdemon. The only way we'd survive another encounter if it's angry is to destroy it completely using that exorcism of yours—which actually means Blaine dies, too, since it was possessing him the last time we saw it. That's kind of a win-win, when you think about it. As long as you can contain it and exorcise it before it mind-fucks you into oblivion and you both die choking on your own blood, you'll be aces. Me? I'll wait in the car, thanks."

Rachel pursed her lips. "Well...we accidentally let it out, so maybe it will be happy with us, you know? We did free it from an eternal skull-prison, that's got to count for something."

Nix skipped past her. "Doubt it."

"Don't you even want to find them?" Rachel asked her.

"Blaine? No. Violet? Don't get me wrong, she seemed like a nice kid, and she could make a powerful ally if she were alive, but she's *not* going to be. This is an archdemon we're talking about. You both should know better. The best thing we can do is stay far, far out of its way and consider ourselves lucky it didn't crush us when it had the chance."

Rachel squared her shoulders. "Well, we're going to try anyway."

"And I'm going to wait in the car."

"She could be the *powerful ally* we need to take on the Order," Rachel said.

"Great, I hope so. Let me know—I'll be in the car."

"So will he." Danny opened the small trailer hitched to the van to reveal Cirrik, trussed like a calf and locked in an iron cage atop a sheet of canvas painted with sigils and sewn with crystals. "You can keep each other company. But I gave my word I'd take care of that girl, and I intend to do everything within my power to keep it. So we're doin' this."

When they climbed in the van, Nix in the back, Rachel turned around to look at her. "If you can't deal with one archdemon, what are you planning to do when we locate the Order? You do realize you can't sit in the car. We have to deal with this. And fast. No way around it."

Nix didn't have an answer. For all her bluster, all her rage and desire for revenge, she had no idea what to do. Finding them was proving difficult enough. But taking out the three archdemons heading the Order, more powerful in the united front they posed, that was a different problem entirely. She'd never been the kind of demon to face problems head on. To figure it all out in three days and three nights—find them, defeat three of them, and dismantle their army? Nix couldn't breathe.

"Whatever," Nix deflected. "Let's get some breakfast. Elliot's starving."

"That's exactly why I went on a supply run yesterday—so we don't have to get breakfast. We've got all the meals we need right here." Danny climbed into the trailer next to Cirrik and spun the combination lock on his massive storage container. "We'll be set up for a few days, at least, while we figure out how to get to the Order." Lifting the lid, he stared inside for what felt like several minutes. Stone-faced, too tired apparently even for Nix's bullshit, Danny lowered the lid and stepped out of the trailer. "We'll pick something up on the way."

They didn't. Elliot's stomach growled.

Chapter 11

Raiding Danny's supplies last night had been a grave strategical error. Nix was beginning to see this now. If Danny had purchased more food in the first place, she wouldn't be in this position. Nor would anyone else be dealing with the hunger-induced rage stifling the atmosphere of the van.

Though Danny promised they'd stop soon for something fresh to eat, that had been hours ago. Rachel handed her a granola bar. Nix bit into it, the stale chunks sucking up the saliva in her mouth with a lingering cardboard flavor. Nix couldn't get it down. In a fit, she threw it out the van window. They sped up. Nix pouted for hours. They took side roads to avoid highway patrol, making their trip even longer.

Every restaurant they passed Danny would dismiss as too busy, saying someone might recognize them from the news, or there could be cops. They were waiting for an elusive fast-food joint dead enough they could speed through, with an easy exit. Elliot did nothing but complain about his imminent starvation until Nix had to shut him down, but that didn't stop the hunger pangs from racking his body.

All along the road, billboards promoting hot and juicy burgers taunted her. Something wet slid down her chin and Nix reached up to brush it away. Drawing her hand back, she inspected it. Saliva. Swallowing and licking her lips, she silently cursed Elliot's overly responsive body. She glanced around to make sure no one noticed the drooling, but it appeared she was in the clear.

With Elliot off in dreamland and Nix herself harboring indifferent opinions at best when it came to fast food, this seemed to be a purely physical response. Nix wasn't hungry. Elliot wasn't hungry. But his *body* was insatiable.

Nix was nine shades of done with this. At first it had been annoying, but now it was getting weird.

They stopped for the night at a little rental cabin outside Santa Barbara that didn't ask too many questions and accepted cash. All she'd managed to eat was an unsatisfying bowl of fruit and something called froyo.

"Oh my god," Rachel all but screamed at her, slamming the private cabin door, "fine! I get it, you're hungry. We all get it. I'll order some damn pizza if you'll *shut the hell up* already."

Nix shuffled over to a polyester couch and plopped down in it, dropping Elliot's black canvas bag on the floor. "Well…all right then."

"Good." Rachel glared, hands on her hips.

Danny slid inside with some more bags, glancing between them. She expected him to argue about the pizza thing, how it would "put us all in danger and we'll surely die, blah blah blah" or some other nonsense, but he didn't say a word.

"Good," Nix echoed quietly.

Sure, pizza. What could go wrong?

Chapter 12

Rachel and Danny argued upstairs in the cabin's small loft where two of the beds were located. Something about demons and *You deal with it then!* and *Don't you speak to me like that!* The usual. Nix wasn't really paying attention. They'd spent hours driving, wasting their very limited time in what Nix was sure would be a fruitless pursuit. To make matters worse, Danny didn't want to search their destination in darkness, and they had no leads on the Order, so they planned to waste the night, too.

The curtain on the cabin's bay window was open and the first-floor lights were off. She was supposed to be keeping an eye on the trailer parked with its doors nearly flush against the side of the cabin. "Watch it like a hawk and see he don't get out till we figure what we're doing," Danny had directed, continuing to labor under the impression that he had any right to direct her. In reality, she was staring out into the dusk with laser-sharp intensity awaiting the pizza guy.

Nix flexed Elliot's hands. She paced.

The tiny cabin was stifling, worse than Blaine's house for heat retention, worse even than the sweltering van. She'd opened the windows but there wasn't so much as a breeze outside and the languid overhead fan did nothing but stir up the dust.

She pulled Elliot's sweaty t-shirt over her head and threw it on the floor, carding her fingers through his short, damp hair. She stood on wobbly legs and went over to the mock-kitchen, pulling out a foggy glass and filling it up from the tap. She downed the liquid in one gulp, refilled, repeated. She nudged Elliot mentally, but he'd been fast asleep since the long ride.

Outside, the night was still. Inside, she was vibrating into pieces.

Elliot's entire body ached as she leaned over the sink with the empty glass in her grip. Something was wrong. Maybe he was sick.

She'd had sick hosts before—usually killed them and put them out of her misery. This could be one of those…what did humans get these days? A flu? Those were common. Spanish influenza had been a little like this. That must be it, a bad flu. If he was sick, Nix was calling a timeout. He could deal with this himself and she'd ride along with Rachel until he'd sorted his issues out.

Encouraged by her new game plan, Nix straightened, only to be hit by a rush of dizziness. She heard the snap before she felt the flash of pain register in Elliot's hand.

Glancing down, she saw the glass shard in her grasp, blood already slipping hot and red into the steel sink. Sighing, she released the broken glass and picked the errant piece out of Elliot's thumb, the hand quickly numbing. The blood slowed to a sluggish crawl.

Sucking her bloody thumb into her mouth, a crack of clarity shook the haze from around her. A jolt of taste lit up her senses and for a second she felt fine again. Better than fine—fantastic.

With a pop, Elliot's thumb slipped from between his lips and a metallic flavor lingered on Nix's palate that was less like blood and more like a rich, smoky wine.

A knock at the cabin door snapped Nix's attention back to the present moment. She stumbled toward the sound even as the argument upstairs registered dimly across her consciousness.

The scent of pepperoni and grease reached her before she opened the door, but beyond that, something else.

She stopped and inhaled. Nix pressed her face to the door.

Sweat. Skin. A beat underneath it, a drum that rumbled through her entire being. A human heartbeat. She could smell it, taste it.

Saliva flooded her mouth. She swallowed. The door was open before she registered opening it and a set of blue eyes were looking into her gray ones.

"Hey, man, you ordered—"

First her hands were around the guy's throat, just to feel the beat beneath her fingertips. But then he was choking, and it wasn't enough to feel it.

The pizzas slipped from his hands as he grabbed at her wrists, scattering down the steps and bouncing out of boxes.

She was so hungry. Everything smelled sharply of pepperoni, and so did he. She needed to eat.

His throat was in her mouth before she realized what was happening. A strangled yip slid out of him as her jaws clenched down, tearing at his trachea.

Fingernails scratched at her skin, but she knew only flesh, only blood. Lowering him to the ground, he stopped struggling. She gulped to keep up with the flow, then ripped and tore. Ravenous gulps became voracious chews, hurried swallows; she couldn't get enough.

The flavor, this was it, this was what she'd been missing—

Nix wasn't sure what finally cut through the haze, but it wasn't until the sense of starvation ebbed and was replaced with sudden, shocking clarity that she even noticed the pizza guy lying still beneath her or the chunk of flesh heavy and wet in her mouth.

Her jaw—Elliot's jaw—was stiff and aching. For a moment, everything was silent. Nix's vision was half red-tinged from the blood spatter staining Elliot's right eye. She blinked it away.

Rachel and Danny stared from the base of the stairs. Quiet now. Afraid to come close. Danny vomited at the sight. Rachel turned ashen.

Nix swallowed, wiping her mouth. Elliot's insatiable hunger lately—it had been an annoyance, but she'd ignored it. It seemed impossibly naïve of her now. This was so far beyond the realm of normal hunger, she couldn't comprehend how she hadn't seen the signs. She stood.

Danny and Rachel skittered back. Danny grabbed a gun, vomit still clinging to his beard and an uncharacteristic tremor in his hand. Would they actually shoot Elliot? Danny knew it wouldn't touch Nix, only his adopted son—and to catastrophic results. Still, he didn't lower the weapon.

"Stay back, demon."

"What did you *do*?" Rachel shouted, shrill.

Nix looked down. Blood, bright and sticky, coated Elliot's naked chest, stained his jeans, covered his hands and arms. She could feel it on his neck and mouth. She lifted one hand and wiped it across his face.

"I…it wasn't me," Nix tried to explain, but even to her, the usual refrain sounded flat.

"The hell it wasn't. We saw you tearing up that boy! Eating him." Danny's aim faltered. He looked queasy. "Why?"

"I swear, it wasn't me, it was Elliot—Elliot's body." She realized distantly he was still asleep in their shared mind. "He was so hungry; I couldn't stop him. There's something wrong."

"Bullshit. Get out of him, now."

Nix looked around. "And go where?"

Danny's gaze fell to the corpse of the pizza boy.

Nix balked. "No way. He's not viable. I won't."

"Seen you in worse. Do it now. Get out."

Nix straightened. "No." Even if she could make the pizza boy work, the second she was out of one of the hunters, she lost all leverage. Danny would exorcise her without a doubt.

Rachel intervened with her hands out. "Now, hold on, let's talk about this."

"Talk?" Danny's eyes widened so far they risked falling out of his skull.

"The demon can share with me until we get this figured out. We don't have the whole story. We need to talk to Elliot."

"No way," Danny said. "Demon's too big a risk in you. It did this and you want to give it more power?"

"I can control it," Rachel said. "Like before."

"Done," Nix agreed, eager to get out of Elliot and be rid of whatever the hell was wrong with him. They might argue constantly, but one thing Nix could be certain of was that Danny would never let anything bad happen to Rachel. Nix would be safe in her body.

Danny shook his head again, handing Rachel his gun. She took it, her brow furrowed. He reached up and removed his anti-possession amulet.

Nix's flesh-laden stomach sank.

"I'm taking it," Danny said. "We can't risk it in you if we don't know what's happening."

Nix groaned. "Fine." Anything to get out of this insatiable cannibal furnace. Even if it meant bunking with this asshat.

Nix made the jump.

Chapter 13

Danny tried to flex his fingers. They remained still, under Nix's control. He struggled instinctively, then desperately, like prey thrashing in a snare. All to no avail.

Nix rolled her eyes and flexed his fingers for him. He calmed, settling slowly as he seemed to orient himself and remember what was happening.

"This is a worse hell than I could've imagined," Danny said within the confines of their shared mind.

Nix raised Danny's bushy eyebrow. *"For you and me both."*

"Is he okay?" Rachel's warm hand landed on Danny's cheek. Her green eyes stared into Danny's brown ones, watery and squinting. She looked younger through these eyes—a child. Softer around the edges. Nix's new chest swelled with a pulse of Danny's instinct: *protect her.* Rachel was shaking her head. "I'm not sure about this. Tell him we can switch if he wants. If it's too much. I can handle it." Her hand fell to Danny's anti-possession necklace, now around her own neck for safekeeping.

An image flashed through Danny's mind in front of Nix: Kevin Rousoe giving Danny this necklace. The dead-boyfriend memory left Danny's heart heavy, his chest tight.

"*Stop,*" Danny said. "*Stop looking at…at me. You've no right.*" He burned—anger, embarrassment, confusion. Nix pushed his emotions down.

"*Stop showing me, then,*" she told Danny. To Rachel, Nix said, "He hears you. He hates it, but I think it's okay for now."

Rachel knelt next to Elliot, who was collapsed on the floor next to the gnawed-on pizza boy. Elliot was still recovering from the shock of the transition, but Nix could see his gray eyes fluttering open already.

"*This is what it's like? Lookin' outta my own eyes, a monster workin' my arms and legs, my voice. Only a demon to talk with.*" Danny grunted in a manner Nix had come to identify as disgusted.

She pursed his lips, crossing Danny's thick arms over his broad chest. "*You're not such a great conversationalist yourself, pal.*" Swishing Danny's tongue around in his mouth, she added, "*Gross. I'm going to brush our teeth. Where's your toothbrush?*"

Danny scoffed. "*Don't you think that's the least of our problems, demon?*"

"*Yours, maybe. Not mine. I have to live in this slum.*" Nix cracked Danny's neck, stretching out the parts that pulled uncomfortably. He was the worst fit yet. She could have predicted that. "*You really don't take care of yourself, do you? You ran this thing hard and put it away wet, all right.*"

"*You're…complaining. About my body? You don't even have a body. You're a thief.*"

"*True on all counts, Danny-boy.*"

"*Don't call me that.*"

"*Usually my rentals are a higher quality, that's all. You know…no offense, or whatever,*" Nix added, because she was conquering the whole human social conventions thing.

"*Maybe it's better we don't talk,*" Danny said.

"*That's what they all say, at first.*"

Elliot groaned, sitting up with Rachel's help.

Immediately, Danny's tune changed. "*Hey, demon, move me over there.*"

"See? Short lived, the no-talking." Nix hadn't noticed when Rachel did it, but at some point during Nix's transition into Danny, Rachel had closed the cabin door to prying eyes—though out here, it was unlikely they'd see anyone for a while. The stack of mangled pizza boxes sat next to the door, too, but there would still be a mess on the steps, the guy's vehicle outside…and the body to deal with.

Nix stooped next to Elliot and Rachel in time to meet with Elliot's reaction to the corpse next to him.

"Holy shit!" He scrambled to the side, shuddering. "What happened? Who is this? Where are we?" He whipped his gaze around the room, blood-shot eyes wide. With the sun set, his eyes had a slight shine to them even in the incandescent lighting of the cabin.

Rachel smoothed Elliot's fair hair back, speaking slowly as she explained, "El, you ate him. Do you remember anything about that?"

"Ate him?" Elliot blanched. Nix expected him to barf, but he didn't. He held up his bloody hands, looking down at himself, then over at the mutilated body. His brow furrowed. "That's insane, Rach. I was asleep in the car and—wait, where's the demon?"

Rachel motioned to Danny. "Nix is in Pops until we can figure this out. We ordered pizza and left you and Nix down here to guard the trailer and wait for the pizza guy. Pops and I were having a conversation upstairs. You'd been really hungry the whole trip—"

"Yeah, I remember being hungry. But, I'm still hungry. Really hungry, actually. So I couldn't have eaten, right?"

Rachel's eyebrows rose. She looked to Nix. "No, you definitely ate."

"You can't seriously think I ate that guy?" He laughed, rubbing at his jaw. "I mean, it was the demon. It wasn't me. Why are you both looking at me like that?"

"Nix says she wasn't in control. She says your body took over. That there's something wrong with you. I'm not saying that's the case, okay? We need to figure this out." Rachel tilted her head toward the body. "And, well…we have to deal with this, too."

Elliot sat stock still, his hands in his lap, mouth red and partly open. Flesh was still lodged in his teeth. Everyone needed to brush their teeth at this point.

"Hey, El? How about you get cleaned up and I'll have a talk with Pops. We'll sort this out. There's a bathroom and your bag is over there."

He licked his lips but didn't move.

Rachel stood and waved Nix to follow around a corner. Nix didn't know how this was going to go, but so far Rachel still seemed to be on her side.

"My girl will see you for what you are," Danny said. *"Damned cannibal. Can't believe we bought into your bullshit this long. Can't trust a demon."*

Nix huffed. *"All right, hunter, let's get this straight. Your boy did this. Yes, I was in him, but it wasn't me behind the wheel. It was out of my control. There is something seriously wrong with him. Even I don't go around eating people."*

Danny's pointed silence was accusation enough. Elliot had been asleep in their shared mind when it happened, but Nix was almost certain she hadn't been the compelling force behind this little cannibalism incident. Ninety-nine percent. It had been a tough couple of months, but it wasn't as though she woke up this morning thinking *Damn, I could really eat a pizza guy today.* Maybe she was slipping. Then again, now she was in Danny, and she definitely didn't feel compelled to eat anyone—or anything, for that matter, possibly ever again. Nix rested a hand on Danny's stomach, realizing what a relief it was to not be hungry.

Rachel stared at her. "What am I supposed to think? You didn't tell us he was asleep. If it wasn't him, it was you. So, what the hell?"

"I swear, it wasn't me. But…it wasn't Elliot, either. It was his body. Only his body."

"That's the most absurd—"

"Hear me out." Nix raised Danny's hands like she was under arrest. "He's been so hungry, constantly, for weeks. I didn't think anything of it at first, but it wasn't normal. Now that I'm out of him and can finally think clearly without the haze of hunger pulling at me, I think I might know what's wrong."

Rachel crossed her arms. "What?"

Nix took a breath, knowing the theory she was about to share was risky—her head would still be firmly on the chopping block if she was right about it, but so would Rachel's and that had to be worth something. "His eyes."

Rachel sucked in a breath. "No. That can't be it. You said he'd be fine."

"We took a risk by putting ghoul eyes in him to replace the eyes he'd lost. Yes, the transplant was successful. But I think it's changing him in other ways. Making him…" Nix wasn't sure how to say it.

"A ghoul," Rachel said.

Nix shrugged. "Not quite. More like some kind of hybrid. Maybe something new altogether. Like the ghoul is merging with the human and mutating into something else. Ghouls are usually as cold as corpses and that's what they eat—rotted flesh. Elliot's burning up like a furnace all the time and, well…seems to like his meat fresh."

"This is speculation. You're basing this on nothing, throwing suspicion off yourself."

"If I'd wanted a human snack, I wouldn't have stuck around for the inquisition afterward."

Rachel hugged herself and shook her head. "I'll ask El if he's experienced any other symptoms. I don't know what's going on, but you're wrong about this."

They rounded the corner back into the main room. There, by the door, knelt Elliot. Elbow-deep in entrails, he shoveled handfuls of guts into his mouth. The pizza guy's dead hands swished against the crusty linoleum floor with every forceful movement. Elliot's animalistic gaze snapped to theirs.

"So hungry..." he said, panting around bites. "Can't stop."

Chapter 14

The verdict was in. Nix was back in Elliot's body—he couldn't be trusted to control himself. At least now Nix knew he needed controlling. Her short trek in Danny's skin left Danny quiet and shaken, though that could have been attributed to a lot of things given the situation. Danny, Rachel, and Nix-in-Elliot collapsed on the couches in the cabin after transferring, arguing, checking on Cirrik, and cleaning themselves up a bit. Nix ignored the body still by the door.

Rachel twisted her head to stare at it though. She huffed. "Shit. Someone will come looking for him here."

Danny handed her the boy's looted cellphone. "Text his boss. Tell him something about a family emergency. Buy us a few hours, at least."

Rachel fiddled with it. "It's locked." She looked at the body again. "Fuck this day." She knelt next to the dead guy, pressing his fingerprint to the phone until it unlocked. "Got it." Her fingers flew across the screen. "Done. The car probably has GPS though, have to ditch it fast." She sighed like a deflating balloon, crumpling in on herself with the effort. "We can't stay here."

Danny leaned forward, head in his hands. Sweat stained the back of his shirt. "What are we going to do with the body?"

Rachel tilted her head, staring at their big white cooler—mostly empty, thanks to Nix. "Well…"

Danny looked up at her. "I don't like your tone."

Rachel's gaze slid away. "It's just…he *is* already dead. We can't do anything about that now. But, Elliot—"

"Oh Jesus Christ," Danny said, "you're not suggesting we…*let* him finish eating the guy?"

"All I'm saying is there's nothing we can do for the man. We need to get rid of the body…and Elliot does need to eat. Plus, we have a cooler." Rachel, ever the pragmatist these days.

"There's no way in—"

"It's at least something we should consider. It did…calm him down a bit. Right?" She glanced at Nix.

Nix shrugged one shoulder in confirmation. Compared to earlier, the hunger was mild. Present, but faint. Something she could suppress with effort, but Elliot alone apparently couldn't manage his own hunger for long.

"If we drive around with a corpse," Danny said, "and we get pulled over—"

"Then what?" Rachel pursed her lips. "We're beyond screwed no matter what at this point. A corpse in the cooler would be like—"

"A cherry on the cake?" Nix offered.

Rachel glared. "Stop helping."

Danny leaned back against the couch. "Absolutely not."

Rachel did the same. "Well, what do you suggest?"

"We'll put him in his car, drive him out to the docks, and light it up. I'm not condoning eatin' corpses."

Wasteful, Nix considered with a sigh. Elliot's stomach growled. Rachel and Danny both turned to her with horrified expressions.

After a long moment, Danny leaned forward, resting his arms on his knees. He exhaled hard. "Get the tools from the van. We'll have to divide him up if we're going to fit him into that cooler."

Chapter 15

Hacking a human body into pieces takes forever. Nix was intimately familiar with this fact. There was a period in her non-life she'd indulged in the activity recreationally, like most young demons, but the sheer time-consumption became grueling. Hacking off a limb here and there was a blast. But tidy body disposal? Packaging? It wasn't worth the effort. Outsourcing was the way to get the job done right.

Nix took on the role of supervisor, due to her expertise and the excuse of needing to keep Elliot's hunger at bay. Elliot, due to his sensitive disposition, was whisked off to dreamland for the whole thing. Rachel and Danny took on the bulk of the work, as was appropriate to the station of mere humans.

Dawn crested by the time Danny returned from disposing of the guy's car in a nearby ravine. They were all ready to get back on the road, too nervous to stay in one place with pizza sauce and blood stains increasingly visible in the sunlight.

Looking up at the sky, Nix's chest tightened with the knowledge that night had passed them by. In her mind, they stood at the base of a mountain, the peak disappearing into the clouds. An impossible climb. Night three had been a wash, and now they were down to two days. In only two more nights, the Order would ascend and their window of opportunity would be closed forever.

After helping Danny load the heavy cooler back into the van since Nix's strength surpassed that of the meager humans, Danny turned to Nix. They were all loaded up and Rachel was checking on Cirrik. Danny dug something out of his pocket and handed it to Nix with a gruff, "Here." He motioned toward the cabin where the blood had stained the ancient linoleum at the front door and the guy's head and some less-edible body parts had been abandoned in the bathtub.

Nix looked down at the object in her hand: Danny's most-prized lighter. A peculiar warmth stirred in her chest, releasing the tightness there. She grinned, standing taller in Elliot's already towering frame. Maybe they wouldn't stop the Order in time. Maybe the world was doomed. But she had this moment right now, a lighter in her hand, and she would suck the remaining marrow out of existence before it ended.

Danny grunted dismissively. "Burn it to the foundation. We don't want anything left."

Was that...an apology? Nix scrutinized him and decided it was. He believed her now about Elliot, that much was clear. And this was an olive branch of permitted arson—given to Nix, no less, not even to Rachel. She'd never had such pleasant internal sensations toward the hunter before. Nix flicked the lighter on, admiring the flame.

The cabin—a rat trap of a building with asbestos peeking out of the cracking walls—sucked up the flame like a smoker trying to quit. Nix didn't even need accelerant. She could have given the place a heated glance and it would have combusted, yet she was still impressed at the speed and enthusiasm with which the flames devoured the small building.

It was all they could do to rip down the long gravel driveway connecting to the twisting lane from which the other cabins sprouted. They definitely lost the $25 safety deposit on the place, but considering it rented cheap hourly or nightly and they accepted cash without a card, it wasn't as if the owners would be surprised to find their cabins burned down with body parts inside every so often.

At the wheel, Rachel glanced into the rearview mirror at Danny's sleeping form across the backseat. His snoring rumbled through the van. She blinked long and slow. The car drifted into the center of the road until Rachel shook herself and corrected them. "Think I need to switch off. I'm going to get us in an accident."

Nix heard her but was playing with her new lighter in the passenger seat.

"You can drive, right? Since Elliot knows how?" Rachel turned toward her, swerved again, and refocused on the road.

"Huh?" Nix asked. "Wait, what? You're going to let me drive? Hey," she added as the excitement faded to offense, "I don't need Elliot's brain to drive. I can drive. I've been driving since cars were a thing, way before you were born or your parents were born or—"

"Shh," Rachel said, "you'll wake Pops. I'm going to pull over and we can switch. Keep straight on this road until the exit, then wake me. The pendulum said Violet and Blaine were here." She pointed at a spot marked on the map between them.

"I can drive literally any vehicle," Nix added. "Vehicles that don't even exist anymore. It would blow your tiny human mind, the extent of my driving capabilities."

"Oh my god, I get it. Shush." Rachel pulled over at the side of the road, muttering about Nix having just the other day run a guy down in a standard transmission. "Do not exceed the speed limit or break any laws. I'm serious. If we get pulled over by the cops—"

"Yeah, yeah, I get it." They got out of the van and Nix jogged to the driver's side. The scent of sage brush swept over them as a gust of desert wind scattered sand across the asphalt. Climbing in, Nix flexed her hands on the steering wheel. It had been a while. The hunters—well, Danny—had a strict policy about demons not being allowed to have any fun whatsoever.

That was part of the deal for working together. Best behavior. It was excruciating, but if it got her closer to the Order, to revenge, it would be worth it.

Rachel got in the passenger's seat. Danny didn't wake and Rachel was asleep as soon as the road evened out under them. The quiet added to the gnawing in Nix's host stomach. She glanced half at the road and half into Elliot's dreams—BBQ cannibal massacre, what a shocker. She prodded Elliot awake, leaned into his wave of relief at seeing the open road laid out before them as opposed to the blood and guts he'd been immersed in. Waking from a dream—she missed the sensation sometimes, but she liked it in her hosts.

"*Shake it off,*" she said. "*We're on the open road again—bet you missed this. Boring as shit.*"

"*It was a dream?*" Elliot asked, bleary.

"*Well. Not all of it. Massacring a bunch of suits at a corporate picnic and gnawing on the corpses with some BBQ sauce, that was a dream—interesting choice of venue, by the way. Specific. Something very Freudian in there somewhere, I suspect. But killing and eating that guy last night...twice...that was real.*"

Elliot's guts twisted.

"*Hey,*" Nix said, squinting into the warm sun, "*don't feel bad about it. Shit happens.*"

A flush of red colored Elliot's arms where they were perched on the wheel. "*It doesn't just happen. It was your fault.*"

Nix pulled down the visor. "*It wasn't—*"

"*These eyes, the ones you helped Rachel put in me, they're the reason this is happening. The reason I'm...changing.*"

She dug around for sunglasses in the door and slid them on, too. She had to admit, his eyes were inordinately sensitive and had remarkable qualities—induced cannibalism might be a side-effect he had to live with. "*Oh. Well, yeah, I guess that's true. But that's as much on Rachel as it is me.*"

"*Both of you did this to me.*"

Nix couldn't help the astonishment in her tone. *"You're seriously mad at her? Not that I'm defending her or anything, but she was only trying to help you get your sight back. You were pretty pathetic, stumbling around blind before. Wasn't long ago you were thanking her for restoring your vision."*

"I was wrong. What she did, what you both did—you made a decision for me and you had no right. Of course I wanted to see, but I never wanted this. You turned me into a monster. Like you."

Nix snickered. *"You're a ray of sunshine. Starting to regret waking you up, doll."*

"It was magic that did this to me, right? So you can undo it." Ah, there it was: bargaining.

Nix considered this. *"It was my suggestion, my knowledge, but it was Rachel's magic that made it happen. I was honestly shocked she even pulled it off. And considering how shaky her powers are in general, I can't imagine she would be able to simply un-pull-it-off."*

Elliot's muscles tensed. *"There has to be a way."*

Nix consciously released them, stretching. *"You say that like I know everything about everything—which, thank you. Compliment accepted. But I'm telling you, I've never seen something like this happen before. Or I guess it would be more accurate to say I've never stuck around long enough to see results like this. Usually, a part falls off, you slaughter a ghoul or whatever else is available, get your replacement parts, and patch back up. You move on, no muss, no fuss. I've never had any issues. Mostly."*

"Mostly?"

"I mean, sometimes you'd get a rejection of the transplant and the host would go all blargh"—she imitated the death throes for him— *"and croak. But generally, it would do the job."*

"Why didn't you do it then? Why Rachel?"

She glanced at Danny sleeping in the back, then at Rachel still fast asleep in the passenger seat. Nix hadn't run them off the road, actively tried to kill them all, or even broken the speed limit by more than ten miles. If anyone had told her she'd end up playing this well with others a few months ago, let alone with these hunters, she'd have called them worse names than fools.

"Why would I help more than I needed to? I was already going out of my way. You were her problem, not mine. Plus, I wanted to see what she could do, and she did it. It was impressive."

"So it was her magic that messed it up?"

Nix shrugged. *"I don't know. Could be. Or it could be something about you."*

Elliot stiffened at that answer. The boy had always believed there was something fundamentally wrong with him. He'd never brought it up with Danny or Rachel, but Nix could see the open wound in his psyche, the way it oozed and festered. It was why he worked so hard to please, why he was such a pushover despite his drive for perfection, why he was so desperate for love and belonging no matter where it came from.

Something about neglectful parents—a father Elliot had never known, a mother who never wanted him. She'd abandon him with relatives and friends for days that became weeks that became months. Finally, he'd ended up with Danny, who wasn't around much himself, and he never saw the woman again. She'd called him once as a teen, asking for cash. News had reached him a few years ago that she overdosed. Sometimes, he would fall asleep by tracing events in his life back to his own failings, to how there was something bad or broken in him that even his mother could see and could never stand. Nix watched the wound pulsate between them.

Elliot asked, *"Can't you fix it?"*

Nix stared at the road rushing beneath them. She didn't think she could fix anything, but somehow she couldn't say it.

Chapter 16

Rachel woke when Nix parked the van in front of an industrial building on the waterfront of San Clemente. Avoiding metropolises and cops had made the trip longer than Nix thought was necessary, though they'd made better time than Danny predicted. Nix leaned back in her seat and stared out the window.

Rachel looked around, hair sticking up and a big red crease across her cheek where she'd been leaning against the door. Elliot would normally offer some inane comment about how adorable this was, but he was silent now. Silent and brooding.

Rachel smoothed her dark locks down and wiped drool from the corner of her mouth. "Where are we? This isn't the freeway exit. You didn't wake me." She frowned.

"We're here." Nix handed her the map. "Where your pendulum pointed you. Well, a block away. In case that archdemon is still around, so it won't see us coming. But it could sense us anyway. It probably already knows we're here. Waiting for us. In there. If it's there at all." With a deep breath, she wiped Elliot's hands against his jeans, leaving damp trails on the denim.

Rachel gave her a look. "Okay, chill. Everything is fine. You're freaking *me* out. Not like this is our first archdemon."

Nix choked on air. She started to ask *Are you kidding me?* but couldn't get the words out. Rachel patted her on the back. Danny continued to snore. Apparently Rachel thought surviving the lunatic archdemon Val back in Yosemite was a point in their favor, not blind luck.

There was no telling how dangerous this new archdemon would be. When they'd come across it in Winterspoon's farmhouse, it had been formidable even when locked up in an enchanted box and bound to the bones of a dead hunter. Nix had a history with archdemons much longer than these hunters did, and none of her experiences had ever ended well.

This Winterspoon archdemon had messed with their perception of reality, tricked them into releasing it, then disappeared with two of their crew. She couldn't have asked for a more harmless experience than that, even though Violet and Blaine were probably dead. Hardly her problem. She'd just rather keep her distance. It was bad enough they were planning on hunting down an Order of archdemons, but a side-quest to rescue a paranormal investigator and his psychic niece from yet another archdemon while the clock was ticking? Frivolous.

"You should have woken me," Rachel was saying. "Quick, switch me spots before Pops wakes up." Nix complied soundlessly and found herself again in the passenger seat. Rachel was all business as she got sorted and started checking weapons. "Pops?" She reached back to nudge him. "We're here."

He grumbled himself to alertness, glaring at Nix like she was the one who woke him. "Huh? How?" He checked his watch. "Should have taken longer." Frowning, he turned his hard glare to Rachel, now in the driver's seat. "I told you: sideroads, no speeding."

Rachel flushed, not looking at Nix. "Sorry, Pops."

"Well," he said, "we're here now. Weapons ready?"

Nix broke her silence. "Guns? Against an archdemon? We're screwed."

"I thought you were staying in the car," Danny said. "What's it to you?"

Nix straightened in her seat. "If it kills you for being stupid, I'm down a whole strike team." *Strike team?* Elliot's brain-leaks were starting to annoy her. Was it hot in here or was it her host? Nix rolled down her window, sucking in the warm air of late May.

"And you're on your own," Rachel said what Nix hadn't. "You'd better come with us. Keep us foolish humans from getting ourselves killed."

Damn. Were they right? Nix knew there was no dissuading them from trying to rescue their friends—she'd been trying for the past two weeks. At least if they confirmed once and for all that Blaine and Violet were dead, they could all move on and go about the real business of tracking the Order, finding a way to bring them down before the full moon. Knowing these hunters, they'd definitely die in there, leaving Nix with a ravenous ghoul-mutant Elliot and Cirrik trussed up in the trailer hitched to the van. Options were lacking.

Danny shoved a gun into the front seat, presumably so she could see it, but she felt the presence of it first. The air around it was heavy and electric—blessed. It nibbled, like invisible ants picking at her skin. Exactly what she needed in this heat.

"This was Kevin's gun," he said, giving her a dirty look. "Some monks forged it in a monastery centuries ago. The bullets are regular but treated with holy oil. Won't exorcise your special big bad demon, but a little nobody-demon like you it would. Kick you out, at least."

Nix swallowed, returning Danny's glare. She was well aware of how this gun worked. "Why bring it, then?"

"It'll hurt the bastard like a thousand stinging bees is why. Give us time to bind it, blind it, or sneak up behind it so as we can perform our real exorcism. End the demon once and for all."

"I don't want to get caught up in that. And if Blaine isn't dead, a few bullets will kill him for sure if the exorcism doesn't."

Danny tucked the gun away. "We're here to rescue Violet. We'll do what we can for Blaine, but if it comes to it, that's what he'd want."

Nix scoffed. "You've got a twisted sense of morality, hunter. You won't exorcise Cirrik because of his poor host, but you'll waste your own friend?"

"He ain't my friend. And your boyfriend is possessing an innocent man."

"He's not my boyfriend."

"Would you both stop!" Rachel's voice echoed through the van. Danny retreated into the backseat. "No one is getting exorcised; no one is dying today. We'll be careful. This isn't a guns-blazing operation. It's recon. Looking around to see what we see, then we back off and decide what to do. You in?"

Nix nodded. "What about Cirrik?"

Danny opened the sliding back door, his heavy boots hitting the concrete. "He's not going anywhere. That trailer is Alcatraz. Physically and supernaturally. Better than we could manage in the attic."

"What if someone steals the van?" Nix countered.

It was Rachel who rolled her eyes. "What a great loss that'd be. We'll lock it and hope for the best. Or you stay here and babysit, I don't care. We need to move, so make a decision."

Nix raised her hands. "Fine, fine. I'll come."

"We won't be long." Rachel wound up the windows and they exited the vehicle to stand on the deserted road, locking the vehicle as promised behind them.

The pavement was hot. Nix could feel it through the soles of Elliot's thick boots. It didn't help that Elliot was already burning up internally. Nix thought about grabbing some pre-packaged pizza guy from the cooler, but she wasn't about to bring it up. Elliot wasn't so hungry that she couldn't manage it.

No other cars passed by along the waterway. No movement could be seen from any of the tall gray buildings. Nix had expected smokestacks filling the air with smog, but although the stacks were blackened and stained with decades of soot, it had been a long time since they'd seen any activity. Atop one, a bird nested. The only inhabitants here seemed to be cooing pigeons—though Nix suspected there'd be rats and other nasties once they started looking inside.

The group walked in a careful line close to the side of the nearest building, toward the spot marked on the map. Rachel had been able to narrow the location considerably when the pendulum proved both powerful and exact. She'd used Violet's robe to try and find her, and when the pendulum responded with a clear location, Rachel grabbed a map of the area it specified, then another, then another, until they narrowed their search down to a building—here. Skeptical of the pendulum after having tried others like it and many spells over the past weeks, all to no avail, Rachel tried to test it other ways.

Using Danny's necklace as a grounding object, she asked the pendulum where they were. Disturbingly, despite the supernatural protection on Blaine's property keeping them safe during their stay, it pointed directly at their location. It seemed nothing was hidden from the prying eye of the crystal. Danny found this upsetting, knowing something like this existed, something that could so easily reveal them and compromise their security. It certainly explained why the pendulum was hidden away, Blaine being so security conscious. Rachel decided this meant Blaine and Violet were alive.

Nix was less hopeful. But if it proved its usefulness on their excursion today, it could be used to find the Order. If it really could bust through supernatural veils and they could find a grounding object from the Order, they might have a real shot at locating them. Of course, this line of thought always led Nix straight into the dead end of *and then what?*

Stepping over windswept garbage and broken glass from shattered overhead windows, the group made its way to the front of a faded red-brick building. The only spot of color in the sea of gray. This was it. No one needed to say it. Danny flagged them to follow with one hand, hunching over as he moved with his blessed gun leading the way.

"No security checking these buildings?" Elliot thought. Nix didn't see any either, though she wondered how the hunters would deal with it.

Rachel adjusted the strap of the backpack on her shoulder—most of its contents, Nix could only guess at, but likely their usual anti-demon paraphernalia which always made Nix feel a little embarrassed these days. A set of bolt cutters peeked out from the top though, a bit too large to zip over.

Danny stepped toward the alcove of the door, waving Rachel to him. She reached around to her bag, her hands landing on the bolt cutters. Danny held out a hand to stop her and she stilled. His flashlight lit up the small, darkened space tucked away from the sunlight heating up the road. The chains they'd expected were absent. Rachel lowered her arms and shrugged.

It was Nix's turn. Did she happen to have a lockpick set on Elliot's person? In fact, she did. Not that she needed it—she could wrench the door apart with her bare hands or simply use what was available to pick it—but they were tools of refinement and Nix took great pleasure in that.

Nix was reaching into one of Elliot's many pockets to extract her set when Danny placed his fingers on the door handle and opened it. The disappointment was crushing. Nix slid the lockpick set back in place. Danny grinned like a dream-killer and slipped inside. Rachel followed. Nix took one last look at the empty road. Her lockpicks wouldn't get her out of this, she knew. Rachel's head poked back out and she mouthed, *Let's go.* Nix turned away from the road and followed her hunters into the unknown.

Chapter 17

There was nothing here. They were wrong. The pendulum was garbage. Nix wasn't sure if she was relieved by the dusty, silent halls, or disappointed.

Elliot was getting hungry again, and though Nix repressed the sensation, she couldn't help the pang of anxiety accompanying it. Nor could she help noticing the way Danny's and Rachel's strong muscles clenched and shifted beneath their clothes as they moved. What would it feel like to sink her teeth into all those tight muscles? She shook off the imagery and kept walking, wishing and not wishing she'd grabbed a snack from the cooler before they entered.

Danny led them down winding corridors. Sunlight streamed in from a few of the tall windows far above them, but others were boarded up, leaving their path dappled in light and dark. The occasional rat skittered past, as surprised as they were by the unexpected encounter.

The floor was caked in grime. Occasional whiffs of putrid air rose up, riding on a draft blowing through the building.

"Still no security here," Elliot said.

"So? Who'd waste money securing a place like this?"

"Something's wrong. A few broken windows. Most of the glass was outside, meaning something on the inside broke it. No graffiti in here at all. Building's been empty probably twenty years, so that should be

impossible. No homeless or addicts hanging out here or anywhere on the street. It may not be clean or operational, but someone was keeping people from defacing the place. There should be security here."

"Maybe they only come at night," Nix said.

"Maybe," Elliot said. Then, *"No. This isn't right. That smell is... Christ, I'm hungry. We should leave."*

"Do you hear that?" Danny kept asking.

"I don't know what you're hearing, Pops," Rachel said. Her tone flattened more every time Danny brought it up.

"A little further ahead. We're getting close."

Rachel shot Nix a look that said Danny was grasping at straws.

"Elliot wants to leave," Nix relayed, ready to get out of here herself.

"A little further," Danny said.

They passed through another set of doors and came to a large room at the center of the building, designed like a conservatory. Sunlight streamed in through the tempered-glass roof. The putrid smell that had been teasing them before emerged in full force.

Nix reared back. "Wow. Shitty housekeeping."

Rachel put a hand over her nose. "Probably some of those rats we keep seeing."

No one mentioned the possibility of finding Blaine's and Violet's bodies now, though it was smelling likely.

Chairs and tables were stacked in one far corner. Below them, black-and-white checkered linoleum cracked with their steps. A faint scent of smoke hung on the air, lingering above the sweet rot. Nix couldn't see anything obviously deceased, but black flies hummed in the windows high above them. Maybe a dead pigeon or twenty.

Nix shrugged. "There's nothing here."

"Can't you hear it?" Danny said.

Rachel huffed. "Hear *what?*"

"Music," Danny finally admitted. He holstered his gun. Quieter, he said, "It sounds like...like a music box."

Nix's eyes widened. "Are you kidding? You couldn't have said that earlier?"

Danny swayed. "It's beautiful."

"Music?" Elliot echoed in their mind. His palms pricked with sweat.

"Pops?" Rachel shook his shoulder.

A rat skittered to a stop at Nix's feet. She glanced down at it. Instead of fur, its fat rat body shimmered with black scales. A forked tongue slithered from between fangs. "Shit!" Nix jumped back. "Nope. I'm out."

Rachel raced toward her as Nix's hand landed on the door they'd entered through. Nix jerked the handle. Locked. Of course.

Mind whirring, Nix reached for her lockpick kit, but it slipped from her hand, clattering to the floor and scattering on the filthy snake-rat-infested linoleum.

"Stop," Rachel said. "Where are you going?"

"Didn't you see the rat?"

"A rat? There's nothing here."

Nix bent to retrieve the picks, but her hands were shaking for some reason and Rachel was grabbing at her. "It had scales, and a tiny, forked tongue—shit!"

"Okay, okay, calm down."

Nix abandoned the picks—what the hell was she thinking, bothering with lockpicking when she could bust the door down? She slammed Elliot's body against the door even as he complained. It shuddered but it didn't open.

"Don't tell me to calm down, it's in here—the archdemon, it's here." Nix pulled at the handle until the metal twisted but the door wouldn't budge.

A pretty melody spilled into the room, like something Nix remembered hearing with Callie at the carnival.

Nix stilled. Each note punctured her skin, slithering up her spine until she shivered at the intimate touch. Rachel spun around at the sound, gasping.

"Violet?" Rachel said.

Nix turned slowly away from the door. It was too late to escape.

Violet stood next to Danny, holding his hand. She looked up at him, her lean five-foot frame much smaller next to Danny's six feet. She was still dressed as Nix had last seen her, in checkerboard Vans, a punk-rocker jacket, and acid-washed jeans. Her short purple hair hung prettily in front of her eyes. Danny stood very still.

"Violet, thank god—" Rachel moved toward her but Nix's hand shot out, gripping her arm hard, jerking her back.

The room breathed around them—soft melody on the inhale, a light draft of buzzing flies on the exhale. Violet looked at them, eyes dark voids. Rachel backed up, stepping into Nix.

"My friends," she said, smile reaching wide. "You came for tea."

Chapter 18

Fingers intertwined with Danny's, Violet's grip tightened until he grunted and cringed. Nix heard a crunch.

Forget this. This was not recon. Nix would run for it—she'd bust the door handle right off.

"You can't abandon them," Elliot complained in her head. *"Don't be such a coward, for once!"*

Nix backed up, but Violet's eyes snapped to hers. "Leaving? You've barely arrived."

She glanced to the door. It was gone. Ice ran through Elliot's burning-hot body. Nix gulped.

Violet led Danny toward the center of the room. He seemed trapped in the daze of the music, but Nix knew he was trapped regardless. He shuffled beside her, his free hand hanging limp by his side, inches away from his holstered gun.

Rachel dropped her own hands to her sides, and Nix saw the question there: regular gun in one holster, machete in the other. If she were successful, she'd only end up killing Violet's body in the process—the person she'd come here to rescue—and probably get Danny killed, too. If she failed, they'd all be killed—maybe Violet, too, maybe not. A shoot-out held a lot of risk and little hope of reward. Seeming to reach the same conclusion as Nix, Rachel's hands relaxed and she moved forward to follow them with measured steps across the room, a straight back, and her head held high.

"Brave as hell," Elliot said. *"You could stand to learn something."*

Nix ground Elliot's teeth together until a spike of pain shot through his jaw. *"Fuck. Off."*

Nix stood still. She could see no way out of this. Her instinct was to jump ship. It occurred to her in a flash that she still could—leaving Elliot behind, leaving all of them, rolling the dice and hoping there was someone nearby she could jump to and borrow their body. Also risky, considering the area, but a possibility if she needed it.

Then there was the chance Elliot would lose control again without Nix in the driver's seat and massacre everyone here, including the other hunters. Not that it would matter, since the archdemon would massacre them all anyway. But she would escape.

Maybe Elliot and Cirrik were right—she was a coward.

Violet snapped her fingers and Nix startled to attention. The girl was looking across the room. "Minion, chairs for our guests."

A movement stirred from the far end of the room— something that hadn't been there before. Nix heard Rachel's intake of breath before she saw him.

Blaine sat hunched over in the corner with his long arms hanging over his knees. It was the first time Nix had ever seen the paranormal investigator so quiet and still. He looked ten years older than she'd seen him only weeks ago, closer to forty-five now, with some gray peppering his black hair. His navy dress shirt and tan slacks were as ragged as Cirrik's and he had a blank, far-off look in his hazel eyes. Nix never expected to see him alive, assuming the archdemon would jump to some other body as soon as it had the chance and kill Blaine for kicks or use him up.

It made sense that it took Blaine at first—it needed a ride out of its cage and Blaine had opened its box. Blaine was convenient and its first tie to freedom. But once it was free, it wanted something better, more powerful. Why drive a Pinto when there was a Mercedes on offer? So it grabbed sixteen-year-old Violet for her psychic abilities. Yet it kept Blaine around after the switch to Violet—why?

Blaine's gaze flicked over to Violet and he rose, head down as he shuffled toward a table in the corner. Dragging a set of wooden chairs over with a prolonged screech, he watched Violet, his eyes narrowed, lip curled in a muted snarl.

Violet smirked. Nix caught the flash of a forked tongue as she licked her lips.

"Why'd you take her?" Rachel was the only one daring enough to ask.

The archdemon ran a hand down its petite feminine form and smiled. "Minion was annoying. Mentally narrating his thoughts." She tsked. "Considered dining on a bullet to make him stop. However, he posed the argument that nobility, such as myself, is to be served. So Minion lives. For now. This one is…a curiosity." It tilted Violet's head to the side, eyes losing focus as though listening intently to the faded music around them. "High voltage." Her gaze snapped to Nix's. "Hungry, are you?"

Rachel threw her a glance but didn't say anything.

Staring at Nix, the archdemon communicated telepathically between only them as Violet had been able to before, *"You changed your mind about your child host. Not so eager to bind yourself to a human?"* Its voice echoed in her skull and clung like sap to the fissures of Elliot's brain.

"It's complicated," Nix confirmed aloud, shifting from foot to foot.

"What the hell?" Elliot said. *"How is it in our head—your head? My head? What is this?"* He stirred inside of himself, itchy and unsteady.

"Stop," Nix cautioned him. *"It's using Violet's telepathy. Calm down."*

Elliot couldn't calm down. He scratched at the boundaries of his mind as if Violet's presence there were acidic. *"As in, it can read my thoughts? It knows everything I'm thinking?"*

"So do I, and you aren't freaking out about that. You're embarrassing me."

Violet giggled. Rachel was staring between them now, her brow furrowed. Nix could feel the heat rising in Elliot's cheeks and chest.

"Oh god," Elliot said, spinning out, *"it does. It knows about me and Rachel? What I did to that man last night? Does it know everything I've ever done—oh shit, it knows my fantasies, doesn't it?"*

"Puppet, you're digging your own grave here. I know your thoughts and fantasies; it's not a big deal. Pull yourself together." Nix made eye contact with Violet and added, "He's a mess, ignore him."

A whirl of images flashed through Nix's mind unbidden, like a malfunctioning television: pictures of training and war, hunting, betrayals, guilt, misbehavior from the most minor infractions to jail worthy, followed by a cascade of masturbatory fantasies, each more perverse than the last.

"For Lucifer's sake, will you get a hold of yourself?" Nix muttered aloud. She did not have time for him freaking out right now. *"I swear I'll put you in timeout."*

Elliot whined internally, but the images started to slow down and he went silent inside of himself. Nix breathed a sigh of relief.

Thankfully, Violet turned her attention away, still chuckling. To Rachel, Violet said, "You once came to me with a wish to resurrect those you'd lost. Yet, the dead do not roam the streets, I notice. Pity. Was looking forward to that."

Rachel flushed, glancing at Danny then quickly to her shoes. Stammering, she said, "I-I didn't want, I mean, I thought—I wasn't really going to."

Violet sighed. "No need to defend. No one follows through. Always think they want their wishes, but they do not. I know this. Better than any."

Lacking a better option or a door to exit, Nix figured there was strength in numbers and eased closer to Rachel. She wasn't sure if the archdemon planned to kill them or wine and dine them, but all she could think to do was play this out.

Another chair screeched across the floor and Violet's hand lifted to her temple. As the chair arrived at Nix's side with one final shriek, Violet shouted, "Enough!" With a flick of Violet's wrist, Blaine flew across the room, smacking hard into the far wall and sliding down.

He hacked and coughed, dragging himself up.

Nix and Rachel tensed.

"Your damsel is more...*distressing* than distressed," Nix whispered to Rachel.

Violet took a deep breath, then smiled a little wider this time. She led Danny to a chair and released his hand. He plopped down into it, shaking his head as if clearing it, then clutched his freed hand to his chest. Rachel moved to his side as he looked up at her with wide eyes.

"Please, sit. Drink. Eat." Violet waved her hand at the empty space before them. "The tea is getting cold."

Nix, quietly, spun her chair around and straddled it. Rachel stood there gawking at the empty space of the warehouse, standing between her own chair and Danny.

"Tea?" Rachel ventured with the delicacy of someone talking to a self-proclaimed time traveler waving a gun around like a magic wand.

Violet stared at her blankly for a moment before breaking out into a laugh. "Oh! Silly me." She snapped her fingers again, and Nix fell right off her chair as the whole world shifted. Elliot's insides sloshed, a pool of swirling half-chewed meat. Pulling herself up, Nix whacked her head on a table that hadn't been there a moment before.

Crawling forward, she dragged Elliot's body clear, stood, and righted the fallen chair to plant herself back in it before she fell over from the vertigo. Next to her, Danny and Rachel were staring around them at a grand ballroom surrounded by a garden that seemed to stretch on forever.

The long table was laden with rich treats, from charcuterie boards and sandwich trays to piles of sweets and cakes. And of course, steaming cups of tea. Nix was fairly certain it wasn't real, but the smell was divine and—shit, the saliva thing again. Nix swiped Elliot's chin with his sleeve, already reaching for the charcuterie board. Rachel slapped her hand away.

"Th-thank you," Rachel said, "but we can't stay. We...um..."

"No time for tea?" Violet's smile disappeared. Only now did Nix notice how pale she was, or the patch of dry skin on her neck that seemed to be flaking away with a peculiar shimmer beneath. "The food does not impress?" She drew out her s's like she was savoring the taste of the consonant on her tongue. "Visitors are a delicious rarity at our table. The last was terribly rude. You wouldn't be rude, would you?"

Blaine came up behind them, limping, and pulled out the chair for Rachel. She stared at him for a long moment, then sat.

Violet lit up, clapping her hands with delight. Her purple hair bounced. Blaine silently retrieved a chair for her.

"Blissss!" Sitting across from them, she clinked a small spoon against a teacup until Blaine came around and filled it. Sipping contentedly, Violet stretched the fingers of her free hand out on the table, drawing patterns.

Nix reached for a treat again even though Rachel pinned her with a look. Nix skewered what looked like a fancier version of a bacon-wrapped scallop using a three-pronged fork and brought it to her lips. She ate it in a single bite, the flavor washing over her taste buds and down her throat in a savory rush.

More, Nix thought. Yet something restrained her from grabbing the whole tray. She stared at the chunks of meat. Violet sipped her tea.

When finished, she swished the remaining drops of water around the teacup and peered inside.

"Hmm. Yes," Violet muttered into the teacup. "I see. Oh, I *see*. Curious." She looked up at her guests. "The tea leaves say you're here to take something from me. They think you've come to retrieve your friends. But they're my friends now. Where would that leave me? Alone again, with the bones again, alone in the bones on my own again," she sing-songed. "But that's impossible! Can't go back there—the bones are all burned up. Where to go? You'd have to kill me somehow. Wouldn't be very fair, would it? Don't think you'd do that. Think the leaves are liars. What do you think?" She looked to Danny.

Standing his ground after shaking off his daze, Danny said, "We don't want any trouble with you, but we do need our friends back. They need to come home."

A chill swept through the room, rattling the teacups. The low hum of music stopped and only the buzzing flies overhead remained.

"I was wrong to call you liars," she told her leaves. "Wasn't a nice thing to say, and I apologize." Fingers trembling, she set the cup in its apple-blossom saucer, staring down at the table with a blank expression. "Home, you say."

The room was quiet for so long that eventually Rachel said, "Yes. Violet's mother, she really misses her."

Violet's head titled, and she met Rachel's eyes. "Mother? Always wanted a mother." Her hands fidgeted with the tablecloth. "They made fun of me." She caught Nix's eyes. "Like they made fun of you. I understand. But always wanted one. And a home. And a puppy." She smiled broad and toothy. "Would you like to meet my puppy?" Mouth dropping to a snarl, Violet turned to Blaine and said, "Minion, get me my puppy."

Blaine stilled. He shook his head pleadingly.

To them, Violet explained, "He won't bite. Sometimes…he might…but probably, he won't." Violet waved Blaine away.

Blaine's head lowered and he left the table, wandering into the verdant garden until Nix couldn't see him anymore.

Tall red and orange flowers towered ten feet over them with fuzzy stalks thicker than tree trunks. Nix couldn't see the walls of the warehouse past the thick green foliage of bizarre plants. Lower to the ground, where the checkered linoleum disappeared beneath their leaves, were golden and black flowers with a beautiful sheen that seemed to flicker in a nonexistent wind. Staring at them, it took Nix a minute to realize the thin pistils stretching out from the center of each flower were in fact twitching antennae. The petal of one flower took flight, clicking its glossy cockroach wings as it coasted over their table. The remaining petals sorted themselves, skittering back into place.

Voice smaller than she meant it to be, Nix asked, "Is that why you helped me? At the farm, telling me how to stay with Callie. Because you understood?"

"Yes. Most creatures have a nesting instinct. For us, maybe this is not so natural. But to desire what we do not have, what is more natural than that? Maybe not all are meant to nest. But every creature *wants*. We are all insatiable, in our own way. Nature is our compulsion, but it need not be our restriction."

Nix shook her head. "I don't understand."

"You limit yourself to what you are. As a granter of wishes and a wisher, I know this: we can have both. What we are and what we could be. Limitations are for the lesser."

Nix leaned into the chair. Was this a riddle? Or was she not following? This archdemon struck her as simultaneously childish and ancient, naïve and wise, terrifyingly dangerous and potentially safe. They were definitely going to die here, probably with their spines ripped out through their throats.

Might as well die with a full stomach. Nix reached for another meat wrap and took a bite, chewing. A drop of rain fell to the table in front of Nix. On the white cloth, a grayish-red drip marred the surface. Her eyes lifted to the warehouse roof, obscured by vines and massive flowers. Far above, strung up in vines clinging to the rafters, a masticated skeleton hung.

Rachel gasped beside her.

Danny said, "What the hell is that?"

"Our last visitor," Violet said. "Very rude. Wouldn't stay for tea."

"I-impossible. It's a skeleton. You've been here two weeks, at most."

The tattered remnants of a black uniform dangled from the body, along with clinging bits of flesh around the joints. Explained where the security guard disappeared to. The bones looked scraped—chewed on. Rats, most likely.

Reading Nix's thoughts, Violet said aloud, "Oh, it wasn't all rats."

Something squirmed against Nix's tongue and she realized she was still chewing. Spitting discreetly into a napkin, Nix glanced down. Maggots writhed inside the meat, tiny white bodies bitten in half and still moving.

Bile rose in her throat. Nix folded her napkin, placed it on the table, and drank the tea in her cup in a single gulp. Bitter. She swallowed, still feeling the squirming in her mouth, throat, stomach.

Violet smiled. "You like your tea?"

"Mmhmm." The delicious smell of the meat from earlier turned foul with the illusion broken. Suddenly the fresh pizza guy didn't seem so bad. Nix hated to admit it, but Elliot's hunger had lessened, too. She wondered if the hunters would freak out about the dead guy, but they both sat very still. The second dead guy they'd seen Nix put in her mouth in 24 hours, maybe it was getting to be old hat for them now. Might have to stay that way—Nix couldn't see a way to fix it any time soon.

"You wish to fix the hunger?" Violet said.

Nix glanced up at her and flushed, embarrassed at having forgotten for a moment her thoughts were still on display. "I, um—"

Rachel jumped in, asking, "Wait, is that possible? Do you know how?"

"Now's not exactly the time for this conversation, darlin'," Danny whispered.

Violet clucked her forked tongue, shaking her head as she looked Nix up and down. "Young demons. Lack of wisdom." From the body of a sixteen-year-old psychic, she advised, "Perhaps if you were more experienced, it would have been avoided in the first place."

Nix bristled. "Eating people is getting to be an inconvenience." She wiped at her mouth. "I admit that. You, uh, know how to fix it?"

"Yes. And no. The body is out of balance. Two eyes of the Other is one too many." Violet lifted a fork from the table and twirled it between two fingers. "To control the hunger, pluck one out." She made a stabbing motion with the fork to demonstrate, causing all three of them to lean away. "The hunger will remain, of course, and must be sated as all hungers must be sated eventually. But the balance of power will be corrected. No longer would the hunger dominate the body; the body would cage the hunger."

Rachel piped up, saying, "We don't want him to have to eat people at all, or be…hungry. Can't we fix the problem completely?"

"Yes. And no," Violet repeated. "Pluck both eyes." She stabbed the air twice with her fork. "Remove the contaminant. Yes, maybe this works. And no, maybe this does not. The Other has merged with the Whole. Passage of time binds. Hunger may be curbed, yet persist, even without the eyes. There is always a cost to blood magic such as this."

She looked long and hard at Rachel. Rachel shrunk back.

Elliot was silent. His eyes itched. Nix rubbed at them.

Danny straightened, his forehead wrinkles creasing. "Back to the matter at hand. Maybe we could all reach some sort of arrangement."

"You *want* your friends," Violet said.

He glanced at the skeleton, then at his hands. "Yes."

Violet set her teacup down. "You see, always the wanting. I invite you for tea. I share information freely, helping you fix your problems." She gestured at Nix. "Asking nothing in return. What about what I want? No one ever asks what I want," she said, her voice rising.

Danny shrank back. "Well—"

"Always wishing, always wanting, always demanding—what about my needs?"

"I—"

"What of my wishes?" she shouted, slamming one hand on the table. One of the large teapots shattered, hot tea spilling across the white cloth. "Why—"

Violet jerked forward, coughing and interrupting herself. She swallowed hard.

No one dared move.

"Why..." she continued, but stilled again to swallow, the swallow turning to a choke. She coughed, then hacked. Pushing her chair back, Violet stood, bracing herself against the table and coughing violently.

A bulge pushed up the fine column of her throat and with one final heave she spat up on the table. A dead dormouse, curled up in a ball of saliva, huddled in the middle of a tray of sweet cakes.

Violet lifted a napkin and dabbed at her mouth.

The dormouse—apparently not dead—shook itself off and scampered away as fast as its little legs would take it. Violet sat back down.

"Apologies. What was I saying?"

"You were going to show us your puppy," Nix offered, before Danny could screw this up. Puppies were cute, right? Surely that would be an improvement on this shitshow.

Violet grinned. "Oh yes!" She clapped her hands as Blaine rolled a massive cage out of the garden, cockroach flowers skittering into the air like confetti to make way.

Inside the cage, an equally massive animal thrashed in a space much too small to contain it, its thick claws darting between the bars. The cage rocked as Blaine dodged the outburst, knees quaking together. The creature's jaws gnashed in fury. Thick fur protruded through the spaces between the bars. It was difficult to make out the beast's full appearance, but even in his current state Nix immediately recognized him.

"Its name is Max," Violet told them. "Isn't that the perfect name for a puppy?"

Chapter 19

Danny jumped out of his chair. "Max?" Violet eyed him as he walked toward Max's cage. A large bear claw reached out and swiped at him, missing by inches, and Violet seemed pleased. Pleased he missed or that he attempted, Nix couldn't tell.

"Easy, buddy," Danny coaxed, hands raised. "It's me. It's Daniel."

Something that might have been recognition glinted in the bear's small black eyes. Danny reached out again and though Max growled—a low, intimidating rumble—he allowed Danny to press his bare hand against his forehead.

"I'm so sorry, my friend," Danny said. "I didn't mean it. Any of it."

Violet didn't try to stop the exchange. "My puppy is your friend also?"

As Danny calmed Max with a hushed voice Nix couldn't make out, Rachel said, "He is."

"You have many friends. Why?"

"Why?" Rachel echoed.

"Admirable qualities or circumstances?"

Rachel's eyebrows rose. "Um. I don't know. Maybe both."

"My Violet agrees." Her head tilted to the side, an internal listening. Nix wondered how much sway the young Violet

100

might retain, still trapped in her own body. "She thinks I should be your friend, too." She pursed her lips.

With Max soothed and now sitting in his cage, Danny turned back to the table. "How did you find him?"

"Rescued," Violet said. "Running loose in the forest. Scared. Alone. Injured. Saved him." She motioned to his shoulder. Though it was covered over with fur now, mostly healed, Nix remembered the last time she'd seen Max, and Danny's gunshot that struck him there.

At Edgar Winterspoon's farm, he'd helped them fight off their enemies—hunters and demons alike. At first, he'd been in human form, but she'd seen him transform into this. Unlike most shifters, Max was a unique type—a bear first, a human second. He'd been born an animal and it showed in his social skills. Nix had assumed he returned to his wilds, but now here he was, trapped in a cage.

With what seemed like genuine emotion, Danny looked Violet in the eyes. "Thank you...for taking care of him. You're right that we should be friends. Allies. We could be." Danny sat and motioned to Max. "And you can let him out of the cage now. He won't bite anymore—he was scared. Animals bite when they're scared, is all."

Violet stared at Danny for a long moment, but nodded, expressionless. She waved her hand and the cage clicked open.

Blaine stumbled back, tripping and righting himself just as quickly. He rushed to the opposite side of the table. This close, Nix could now see a rip in Blaine's pant leg that looked to be caked in dried blood. An earlier run-in with the bear.

Max nudged the cage door open with his nose and stepped out, stretching.

He plunked down next to Danny's seat at the end of the table and Nix vaguely felt as if she were having a tea party with Callie's Winnie the Pooh. The absurdity of the situation struck her like a slap across the face. Had Danny—the belligerent asshole hunter—salvaged a rapidly derailing situation with an archdemon by making *friends?* Nix knew she was gaping but couldn't seem to stop.

Everything in her nature compelled her to sabotage this, but that appetite for chaos was currently at war with her instincts for self-preservation—always a dangerously close battle. Maybe the archdemon was right though, maybe she could have both her nature and what she wanted.

She wiped perspiration from Elliot's forehead. He was boiling. Nix didn't know what to do with any of this right now. She was an unmoored ship in the ocean having a tea party with Pooh and a Mad Hatter, craving pizza guy à la mode, and quite probably losing her sanity.

"Friends," Violet tested out the word. She picked up her empty teacup and Nix watched as it refilled itself in a dark swirl, splashing over the edges. Violet cupped it in both hands, her fingers damp and no doubt scalded. "My Violet tells me you're a man of honor, Daniel Whipsaw. A man of legend and great honor. Yet, you lie." She looked up at him. "You speak of friendship, but your heart decries me an enemy. All demons, your heart says, are enemies. Why is this?"

Danny sat forward, his brow furrowed. "I meant what I said."

Violet giggled, dropping her chin to her chest. Her eyes met Nix's.

"She can read minds," Nix said.

Danny leaned back, huffing. "I'm…I'm tryin', all right? I guess—my whole life I've been a hunter, okay?" He puffed his cheeks out. "It's all I know, this war between our kinds. You've always been the enemy. This one"—he thumbed at Nix—"killed some of my closest friends, but ya can see I put it behind me for the greater good. Last time I made a deal with an archdemon, I didn't know and I got burned. Someone I thought was a friend was an enemy. And…when my girl ended up havin' abilities I thought only my enemies could have, I struggled. I still struggle. But I see now it isn't all black and white. I've worked with adversaries against greater foes, and maybe we ain't never gonna be friends, but we ain't exactly enemies anymore, either. So it's all messed up in my head, but I'm tryin'." He sighed.

"Yes," Violet said. "I do see that you try. A difficult road to friendship. Many a hunter has traversed it."

"You were friends with other hunters?" Rachel asked.

"Oh yes. Dear friends. Family. You used to call my friend Uncle Edgar, visit him at feast times. Of course, I had to hide deep down then. No one was the wiser." She giggled again, sipping her tea.

Nix raised an eyebrow, thoughts returning to their battle at Edgar Winterspoon's farmhouse. The archdemon had been bound to the bones of the dead hunter—his skull—and trapped in a box. It had manipulated them into releasing it, but Nix never considered the archdemon could have had a mutual arrangement with Winterspoon.

Rachel frowned. "You mean, you knew what was going on when you were bound to Uncle Edgar? You were friends with him? I don't understand."

"Certainly. Ours was a chosen bond. Edgar, Lizzie, the girls and I, we were very happy. I had a family and could protect them. Assist on your hunts, as you call them, against the dangerous animals. But when Edgar died…" She looked at the flowers. "I could not save him from a mortal death, only prolong it. And my family, they could not release me, could not speak to me in the bones. So they hid me with promises to return with answers."

"I—we didn't know," Danny said, sounding only half-convinced. "Why didn't you return to them?"

She shrugged, eyes downcast. "You haven't touched your tea."

Danny reached for his cup. He drank. "Sincha?"

Violet met his eyes and hers widened. She smiled. "You know your teas. A man also of mystery."

Danny reddened but he didn't back down. "Cards on the table, since ya'll can read my mind. You haven't hurt my friends." He glanced at Blaine, who was worse for wear, and his gaze flickered for an instant toward the skeleton in the rafters, but his expression didn't falter. "And any friend of Edgar's is one of mine. If we can come to some agreements— the we-don't-attack-you, you-don't-attack-us kind." He cleared his throat. "Or kill anybody else. Maybe we can help each other out."

The man was so verbose at this table, Nix could hardly keep up. This was easily a 1000% increase in word output in the last forty minutes of awkward tea party compared to the entirety of the last two weeks.

Violet's head titled. "You, help me? How?"

At this, Danny seemed to run out of steam at long last, looking to Rachel.

"Maybe we could get into contact with Lizzie for you," Rachel said. "See about returning you to your family. Then our friend Violet could return to hers."

Violet ran her hand along the tablecloth, silent.

"Our Violet—your host—she isn't a willing bond like Edgar was, is she?" Rachel asked.

Violet shook her head, purple locks fluttering over her eyes.

"Okay. So you couldn't stay with her a long time like with Edgar, is that right?"

A nod.

"And that's why she's so pale and her skin is…" Rachel trailed off. "She's fading."

Violet touched the flaking skin at her neck. A quick jerk of her head confirmed Rachel's words.

"We don't want our friend to fade away. Maybe you don't want her to, either. But Uncle Edgar, he never took on aspects of his…*passenger* like this. He never faded. Just had his liver condition. If you had a willing host to bond with, it wouldn't have to happen?"

Violet looked up, meeting her eyes. "We would fit. Like a water dance, great ease."

"Do you think Lizzie would take you if we reached out to her?"

Violet scratched at her neck. The skin flaked away, revealing scales beneath. "She claimed she would. But she left. Didn't return. Abandoned. Alone in the bones. Cold." Her gaze drifted away.

"You said she was looking for a way to release you. But you told us how to release you in the farmhouse—manipulated me into burning the house down, in fact, to set you free. Why didn't you tell her to burn the bones?"

"Didn't know. Couldn't tell. Not then. The bond weakens the passenger, even one such as me. Edgar died and, for days, I slept, unaware. No energy without him to hold me aloft. Only the dark sleep. The flesh rotted off my bones. My tongue, my lips, slackened." Violet touched her lips. "The worms came. Couldn't speak. No mouth to speak with. Couldn't see. No eyes to see with. But the bones, they could hear. Listening bones, in the dark sleep. Listening to my family leave the farmhouse, leave me inside deep, deep down in hidden places. Alone in the bones."

"Not all the bones," Rachel pointed out. "We only found the skull."

"No, not all. After many days, Lizzie tried the burning to release me. Burned the other bones to ash. Heard the bones screaming as they burned. Perhaps she thought it was destroying me, so she didn't burn them all. Left the skull, locked me in the box. The last of me, still bound. Left to find another way, she said."

"So she didn't go far enough. Sounds like she didn't want to risk destroying you completely by burning the skull. When we were there, you managed to manipulate our dreams, our minds, and get us to burn the box with your skull in it. Why didn't you do the same to communicate with her?"

"Didn't know it would work, the burning. Such pain to break the bond. Isolation made me stronger, in the bones, in the dreams of the dark sleep. To touch the minds of others. This took time. The decision to burn completely, this was desperation."

"If Lizzie knew it were possible to free you, she might have done it herself, and earlier. She could still be looking for a way to release you from the bones right now."

Violet looked unconvinced.

"You don't know she abandoned you," Rachel whispered. "You don't know until you ask."

Curious, Nix said, "How long were you bonded with your host?"

"Forty human years," Violet said.

Danny gasped. "That's longer than I knew Edgar. You were always there? You knew us?"

"But you did not know me. In many ways, I was always in that box. Alone in the bones." She shook her head. "No, not always alone."

"That's why you said the bond couldn't be broken," Nix said, thinking of Callie, "once made."

"Not easily," Violet confirmed. "Host must die, passenger must burn."

Nix had worn the dead before, the ones with a fresh spark of life still lingering within them. But to be trapped in the dead by such a bond, weakened and unable even to move, to speak, that would be a fate worse than any Nix could imagine. She was relieved now that she hadn't made that choice.

"And Edgar chose it?" Danny's eyes squinted.

"Only the host can initiate the bond," Violet said. "The host must be willing."

Rachel asked, "What about the demon—er, archdemon. Does it have to be willing?"

"No. The free will of the passenger is irrelevant. In my case, I was willing. Ours was a mutual bond."

"So this is some sort of binding spell?" Rachel said.

Violet looked to Nix.

"It is," Nix confirmed. "I have it. She gave it to me at the farmhouse. I was going to use it with Callie, to stay with her—if she chose it. But I decided not to."

The hunters didn't comment on this. Instead, Rachel said to Violet, "If we help you get back to Lizzie, you could stay with her and let Violet go so she doesn't fade."

Violet set her teacup down. "And your terms?"

"Well, you don't harm us, of course. Any of us—including Max, Blaine, or your host. You don't kill any other humans, either. And we have to finish something first. We need some help. Have you ever heard of the Order?"

Chapter 20

Violet swished the dregs of tea in her cup. "I know many Orders. You refer to the Order of the Ram."

Nix shivered. Danny nodded.

Flipping her empty teacup upside down on a cloth napkin, Violet tilted it up and peeked inside. "The leaves have been most talkative of late."

"About the Order?" Rachel asked.

Violet looked up. "They speak of great change. Shift in balance. Thorny roses choking out the garden."

"Sounds about right." Nix stared at her hands.

Rachel leaned forward. "What does that mean for someone like...like you?"

"The Order of the Ram abhors competition. That which slithers underfoot will be crushed by the hoof if spotted."

Danny's lips twisted in his bristly beard. "Ain't you one of them, bein' an archdemon?"

Violet's eyes widened and she laughed. "We all look the same through your eyes, I suppose. We have many Orders, many casts."

Forever searching out common ground, Rachel pressed forward, saying, "So you're enemies?"

"Not friends," Violet said. "At one time, acquaintances. Long ago. Far ago. The leaves warn the Order—your Order—

searches not for friends in this conquering." She stared into her cup again. "Their trust misled them in the past, right into a glass cage." Violet held one hand up, as if miming pressing it against an invisible curved wall. "Trapped like I was, but much longer. They will never make such mistakes again. Many years to plan in the cage of sky glass."

"They want revenge?" Nix asked.

"No. And yes. More than revenge—revolution. The betrayers are long dead. Revenge cannot be exacted against them. It must, therefore, be exacted against all."

"All?" Rachell asked.

"All," Violet confirmed.

"As in humans," Danny said.

"And any who get in the way."

"The tea leaves told you this?" Rachel worried her lips between her teeth, no doubt wondering what else the leaves were telling this archdemon.

"Oh yes. The leaves see much."

"Do they see the future?"

"Naturally."

"So you know how all of this ends already?"

"Yes. And no."

Nix groaned before she could remember to censor herself.

Danny asked, "How does it work?"

"The leaves whisper. As with all those who Know, I cannot know my own future—a violation of natural order. But that of others, the leaves offer a glimpse." Violet peered into Danny's eyes. "Would you like to know how you die, Daniel Whipsaw? At whose hands?"

Danny stilled. He ran his fingers through his scraggly beard, not looking away. He inhaled deeply. "No. I'll take the surprise."

Violet turned to Rachel. "And you, witch?"

Chapter 21

Rachel straightened at Violet's offer to tell her how she would die. "All right."

"Very well." Violet's eyes glazed over and Rachel paled as something passed telepathically between them. When Violet snapped out of it, Danny reached out and placed his hand atop Rachel's. She pulled away, staring at the table.

Violet's gaze turned to Nix. "What of your host?"

In the quiet expanse of his mindscape, Elliot whispered, *"Yes."*

The archdemon's voice unspooled in their shared brain.

"Your great love will be the death of you. Yet I suspect you did not need me to confirm this. Did you, young hunter?"

"N-no." Elliot went silent and still.

"And you, Nix? Do you wish to know how it ends for you?"

"I'm immortal," Nix argued. *"I can't end."*

"You know that's not true. We all end, eventually. That is the natural order. I can tell you, if you choose. For some, knowledge is paralyzing. For others, it is reassuring, emboldening. It is what you make it."

Nix knew what it would be for her. She thought of Elliot calling her a coward, her impulse to flee. She thought of Cirrik accusing her of being a traitor, always running. This battle with the Order wasn't one she could run from, even if it proved to be the end for her. She couldn't afford to be a coward anymore.

They'd taken enough from her—she thought they'd taken everything. And they could take her disgustingly unsatisfying non-life, too, but they wouldn't make her a coward any longer. She couldn't go into this with hesitation.

"No. I don't need to know."

"Very well."

The presence departed.

Rachel was watching her from the corners of her eyes. Nix wondered what she'd been shown.

Danny asked, "If you can see how we die…can you see if we win this—and skip the yes and no answer. Give it to me straight."

Violet tucked her purple hair back behind her ears. "There are many possible paths."

Danny huffed. "But can we win?"

"In all the paths, failure. All but one."

Danny sat forward. "So what's the one path?"

"If I tell you, the path closes. The one path, you must find half-blind."

"Well that's bullshit," Rachel muttered.

"The path is the path," Violet said in her pseudo-sage voice, and Nix had to agree it was bullshit. Maybe she was jerking them around and all of this was bullshit.

Rachel crossed her arms. "Can't you give us anything to go on?"

Violet peered into her teacup once more. "I see witches in crimson robes. A coven. And a sprawling mass of vines sprouting roses as red as a sea of blood."

"A coven?" Rachel's eyes were wide, perhaps with the prospect of encountering others like herself.

Nix turned the idea over in her mind. An image of Maria's rose garden sprang to mind. *Bruja.* It wasn't a coincidence after all.

"You know the witch's garden," Violet said. "Good. The leaves say you'll need a trinket from the witch."

Danny turned to her. "What does she mean?"

Nix flushed. "I, uh, thought it was a coincidence. But the house I landed in after our experiment on Cirrik, the little old lady, she was a witch. It seemed so random, landing there."

Danny's face reddened. "You didn't think to tell us?"

"She was harmless," Nix said. "I'd have noticed. You have my word."

Rachel glowered. "That's not worth much, is it?"

Running his hands down his face and puffing out a breath, Danny's shoulders visibly relaxed. "We need to go back, then." He looked to Violet. "You're willin' to work with us to take the Order down? And we'll help you get back to Lizzie after?"

"It is to the benefit of all for the Order of the Ram to be destroyed."

This brought Rachel out of her ennui. "You think that's possible? We don't even know how to find them."

"You found me."

"Yes," Rachel said. "With a scrying crystal. A pendulum."

Blaine glanced up, eyes wide.

To Blaine, Rachel explained, "We found it in your office and—"

"My office?" For a moment he looked affronted, like the old Blaine. "You shouldn't have gone in there. You didn't touch anything, did you?"

"Um…" Rachel glanced at Nix. "A few things."

Blaine paled.

"Hush, Minion," Violet said.

Blaine returned his gaze to the floor.

"To scry, more is needed than a pendulum," Violet said.

"Well, we had some of Violet's things, too, as grounding objects. But we don't have anything from the Order," Rachel said.

Violet touched a finger to her lips. "Hmm. What of their prison? An enchanted roman glass orb, correct?"

Nix perked up. The blue glass ball had indeed been shattered during her confrontation with the archdemon Val, but if the Order had been imprisoned in it for centuries prior to Val getting her hands on it, perhaps their powerful energy signature was still present in it. "We could find the pieces—I bet they're still in that burned-up house. Wait, how did you know? Never mind—the leaves, right?"

Violet nodded.

Nix deflated as thoughts flew through her head. "But there were scores of other demons and human souls stored in that ball, too—wouldn't using it as a grounding object direct us to all of them?"

"The strongest energy signatures will be those present the longest—but if others were present, yes, this is a problem."

Rachel said, "Maybe we could combine the shards with something else. We also have two things the Order created."

"What do you mean?" Nix asked.

"You and Cirrik. A direct connection."

"I'm not so sure about this," Nix said. "How would it work?"

Rachel shrugged. "A few drops of blood from both of you—your presence corrupts your host's blood, right? Nothing's more powerful than blood magic. Would it work?"

"It would," Violet said. "One might not be enough, but two demons born from the Order of the Ram combined with the glass and a trinket from the witch's garden—this could work."

"So we recover the shards. Visit this witch's garden. Find the Order."

"Great," Danny said, moving to stand.

Rachel placed a hand on his shoulder to stop him. "We shouldn't all go back to Yosemite to find this witch's trinket and the broken orb. We can't risk bringing Cirrik with us and someone needs to watch him. If a bunch of us go road-tripping, we'll draw more attention than we need."

Danny frowned, but he didn't argue. Turning to Violet, he said, "Is it okay if we bring our trailer in and stay awhile? Don't want to exhaust our welcome."

"Your welcome is inexhaustible, Whipsaw, friend of Edgar. Minion will assist." Violet waved Blaine to help Danny sort out the trailer. Max whined at the end of the table, and Danny patted him as they passed. Nix noticed Danny slip something small into Rachel's jacket pocket on his way out the door. Violet didn't seem to.

Rachel turned to Nix, not making eye contact as she said, "You and I are going to take care of this before the end of the day. Long drive to Yosemite and back again. Let's not waste time."

Nix grabbed her arm. "What did she show you?"

Rachel shook her off. She didn't answer.

Chapter 22

Nix found herself in the ugly van with Rachel. It soon became apparent this was by design. The road opened up again when they reached the highway on their way from San Clemente back toward Maria's house in Yosemite and Val's farmhouse where they'd last seen the roman glass. It seemed like a needless retracing of their steps, and Nix wasn't completely convinced they'd be able to find the Order's location with the pendulum, but they were also facing a ticking clock and few options. Nix rolled the window down to let the heat out.

Rachel slipped a small phone out of her jacket pocket. It looked like something out of the nineties. She flipped it open and jabbed at it. The car swerved.

"Is that what Danny handed you?" Nix asked.

"Shh," Rachel said. The tinny sound of a ringtone carried on for a few minutes as she repeated the process over and over again, her driving degrading steadily. Finally, Rachel said, "Hey, Lizzie. It's Rachel Whipsaw. We need to talk. It's urgent. Text me back at this number—don't call. You know the drill." She hung up.

Nix was stuck in a whirlwind of thoughts about Cirrik. Had he bounced her to the old witch's home on purpose? He must have. But why? Was he giving her a clue or setting her up?

He'd seemed to think he could sway her into escaping with him earlier. Maybe he hadn't given up on her completely. Or, it was a trap. But if it was a trap, why hadn't anything happened when she was at Maria's the first time? Her thoughts swirled in circles.

Elliot was yammering, *"I wonder why the archdemon was hiding out in San Clemente. Were they there the whole time, do you think? Seems out of the way. The security guard could only have been dead four or five days, but I guess they could have been there longer. But why the factory district?"*

"What does it matter? We found the teen psychic and even Blaine. Alive, no less," Nix said. *"I can't believe we walked away from that. Not how I imagined it going at all."*

"Something still isn't right," Elliot said. *"We shouldn't have left Pops there. Or Max. Any of them, alone with that archdemon. It killed a man and hung him on the rafters for being rude—and we're trusting it."*

"You're trusting me."

"My point exactly. But at least you've proven your willingness to work with us. An archdemon is a different story. You were human once. It never was. I can at least understand your motivations—you've experienced human emotion. Love. Loss. It talks a good game, but I don't trust it."

Nix wasn't sure if she trusted it, either. But in a way, it understood her. She'd never met another demon who broke the mold in the same ways she did. *"Rachel will check its story, right? She's getting in touch with that Lizzie person—Edgar Winterspoon's wife. If she confirms the story, then we'll know it's legit."*

"Yeah. If we can get in touch with her. I don't think Danny's heard from any of them since they moved to New York after Edgar's death. I've got a bad feeling about all of this. Can you talk to Rach?"

Nix opened her mouth to relay Elliot's concerns to Rachel but didn't get the chance.

"I need you to put El to sleep for a minute." Rachel pocketed the phone. "You and I need to talk."

"What the hell, Rach?" Elliot said, but Nix ushered him off to dreamland before he could get annoying about it.

"Done," Nix said.

"For sure?"

Nix nodded.

Rachel whipped around a car in front of them. "When the archdemon asked Elliot if he wanted to know how he died, what did he say?"

Nix stilled. With Elliot asleep, she couldn't ask his permission to share. They had an agreement about sharing and permission that kept Nix in the driver's seat. She was supposed to be honest about Elliot but also only share with his permission. She wasn't quite sure how to answer without violating both agreements here. She hedged her bet with a lie. "He said no."

"As if you'd tell me anyway. And you? Did it ask you?"

"I declined, too."

"Why? Why wouldn't you want to know that?"

Nix shifted at the rise in Rachel's voice, the unfair hostility. Was she mad? Her face was all red, eyes hard, jaw clenched. "I didn't want anything to get in the way of what we have to do," Nix said. "Um, are you...okay?"

Rachel's hands gripped the steering wheel and she stared straight ahead. The odometer clicked upward. "Don't."

"I just—"

Rachel swallowed. "It told me how I die. Is that what you want to know?" Rachel cut her eyes to Nix, a cold glare. The car swerved over the center line again. "Judas' kiss. It said you were going to kill me. Said a bunch of weird shit, but that's what it came down to. *You* kill me. So this whole truce thing," Rachel said with a biting laugh that forced Nix back into her seat, "I guess this has been a big fucking joke, hasn't it? You didn't even tell us the old lady you happened to fall into was a witch. So much for being on the same side."

Wind whipped through the van as Nix processed being accused of something she hadn't done yet. "Rachel, I wouldn't hurt—"

"I convinced Pops you were safe. Such an idiot, putting him in danger—putting El in danger. I can't even look Pops in the eye now." She slammed her hands against the steering wheel. "Damn it. I vouched for you. I've been hanging out here on a limb for you this whole time and you...you—"

Nix raised her hands, palms outward. "Wow, can you stop? I'm not going to kill you. I haven't done anything and you're freaking out."

"Haven't done anything? You withheld information."

"There are witches all over the place. I didn't think anything of it. And I was in her head, she's not evil. I didn't—"

"You killed Joan and Jake. Kevin and Rodney. You killed people I loved in *my* body. That's nothing? How could I have been so stupid as to think things could work out. Of course you betray me. Of course you do. You're a monster."

The words hit like a sucker punch, though Nix didn't know why. Sure, she hadn't been planning to kill these hunters. Maybe she'd even grown a little weirdly fond of them. If anything, she was more concerned about them betraying her, but at the end of the day they were hunters, and she was a demon. Cirrik was right, they weren't her friends. She was naïve to think they wouldn't turn on her. This was always coming.

Nix folded in on herself, tucking Elliot's long legs up against the dashboard and turning away. "So all it took to convince you to throw away everything we've worked to build was the word of an archdemon? I've proven myself over and over. I don't know how else I can convince you I'm not a danger to you or your family now. Has it occurred to you this archdemon might be messing with us? That it planted this in your head for exactly this reason—so you'd spin out and stop trusting me like this? To pull us all apart right when we most need to present a united front?"

Rachel's fingernails dug into the faux leather of the steering wheel. She breathed out in a huff, then roared, "I don't know what to do."

"I am not going to kill you."

She laughed bitterly.

"I won't," Nix said. "I swear to you, I won't. I will not, under any circumstances, kill you or Danny, or Elliot. I swear on…on Callie. On my sister's grave. I wouldn't do that. I promise."

Rachel side-eyed her, fingers relaxing a little on the wheel. "Maybe you do kill me, maybe you don't." Her eyes welled up. "But please, don't hurt them. They're all I have."

"I promise, I won't."

"I don't know how to keep them safe."

Nix stared out the window. "Neither do I," she admitted.

Chapter 23

By the time they pulled up to the burned-out farm in Yosemite, it was past dinnertime. Another day burned up. Nix couldn't help but wonder if they were wasting precious time on a fool's errand, but it was the only lead they had. Torn police tape waved in the breeze, some caught up in the razor-wire fence surrounding the property.

Nix hadn't been here since the incident with Val. As they stopped the van in front of the pile of sticks that had once been a house, Nix remembered crawling out the basement window in the charred body of an Ohio Realtor who had once been an archdemon's host. She'd ambled all the way from this farm to a playground in Sonora, back to Callie. Nix smiled at the memories of the terrified townsfolk scattering upon seeing her shamble down the street.

Rachel pulled open Nix's door and handed her a pile of meat packages from the cooler in the back. "Eat these. All of them. Before we go in. I don't want El getting hungry."

Nix didn't argue. Rachel had some froyo and granola while they picnicked on the charred front porch. The acrid scent of smoke still hung on the air here even though it had been months since the house burned down. To be fair, parts of it were mostly intact. It was the basement that was hit the worst, followed by the stairs and the back of the house.

Unfortunately, they needed to go down those stairs and into the basement to find what they were looking for, if it was even still there. Presumably, the firefighters would have made a mess of the place. Could be here awhile.

Nix chewed through the last of the pizza guy's left thigh, handing Rachel the garbage to return to the van.

"Is El still asleep?" Rachel asked.

"Yep."

"What we talked about stays between us." She stood, hands on her hips. "Okay, we'll need some tools. Looks like there are shovels and garden stuff in the shed still."

Nix helped out, grabbing a shovel from the mound of various tools covered in cobwebs at the edge of the property.

"We only need the one," Rachel said.

"But—"

"Elliot's eaten, so I want him on lookout. Nix, I want you with me now."

Nix leaned against the shovel. "Uh, I'm not so sure that's a good idea. What if he...you know?"

"He's full, isn't he?"

Nix checked in with Elliot's stomach and had to admit he wasn't feeling overly hungry now. Satisfied, even. "Yeah."

"And it's only the two of us out here. He can't take me on with your strength behind me."

"True."

"I don't want you in him anymore." Her gaze was unwavering.

Nix twisted the shovel into the caked earth. "You'd rather bunk with me yourself? All things considered, I would think you'd want to be as far from me as possible."

"I can handle you better than El or Pops can. You can't control me like before. You can't control me like you can either of them. And right now, I don't trust you with them. You said the archdemon didn't tell him how he died. I want to hear it from him. Make the switch."

Nix sighed. She pulled herself in tight, swelling up into Elliot's throat and detaching from his senses until the familiar freedom of floating overtook her. Nix's dark vision latched on to the bright-red light of Rachel's form and she channeled herself into her host body.

Coming to, sulfur tinged the air. Nix flexed Rachel's hands, her arms. She stretched the muscles of her neck.

Elliot shifted and groaned on the grass across from her.

Rachel's familiar voice touched Nix's consciousness in their shared mind. *"El."*

"I'll check on him," Nix said.

She knelt over Elliot's supine form, helping him to sit up.

"What's going on?" Elliot said.

"Rachel thought you could use a break. You're on lookout duty. Think you can handle it?"

"Yeah," he mumbled, carding his fingers through his hair and rubbing at one eye. "Got it."

"Ask him."

Nix sighed. "Rachel wants to know…when the archdemon asked you if you wanted it to tell you how you die, what was your answer?"

Elliot looked into her eyes, silent for a long moment. "I said no."

Nix's eyebrow rose.

The tension in Rachel's shoulders released a bit.

He blinked up at her with his silver-gray eyes. "What did it show Rachel?"

"Well?" Nix asked.

"Don't tell him. Say…say I live until I'm old and die peacefully."

"She dies peacefully in old age."

Elliot's eyes narrowed. "Bullshit. I saw the look on her face."

"Don't tell him anything."

"That's what she says. We're burning daylight. You good to be lookout or not?"

Elliot pursed his lips but nodded, rubbing at his eyes again.

She helped him to his feet. "Great. We're heading in. If you get hungry, there's meat in the cooler. Don't get weird and eat anyone in the ten minutes I'm not watching you."

Elliot shrugged vacantly, staring at the toolshed.

Nix shook her head and grabbed the shovel. *"Good?"*

"Thanks," Rachel said.

She headed to the front door and forced it open with the shovel. A puff of dirt and dust hit Rachel's lungs and left Nix coughing. Ash coated her tongue and nostrils. Dim light leaked in from a few shattered windows, but the place was dark.

"There's a flashlight on my belt," Rachel said.

"Right." Nix didn't have any handy night vision in this body. Inconvenient. Would have been better doing this in Elliot, but Rachel had to be all sensitive. Nix huffed.

She pulled out the flashlight and the house lit up.

Oh. She remembered this place. The kitchen table still stood. And the broken bookshelf the archdemon had telekinetically thrown her into while in Rachel's body. Nix watched the flash of Rachel's remembrance accompany the images alongside her own. The door to the basement was gone now—busted down. Looking at those steep stairs made Rachel's shoulder ache. Nix moved to the top of the steps and stared down.

Most of the steps were destroyed. She'd have to jump down and climb back out. She remembered standing at this angle and watching as Cirrik was strapped to a chair with invisible ropes in the center of the basement. His mail carrier host's skin peeled back as his muffled screams bounced off the walls. *Real death, my love.* Nix shivered. At the time, she'd thought she was watching him die. Lucky bastard that he was, it didn't stick. Never did with him. He could get out of anything. Nix smirked.

She crouched, then leaped to the bottom of the demolished steps, sticking the landing. Pools of stagnant water filled the corners of the basement. Since California hadn't seen rain in ages, Nix could only assume it was left over from the firefighters, but that had been so long ago—maybe a pipe had burst. Nix swept the beam of the flashlight around the destroyed space until she found where the showdown had been.

"I don't see any glass," Nix said.

"Firefighters were down here with hoses. Probably got washed under something."

Nix's eyes followed the beam of light along the edges of the basement floor, checking beneath the sparse furniture and poking around with the shovel. Under the tool bench, the light bounced off something. "Hold on." Kneeling on the filthy concrete, Nix reached under the bench, fingers stretching out and contacting something sharp. She rolled it out. Blue glass caked in grime.

"Perfect," Rachel said. *"It's almost all in one piece. Where's the rest?"*

Nix pulled out a few more fragments, stacking them inside each other. *"Looks like they all fit."*

"Let's get out of here."

"Finally."

Nix brushed Rachel's black jeans off as she stood, gently tucking the glass into her inside jacket pocket.

Elliot's scream shattered the silence of the basement.

Chapter 24

Nix stumbled into the bench, dropping the shovel. She tried to locate the source of the sound. *"What's happening?"*

"Elliot's hurt," Rachel said. *"Find him."*

Nix oriented herself in the darkness, fingers tight on the flashlight. *"It came from above us. Outside. We must be under attack."*

"I didn't hear any vehicles pull up."

Nix glanced at the broken staircase, then the broken window. The window was lower, faster. She'd climbed it before in worse shape. Nix grabbed the edge and hefted herself through the small opening, shimmying over the threshold and into the clean air. Rachel's belt and all the junk looped into it kept getting caught, halting her progress. As another shout pierced the air, Nix managed to get loose. The sound of the glass bauble in her pocket cracking a little more made her cringe, but there was no time to think about it.

She tossed the flashlight into the dirt ahead of her as she dragged her legs out. Scooping up the flashlight with gritty palms, she tucked it into Rachel's belt, vision adjusting to the evening light.

"I don't hear him now," Nix said.

"Check the van."

Nix ran to the front of the house. No sign of Elliot. No other vehicles. No indication anyone else had been here. *"Was he taken?"* Then she shouted, "Elliot?"

A groan from far away. The toolshed.

Nix darted across the property, shoving the door open. She gasped.

In the dim light of the shed, Elliot sat cross-legged on the floor. In one hand, he gripped a rusted two-pronged weeder. His other palm clutched his right eyeball.

Blood dripped from the cavern of his empty socket as he stared up at her.

"What did you do!" Rachel shouted in Nix's head.

Quieter, Nix echoed aloud, "What did you do?"

When his mouth opened, blood dribbled from his top lip to the bottom one. "I fixed it," Elliot said. His voice trembled as he gripped the eyeball, the thick ocular stalk poking out between his fingers. "The hunger. I can control it now."

Rachel cursed, *"Shit, shit, shit…"*

Nix dropped to her knees beside him. She took the weeder from his grip and tossed it on the floor. His skin looked pale against the bright shade of red. His remaining gray eye blinked slowly.

"You're in shock."

"The eye," Rachel was saying, *"it's still intact. We can put it back, right? Jesus. Just…put it back in."*

"Yeah, okay," Nix said, thinking aloud. "We can figure this out. Maybe we can fix it. Put it back in."

Elliot's one eye went wide and his mouth opened. He skittered back. "No!"

"Wait," Nix said, hands up, "I was—"

Elliot popped the eye in his mouth and bit down. It spurted like an unripe tomato, torn and mutilated but so tough it was still mostly whole. He spat it out into a corner and it rolled, wobbling through the cobwebs before stopping to look back at them.

He tucked his knees to his chest.

"Okay," Nix said after a moment. "We'll...leave it out. That's fine." Internally, Nix asked Rachel, *What the fuck? What am I supposed to do with this? I told you it was a bad idea to leave this basket case alone.*

Through the chorus of *shit*s Rachel said, *"Oh god, what am I going to tell Pops, coming back with him like this? He's going into shock. You need to swap again. Then I can clean him up—you, in him."*

Nix recoiled. *"I need to swap? Suddenly you trust me with your precious family again? Did I stop being a monster in the last hour? That's a fast rehab."*

"Please," Rachel said. *"We don't have time to argue."*

Nix watched Elliot rock back and forth, shivering. *"Fine."* Nix wasn't looking forward to the pain of a gouged-out eye. *"You owe me, and I expect payment in the form of a little damn trust. I've earned it."*

Rachel sighed deep within herself. *"Agreed."*

Nix made the swap. She wasn't disappointed. A gouged eye was the worst kind of migraine. "Motherfucker," she said, lifting Elliot off the ground and wiping viscous eye juices and blood off on his pants. "Argh." She spat repeatedly on the floor of the shed, unable to get the salty, turkey-giblet taste out of her mouth. Something crunched between her teeth and she dug it out. The lens. She spat again. "Foul."

Elliot said, *"I couldn't do it again, I couldn't kill a man—I had to do what the archdemon said. Restore the balance."*

"I'm not having this conversation with the taste of your eyeball in my mouth, puppet." Nix swept Elliot back to dreamland so she could concentrate on getting his bodily functions under control and counteracting the effects of the shock.

Rachel was shaking herself off. She took a deep breath, hands on her knees. Nix wondered if she'd vomit this time, but she didn't. Her eyes welled and she swiped at them, turning away. "I've got a bottle of Cutty Black in the van," Rachel said in a strained voice.

"Sold."

Rachel blinked away the emotion in her eyes. Nix watched her push it down. She stood straight, shoulders back, chin tilted high. Moving close, Rachel peered into the empty socket with a forced air of clinical detachment. "Bleeding isn't actually terrible. I'll patch the eye up."

"Speaking of patch, do you have one?"

"Still have a bunch of stuff from when he lost his eyes the first time. Serious meds, too. Painkillers. Antibiotics. Though I doubt there's enough in the world to stop this from getting infected. Fuck." Her gaze wandered. "You don't think we can put the eye back in?"

Nix glanced at the mutilated eye in the corner of the toolshed. The eye stared back at her. "Nah. Some lost causes should stay lost." She closed the door behind them as they walked to the van.

"El awake?" Rachel asked.

"Figured he could use some quiet time. You want me to pull him out?"

"No. Let him rest." Rachel stuck her hand in her jacket pocket and jerked it back out. She hissed, sticking a finger in her mouth. "Glass got crunched. Shit. Think it will mess up the scrying?"

Nix shrugged. "Don't see how. It was already broken. Nothing to do about it now."

"Maybe it won't even work." Rachel slammed the side door of the van open, then punched the metal hard enough to split her knuckles. Blood smudged the side of the van. Rachel leaned her forehead against the window. "The archdemon's probably jerking us around. I shouldn't have left Pops with it."

Nix dropped onto the footboard of the open backdoor next to her, sitting. "Can't know unless we try, right?"

Rachel dug a bandana out of her jacket pocket and wiped the blood off the side of the van. Next, she opened a half-empty bottle of 100-proof whiskey from under the passenger seat and took a swig. She splashed some on her knuckles, then handed the bottle to Nix.

Rachel stared at her as she took a hearty swig. "That archdemon put it in his head to mutilate himself like this."

"He didn't seem like he was dwelling on it or anything. If I thought he was going to do something like this I'd have talked him out of it. We don't know if it'll work or not. He isn't hungry, but he did just eat. Plus, it said it wouldn't stop the hunger, only give him control back."

"There were a lot of caveats in that little speech. Plenty of ways for it to hedge its bets and dodge responsibility for crappy advice if it didn't work out."

"Exactly."

"So what, the only way we know if it makes a difference is if he doesn't compulsively cannibalize someone?"

"Seems like," Nix said.

Rachel unpacked a first-aid kit. "And in the meantime, El's missing an eye. Maybe he decides to gouge the other one out, too. Christ." She took Nix's chin between her fingers and tilted her head—Elliot's head. "Look at that. No hesitation marks. He just went for it. How's that even possible to do to yourself? Bleeding has basically stopped. Did you do that?"

"No, it stopped on its own. He heals fast."

"Faster than normal now, you mean?"

"Yeah. His broken arm healed way faster than it should have when we got back to Blaine's, not that I'm complaining."

Rachel wiped the blood off Elliot's face, the cloth cool against Nix's s hot skin. Considering Elliot seemed like he was going into shock, the furnace-like quality of his internal temperature regulation boded well to her. The shivering had stopped. Maybe he'd dodge an infection from the rusty garden tool, though it seemed unlikely. Nix wasn't interested in sticking around through more of Elliot's inconvenient bodily functions, yet here she was again, helping. Trying to prove herself. There didn't seem to be a light at the end of that particular tunnel, but she kept chugging along like a sucker.

"Maybe you were right," Rachel said, dabbing. "Maybe it was lying about everything. About you killing me. Sowing dissent among us. Getting Elliot to do this to himself. Could help, could make it worse, who knows. And scrying to find the Order." She pursed her lips, shaking her head. "I don't know what to think. What should we do?"

Nix didn't know. What she did know, was that they didn't have options or time. "The archdemon seemed to confirm some of what Cirrik told me about the Order's plans—in a vague, Greek-prophesy kind of way. That could mean Cirrik's telling the truth and his information is accurate, or it could mean the archdemon was reading one of our minds about what we know of the Order's plans and parroting it back. We can't trust anyone here. But at the same time, what other choice do we have but to move forward with the information we've got?"

Rachel pressed something Nix couldn't see with her one good eye against the empty socket and said, "Hold this." Nix patted around until her fingers came into contact with some gauze and pressed down. Rachel ripped off some tape and stuck it on. "I guess you're right. If we don't move on this and it is legit, our window closes. Then we aren't the only ones screwed. So we go back and hope to hell it hasn't slaughtered Danny and the others. Guard our thoughts and suspicions. Proceed as normal. At least check in on that old witch while we're out here, see if she has anything to do with the Order."

Nix grabbed an eyepatch and snapped it in place overtop the gauze. "A blind leap."

Rachel ignored her pun. "Demons lie, right?"

"Of course. Same as humans. You know that."

"It could be telling the truth, though."

"If the truth served it. Or if it knew the truth would hurt more than the lie. Same as humans."

Rachel dropped down next to her on the footboard. "Damn."

"Exactly."

Chapter 25

The sun was nearly set as they drove up to Maria's now familiar gravel lane. Nix tried to remember how many days it had been since she'd run down Maria's asshole grandson in this driveway. Was it only the day before yesterday? Yeah, that's right, because it was their last day at Blaine's and the next night Elliot had gone all cannibal and eaten the pizza guy instead of the pizza. It all blurred together in a swirl of poorly planned disaster. As of tomorrow night, the Order would be unstoppable.

The old witch's grandson wasn't rotting in the driveway, as far as Nix could tell, so someone dealt with him. They'd need to pull in closer to determine if any pool of blood remained. There hadn't been any rain for ages, so who knew. Nix sighed. This was one mess she hadn't expected to be forced to deal with any further. Everything seemed to be coming back to haunt her lately. She missed the old days where she could pull the pin, toss the grenade behind her, and walk away without consequences.

"Are you sure this is it?" Rachel asked.

"I'm sure," Nix said. "I got pretty familiar with the place."

Rachel seemed to take Nix's morose mood for an accusation. "You were only there a couple hours, at most."

Rachel looked out her window, chewing on her lip. "Technically, the spell worked."

"True. I'm just shocked Cirrik...helped. Sort of. In his own weird, indirect way. Which is actually the opposite of helping, since it was so damn convoluted. But maybe he was giving me a hint." Nix scratched at the edge of the eyepatch. "Or he was setting me up."

"What if it's not about him? Maybe you were meant to find this place, this witch, whatever she has that could help us stop the Order from ascending."

"What do you mean?"

"Fate. Maybe it's fate, how all of this worked out. The good and the bad. Life and death."

"You believe in that?"

Rachel didn't answer.

Nix thought about it, but she didn't have time for the spiral of what-ifs. It wasn't ideal, coming here right after Elliot had mutilated himself. Not like they could go to a hospital though, and if the archdemon was right about witches being involved in this equation—Maria being one of those witches—then they had to know for sure how the woman factored in. With all the driving they'd done lately and the deadline swooping closer, it might be their only chance to find out.

"What do we do?" Rachel asked. "Should we talk to her? Or, like, sneak onto her property."

A few black puffs bounded across the grass, barely dots from this distance. Nix couldn't see any movement through the windows of the house, but equally couldn't imagine Maria leaving her cats alone for long. Still, if she got in trouble about the grandson thing... "She may not even be here. Let's play it by ear."

Nix slipped out of the van and opened the gate leading onto Maria's property—closed now, though it hadn't been before. Rachel drove the van forward. Nix thought for a moment, then closed the gate behind them. If they really needed a quick escape from the sweet little old lady, the gate wasn't so serious they couldn't drive through it. It was a gate of pretenses, much like the rest of Maria's life, apparently.

Gravel crunched under their tires as they pulled up to the house. Cats darted out of the way of the slow van. Still no movement from inside.

Rachel parked and killed the engine. "Do we knock? Will she even hear us if she's in there?"

"She's not deaf. Not *that* deaf, anyway."

They exited the vehicle and stepped up the geranium-dotted stairs to the front door. Nix glanced back at the gravel driveway—no obvious blood stains. Someone must have cleaned up. Rachel's hand landed on Nix's arm and she leaned in. "Is she dangerous? I mean, what do we do if she attacks? I know she's a witch like I am, but...she's human, right?"

"Yes, she's human. I don't think she'll attack us. She was pretty nice."

"But if she does..." Rachel's grip tightened. "She must be powerful if she was working with the Order. And...evil."

Nix laughed and knocked on the door. The welcome mat sported an image of a cat in a heart.

"I'm serious," Rachel said.

"If she was, she's something else now. I would have picked up on it. It's equally as likely the archdemon was messing with us and she has nothing to do with anything."

A shuffling sounded from inside, but no one answered. Could have been the cats, or Maria didn't want company. Nix knocked again.

"Hey." Rachel nudged Nix's side as an SUV drove up to the gate. A petite woman got out, opened the gate, and looked at them. She tilted her head and waved before jumping back into her car and repeating the elaborate gate closing process a second later.

"What do we do? Do you think it's someone with the Order?" Rachel said.

"Be cool," Nix said. Realizing her error, she added, "I'll do the talking."

Rachel glared at her but turned a wide smile on the small blonde woman walking up to them. She wore cat-print scrubs, her hair back in a high ponytail, and carried a large pink bag.

"Well hey there!" the woman said. "Are you Mrs. Mora's family—oh my..." Her smile fell as she closed in on them. "Sweetie, your eye! Are you all right? You need an ambulance?"

Nix lifted her hand to the haphazardly tapped gauze covering Elliot's eye. Rachel looked to her with lips pressed in what Nix could only interpret as a sarcastic smile.

"Uh...no, thank you, ma'am. I'm fine. A little accident. It's nothing."

"Oh. You've got some blood...all down your shirt." The woman took a step back like she might vomit in the geraniums.

Nix glanced down at Elliot's shirt, noticing for the first time that it was, indeed, bloody. A detail they'd both entirely overlooked before knocking on a sweet little old lady's door, prepared to give her a heart attack. "I...um..."

The woman glanced back at her SUV, taking another step backward. It was starting to look like they'd have to kill her when Rachel burst out laughing.

Nix and the woman both turned to her in shock.

Rachel smacked Nix in the chest with the back of her hand. "Don't mind my brother, ma'am. He's a real joker. It isn't real blood. He's helping me make a video for a college project."

The woman took a breath and visibly relaxed. "Oh. Well, you certainly know how to make convincing special effects, or whatever you young people call it. But uh, maybe you shouldn't be dressed like that visiting your grandmother? You're liable to give her quite a fright."

"You're probably right. We weren't thinking, Miss—uh, I don't think we've met?"

"I'm Mrs. Mora's new care aide. My name is Lainie. I was assigned a couple days ago to check in on her twice a day—you know, make sure she's eating and taking her meds and that sort of thing. She's a lovely lady."

"We sure appreciate that, Lainie. Our parents don't like to worry us, so they don't tell us much. But we still worry, you know?"

"Of course, dear. I can only imagine the past couple days have been terribly stressful for your family. The man in the hospital after the incident here, was that your cousin? If you don't mind me asking."

"Yes, ma'am."

"Well, I've been praying for his speedy recovery. The Lord is good. Praise be."

"Yes," Rachel agreed. "Praise."

"Maybe I should change?" Nix suggested.

"You do that, El." Rachel handed her the keys to the van. Nix left the two chatting on the porch and dug around the back until she found a clean enough t-shirt for Elliot, swapping it out. She knelt to check the side mirror, rubbing out a bit of drying blood from under Elliot's chin. "You owe me, puppet," she muttered to her sleeping host.

Hopefully this Lainie person and her cheerful cat-print scrubs wouldn't be sticking around long. Rachel walked into the house behind her and Nix jogged to catch up. The heavy cat smell of the house hit her as she entered. Glancing around, she didn't see Maria.

"I'll take care of her meds and get her up for you, then I'll leave the three of you to catch up in the living room," Lainie said.

Nix and Rachel scoped out the house while Lainie did her thing. Same indeterminate quantity of black cats. Same innocuous decorations as before. Rachel snooped in drawers but Nix had already done this song and dance. She plunked herself on the dusty-rose velvet couch in the living room, across from a well-worn La-Z-Boy.

As voices reached them, moving closer, Rachel snapped a drawer closed and dropped onto the couch next to Nix.

"But my other grandchildren live in Nevada," Maria was saying. "They didn't say they'd be coming to visit. Only Charlie lives nearby and he's in the hospital."

"I know it's hard to remember sometimes, Mrs. Mora, but I'll get some tea for you and your grandkids and you'll have a nice little visit, okay?" Lainie led Maria into the living room and set her in the chair.

Maria stared at them long and hard. "I don't know you."

Rachel looked at Lainie and smiled. Lainie matched her smile, understanding. She left the room and clattered around in the kitchen.

"You aren't Davy and Kiki," Maria said. "They're only small. Kiki just turned eleven, you know."

"Wow, eleven," Rachel said. "She must be getting big. Was she excited for her birthday party?"

Maria lit up. "Oh my, yes. She's a ballerina. Pass me that photo album, I'll show you pictures."

"I'd love that." Rachel pulled an album off the shelf and passed it to her.

Nix side-eyed Rachel with a frown. They'd be making faster progress if they'd killed the nurse.

"See how talented she is?" Maria pointed to a picture of a little girl in a tutu. "I used to dance, too. Oh, but that was a long time ago."

Laine set a tray of tea on the table in front of them. "I'll leave the three of you to catch up. Mrs. Mora, I'll be back in the morning, okay? You take care of yourself and have a lovely time."

"We will, thank you, cariño," Maria said, now apparently unconcerned that these not-grandchildren were in her home. Rachel really was a witch.

Lainie left. Maria flipped through her album, glancing up to point things out to Rachel, then she suddenly looked at Nix as if seeing her for the first time.

Maria lifted her hand to her face and asked, "Young man, what happened to your eye?"

Nix had the sinking feeling she'd be answering this question endlessly for the duration of her time in Elliot's skin. She sighed. "I gouged it out with a garden tool."

Rachel glared at her. A bird-song clock chimed the hour with the warble of a Ruffed Grouse. Another hour lost. The cute clock didn't soften the blow of the sunset beyond the witch's curtains.

"Oh." Maria blinked. "I love gardening. Did you see my rose garden?"

"Very impressive," Nix said. The woman was sweet, but they were wasting time here. Nix was ready to push things into a higher gear. "Though I'm not so partial to roses myself. Too many thorns."

"Oh yes, you have to wear gardening gloves," Maria agreed.

"The demon worship can be problematic, too. Taints the soil."

"I'm sorry?"

"Nix!" Rachel stood.

"I think you know what I'm talking about, Maria. We know you're working with the Order—the Order of the Rams. All those roses. Kinda their brand." Nix wasn't certain of Maria's involvement, but she pushed anyway because she knew Rachel wouldn't.

Maria stared at her for a moment, blinking. "Can I get you some more tea, cariño? How about some cookies?"

Nix leaned forward. "These are serious accusations, Maria. We need to know about your involvement with the Order."

"Order?" Her jaw worked. She seemed to be chewing on the word. "Are you from the municipal office? I pay my taxes." She reared back. "I don't know you."

"Maria," Rachel said soothingly, "I don't suppose we could have some of those cookies?"

Maria brightened. "Of course, let me get them. They're fig newtons, you know." She got out of her La-Z-Boy and shuffled over to the china cabinet.

Rachel shot Nix another glare, mouthing, "She doesn't know anything."

Nix set her head in her hands and exhaled. Even if Maria had been involved with something sinister, there was no way she was anymore. Not like this.

Maria set the tin of cookies in front of her and rubbed her back. "Are you all right, cariño? You feel okay? Have a cookie. Everything is better with a little sweetness."

Nix glanced up at her kind eyes. How could she have been involved with the Order? Maybe this was a mistake. "Thanks, Maria." She reached out for a cookie.

"Hey," Rachel said. "This is you, right?"

Maria shuffled back to her La-Z-Boy where Rachel was propped on the arm holding her photo album. "Oh yes!" She grinned. "Me and the coven."

Nix set the cookie back down, standing and walking over to Rachel. "Coven?"

"Yes, my girlfriends and me. Many years, our group has been together." The photo on the page showed a group of thirteen women, various ages and ethnicities, all wearing long red robes. Smiling at the camera. Maria was standing straight, looking healthy, happy, alert. No cane.

Rachel hummed under her breath. "You look like a choir."

"Choir on weekends. Coven meetings Thursday nights. I'm a soprano."

"Of course," Nix said.

"This was dated two weeks ago," Rachel pointed out, finger on the label.

"Our last performance," Maria confirmed. The Maria in the photo looked a decade younger. Whatever had happened to her in the intervening time had burned her out.

"When's your next meeting?" Rachel asked.

Maria leaned back and sighed. "We had to disband not long after."

"Why? What happened?"

She pursed her lips, shrugged. "I don't remember."

"Maria," Nix said, "it's really important for us to figure this out. I have a way to help you remember. Would it be okay if we tried it?"

Maria looked to Rachel. "All right."

Rachel set the photo album back on the shelf and pulled Nix aside. "What are you thinking? Possessing her?"

"It would be easy and fast."

"I'm not sure about this. What if it hurts her? It's stressful enough, but on someone elderly? You've already put her through it once, what if she can't take a second go-round or she has a bad heart or something?"

"It's not like I possessed her on purpose the first time."

"I'm not saying that. But what do we do with El in the meantime if you aren't in him? He could gouge another eye out, or worse. What if he attacks us or something?"

"Well, we could try your spell again from before…if you could recreate it. Do you remember it?"

"Of course I remember it. I memorize all my spells, I'm not some fly-by-night." Rachel exhaled. "Okay. That one required a potion. But it was nothing special, just boiling some fairly common ingredients. I'll check the kitchen and garden, see if it's feasible."

Rachel disappeared, leaving Nix with Maria in the living room. A cat jumped up on Maria's lap and settled. Twenty minutes of hearing about Maria's collection of tiny spoons later, Rachel re-emerged with two teacups.

"Oh," Maria said. "The tea is right here. You didn't need to make more."

"It was getting cold," Rachel said. "I made some fresh. This is a different kind. I thought we could try it together." She handed Maria a cup.

Maria sniffed it. "Why, this smells like a memory elixir." She frowned, setting the tea down and taking Rachel's hand. "Cariño, you really shouldn't give people elixirs without consent. Who taught you the craft?"

Rachel blanched. She knelt next to Maria's La-Z-Boy. "Um...sorry, ma'am. You're right. That wasn't cool. The thing is, we really need some information that we think you know—but we also think someone might have done something to your memory to make it hard for you to remember that information. It's really important. If we don't figure out what happened to you, other people might get hurt. Do you think you could help us?"

Maria patted Rachel's hand. "I *have* had some memory lapses lately. Lainie said my grandson was here to visit me the other day and"—she leaned close to Rachel's ear—"I took his car! And...and hit him. With the car, I mean. Though he said I hit him with my cane, too. I don't remember a thing. I don't even know how to drive those fancy sports cars. I think it's my meds. But if it will help you, maybe you can sort this out."

Rachel exhaled. "Thank you so much." A kitten rubbed against Rachel's leg as she stood.

Maria smiled, taking a sip from the teacup. "Eduardo likes you," she noted.

Rachel handed Nix the other teacup. Nix waved her away. "You do it this time. I don't know if it was Cirrik's fault or a complication of the spell, but I don't want to risk getting booted again—especially with Elliot in sleep mode right now."

Maria gave her a funny look but didn't comment. Rachel bit her lip. "Okay. I'll try it. You can do the spell?"

"Write it down."

Rachel scrawled it on a pad of paper on the cluttered coffee table. She threw back the potion and held Maria's hand. Nix read off the words. The two sat perfectly still, eyes glazed. Nix waited. And waited. Hmm. Was this what it was like on this side of things? Boring. A cat hopped up on the table and Nix carded Elliot's thick fingers through its soft fur. She grabbed a Reader's Digest. Several minutes later, they gasped, snapping out of it.

"About time," Nix said.

Maria blinked slowly. "Who are you? I'm sorry, young lady, I'm feeling quite tired. I don't think I'll be buying any Avon today."

Rachel patted her shoulder. "That's all right. Why don't you go get some rest. We'll see ourselves out."

Maria lifted herself out of the chair with Rachel's assistance. "You don't mind? Maybe come back tomorrow and I'll make us some tea."

Rachel stood. "Sure. Uh. Thanks."

Maria ambled off down the hall with a flock of cats, mumbling.

"Well?" Nix demanded after a moment.

Rachel ran a hand over her face. She blinked. "It was confusing. I'm not sure what to make of it all."

"Try."

"Okay. At first there was a lot of random stuff—like, about her life. And then I saw those women in the red robes."

Nix stepped closer. "The coven."

"Yes. Turns out they are a choir, too, like Maria said. The coven thing was like a side gig, how they met. They called themselves the Coven of Thorns."

The name clicked in Nix's memory like a train coming into the station. "That used to exist when the Order was around the first time, before they disappeared—or were imprisoned in the roman glass, I guess. There were a bunch of Covens of Thorns all over the place."

Rachel's eyes widened. "Were they demons? These ladies didn't seem like it."

Nix sighed, walking back over to the velvet couch and dropping down. "No, they weren't. They were only witches. Worshippers. They got some of their power through worshiping the archdemons of the Order. Some demonolatry covens choose patron demons to worship, and they were that kind of sect. Not like the nature-worshiping pagans. The Order seemed to find it flattering. By worshiping the Order of archdemons, the coven was made stronger than a regular group of witches, but by being worshiped by witches, the Order was also made stronger than other archdemons without worshippers. A symbiotic relationship, I suppose. The Order didn't really have to do anything but benefit from it, though they favored the covens, so sometimes they'd grant wishes or curse their enemies and such. Only for fun though, not out of obligation. Whenever a coven pissed them off, they'd get the same treatment as any other enemy."

"But that was a long time ago," Rachel said. "If the Order was AWOL for so long, why would the covens still be around?"

Nix shrugged. "Lots of those covens are Legacy. They probably passed their traditions down within families. With the Order locked up though, they likely had restricted powers until recently, comparable to regular witches. Maybe once the Order was released, everything amplified for their coven and with their continued worship the Order realized there were still Covens of Thorns out there. This was probably the closest geographically. There could be dozens all over the world."

"From what I saw, there were thirteen women in their coven, but Maria was more in it for the choir aspect. Most of them weren't serious practitioners."

Two mewling black kittens tumbled over each other on the carpet in front of them. They didn't strike Nix as a witch's familiars—more like a crazy cat lady's hording tendency.

Having dozens of familiars didn't seem practical, but what did Nix know.

"But some were?" Nix said.

"There was a core group of six who were really serious. And pissed that the others weren't as dedicated. I saw the whole group approached by some demons to meet the Order. This was during a choir practice at a community hall. The core six were honored, but the others were scared. None of them had ever actually met a demon before, it was all theory and kind of play-magic for most of them. When they realized what they were dealing with was the real thing, they freaked."

"Freaked?"

"They were talking about disbanding the group—some even wanted to convert their religions—but the six said they needed the full power of the group. They were more convinced than ever that they were on the right path and needed to be more dedicated. Some of the ones who weren't as dedicated were more powerful than the six though, like Maria. The six convinced everyone to gather for a meeting and that's where Maria's memory gets fried."

"What happened to her?"

"She saw her friends falling around her. Some of them died. Some were like her and suffered an extreme energy drain. I think the core six must have siphoned the energy of their coven into themselves so they could continue with the Order without them."

Nix leaned back. "Well that sounds like something the Order would condone. Did you see what the Order was planning to use the coven's amplified power for?"

Rachel twisted her shirt sleeve. "No. But they needed a lot of concentrated power."

"So the coven might be playing a role in their endgame."

"Could be." From the kitchen, the bird-themed clock chimed the hour again with the call of a Wood Duck. It was dark out now.

"All right," Nix said, slapping her hands on her thighs. "We still need to find the archdemons. Did you see the coven meet with the Order?"

Rachel sighed, dropping into the La-Z-Boy. "No. They were only ever at each other's houses or a local community hall. It'll take us ages to investigate all those locations. No way we have that kind of time to play detective. And the two demons who came to meet them seemed like regular-Joe demons, you know? They talked about the Order requesting these ladies' presence, they weren't the Order. Maria definitely never met the archdemons."

"There has to be some connection back to the Order from here, or else why would the archdemon's tea leaves have sent us here?" Nix paused, looking away. "I can't believe I just said that. Chasing tea leaves. This is idiotic."

Rachel rocked back and forth. "Coven of Thorns…what connects them to the Order? What would make the Order know they're members?"

"Book of Shadows, maybe."

"True. I saw Maria had one of those." Rachel looked around, eyes landing on the tall china cabinet taking up one corner of the living room. "This is where she kept it." She stood and rooted through the bottom drawer, lifting out a false bottom after a moment and pulling out a thick book. "Wow, this is old. Maybe we shouldn't take it. I'll look through it." Rachel brought it over. "It's only her family name in it, and it looks like the names of her relatives before her, maybe. Personal, not communal." She bit her lip.

"Not exactly part of the coven, then."

"Oh!" Rachel looked up. "I did see them all wearing those red robes, right?" She touched her clavicle. "And I think they were all wearing necklaces, too. Yeah, like, medallions or something. Gold. Oh…what were they…maybe gold coins?"

Nix straightened. "Coins?"

"Yeah, sort of, but thicker. They looked old. And everyone was wearing the same kind. Not sure what the image was on it though. I should have paid more attention. Maybe we should search the house? But…quietly?"

"I might know where that is." Nix led Rachel out to the extensive rose garden. The light of the nearly full moon was enough to navigate by, though it left Nix's stomach in knots as she mentally counted down. The scent of the flowers was as thick as a syrup on the air, leaving a sickeningly sweet taste at the back of Nix's throat. They trekked through the rows of flowers and over to where the property met the woods. Maria's altar. The wine goblet sat where Nix had left it. Beside it, a bowl of coins.

Nix dumped them onto the tree-stump altar amid the other offerings. She sifted through, fingers catching on a chain. Nix pulled it out. On the end, a heavy, ancient coin dangled—one side the head of a ram, the other a rose. The weight felt familiar in her hands, like it was calling to her.

"I think we found the trinket we came for."

Chapter 26

When they pulled back up to the factory district in San Clemente, it was after four in the morning. The sky was still dark. They'd driven straight through the night, speeding a little and avoiding the cities. Rachel tucked into a side street nearby, but still far enough away they'd have to walk.

Half the streetlights were broken along the road. Moths fluttered around a lone yellow lamp above the van.

"No one on this street again," Rachel commented, reaching into the back and grabbing her bag. She dragged it into the front. "Not even passing vehicles. Maybe it's got some sort of illusion going here—a glamor, like it did at the farmhouse. We aren't seeing what's really going on."

Nix adjusted Elliot's eye patch. "The bizarre garden in the warehouse is a glamor."

"I mean in the street, too. Now that it's loose, who knows how far its influence can reach."

The thought made Nix's palms prickle with sweat. "If that's true, then it *let* us find it. Pendulum or no pendulum. It could have made the building disappear until we stopped looking. Instead, it let us walk right in."

"So it wants something from us, like it said. Maybe to get back to Edgar Winterspoon's wife, Lizzie." Rachel checked the flip phone in her pocket and shook her head. "Nothing." She turned it off and slid it into her jacket. She pulled out a book from her bag—one of Blaine's collection of grimoires. "Maybe we can run a counter glamor or something."

Nix shifted in her seat, one of Elliot's knees whacking the dashboard. Rachel had given her a handful of meds, but they barely took the edge off the pain in her eye. "It'll be suspicious if you aren't playing along. You'll piss it off. It may be playing house with us, but you saw that security guard. It'll gut any one of us if it feels like it."

Rachel flipped through a book. "An anti-mindreading spell? If it reads our thoughts now, it'll know we're not buying its story."

Nix dragged Elliot's bulging bag from the back, too, and dug through it. "If it suddenly can't read your mind, that'll draw suspicion. I might have something better."

Rachel glanced over at her. "What do you have in there, the kitchen sink?"

"Blaine's forbidden office."

Rachel cracked a smile.

"Here." Nix handed Rachel a baggie containing three small, smooth rocks. "They're black jade. They can be used like a psychic barrier—with a psychic niece, I can imagine why Blaine would have a couple on hand to get a little privacy." Nix held up a piece of paper. "These might be more powerful than usual though. They're supposed to 'protect, muddle, and refract psychic communication,' whatever that means. At least, that's what the handwritten label says. They sparked when I touched them, so I think they're legit—guess we test them to find out."

Rachel palmed the stones. "You don't think it'll notice something's up?"

Nix shrugged. "Hard to say. Hope not. This should be subtle enough to throw it off and give you some control over your own thoughts. Take one and slip the other two to Danny and Blaine, but don't let them see. The less any of us are thinking traitorous thoughts, the better."

"What about you?"

"I'm practiced in controlling my thoughts. I'll feed it lines I think it wants to hear so it doesn't get too suspicious of all of us, and I'll keep Elliot out as much as possible around the archdemon. He hasn't heard us talking, anyway, and seems to be buying into it. That'll be in our favor."

Rachel tucked the bag into her pocket. "All right." She sighed. "I guess we go explain what happened to Elliot to Pops."

"You've got the blue glass and Maria's medallion?"

Rachel lightly patted her jacket. "They might be asleep in there right now."

"Well," Nix said, "not all of them."

They wandered up to the warehouse. Rachel raised her hand to open the door, but it swung open for her. Danny embraced her, pulling her inside, as if he'd been waiting at the door for them to return the whole time. "You were late, darlin'. I was startin' to worry—but of course I don't want ya speeding, either. You find the glass and the witch?"

Rachel nodded mutely, looking at the ground. Nix followed them in, the heavy door closing behind her. She moved out of the shadows and Danny gasped.

"No," he said. "What happened? My boy." He placed his hand on Nix's cheek tenderly, then pulled back and scowled. Danny shook a finger in her face. "The demon did this. Didn't you, demon? You hurt my boy?"

Rachel stepped between them. "No, Pops. Elliot did it to himself. Intentionally. Nix was with me searching the house."

Danny's mouth flapped. "Why?"

"He needed a break and he'd recently eaten, so we thought it'd be fine. I took Nix for a few minutes. A few minutes, to go through the house—"

"No, why would *he* do it?"

"What the archdemon told us," Nix said. "He wanted to control the hunger on his own."

"He didn't want to hurt anyone again," Rachel added. She burst into tears.

Nix and Danny both stepped back, wide eyed.

"I'm so sorry, Pops. I did this to us. I made him this way." She sobbed into her hands. "I'm sorry."

Danny shook his head, his expression fallen, and wrapped his arms around her. "Shh, darlin'." He carded his fingers through her hair and held her tight to his chest. "We'll get through this. Together."

Nix looked away to grant them some privacy. Elliot slept peacefully in his dreamscape. Fishing this time, Nix noticed. The water was a silver-black, the sky cloudless and blue.

"You need some rest," Danny was saying. "We'll sort it all after. I ain't mad, baby girl. It'll all be okay."

From the corner of her one good eye, Nix noticed Rachel slide a stone into Danny's inside jacket pocket.

Danny reached out and tugged Nix forward, urging her to follow as they moved down the hallway. In the main hall, the low rumble of a snoring bear rattled the windows. Blaine was curled up asleep in one corner on the floor.

Violet perched in the lotus position in the midst of an array of flowers, eyes shut and a contented smile painting her lips as they walked in. The grand table had disappeared and all that remained was the illusory garden.

Sniffling, Rachel knelt in front of Violet and turned out her jacket pocket, setting the shards of blue glass on the checkered linoleum. She pulled out the medallion next, the shiny coin dangling between her fingers. She placed it next to the glass pieces. "Will these work?"

Opening her eyes, Violet glanced down. "We shall see. For now, rest."

Rachel stood, walking over to the far wall to lie down where Danny had spread some sleeping bags.

Violet met Nix's good eye. "A bold choice," she said evenly. "I hope the corruption was not already too far spread."

"Yeah," Nix said, scratching at the gauze under her eye patch. "Hope so."

Nix laid next to Rachel on the hard, grimy floor, a barrier between the sleeping hunter and the archdemon. Danny soon joined their makeshift camp and Nix stared at the body swinging in the rafters until the sun came up.

Chapter 27

When the others woke after the brief nap, they prepared for the day ahead and for the scrying. If it worked, they could have a bead on the Order before lunch. The archdemon recreated her magic table, which was surprisingly stable for something that didn't actually exist. Nix couldn't stop touching it to test its consistency, but, damn, it was solid.

Rachel pulled a world map out of her backpack, along with several others. She delicately unwrapped the scrying crystal and laid it out on a piece of velvet as Blaine looked on with a scowl. Danny conferred with the archdemon on the other side of the room.

Nix leaned toward Blaine. "Don't look so glum, chum. You realize we wouldn't have found you if we hadn't snooped through your office, right?"

Blaine's gaze flicked to Violet. His jaw tightened.

Rachel slipped behind him, hand on his waist as she reached across the table to shift things around. "Excuse me," she said. She slipped a stone into the pocket of his pants.

Blaine's eyes widened and the scowl faded. A light returned to his gaze. Rachel smiled as she continued her busy work around the table.

Violet and Danny walked over to the table and sat. Rachel and Nix followed suit. Blaine stood at the end of the table as

Max stalked through the garden on the other side, huffing and scratching at the floor. Cockroach flowers scattered in the air as he sniffed them. Max chuffed, pawing at his snout and shaking his furry head.

"So is he going to stay a bear, then?" Nix asked.

"He is a bear," Danny said. "Are you going to stay a demon?"

Nix pursed her lips. "Point taken."

"We require the prisoner's blood," Violet said, looking to Nix. "Then yours."

"Right. Got it." The others stared at her. "I'll go...poke Cirrik with a stick or something."

Danny dug around in his duffle and handed Nix a gravity knife and a facecloth. "A few drops should do it?"

Violet nodded.

"Darlin'," Danny said to Rachel, "make sure he stays locked up, would ya?" Danny handed her a set of keys.

"Sure, Pops."

Rachel walked Nix out a new set of doors tucked around a corner. "Trailer's parked around back. Shipping and receiving dock. It's locked in—brick walls on three sides, and a chain-link gate on the fourth."

"Why are you telling me?" Nix said.

"So you know we didn't leave him out on the street or something, unsecured."

"Like I care."

"Sure. Of course not."

When they walked out into the open air, Nix sucked in a deep breath. "Think we can be out of this creepy dump before lunch?"

"Better be," Rachel said. "The Order's ascension is tonight. You going to slice him with that knife and move on, or do you want a minute?"

Nix wasn't sure why she was asking—the knife was the obvious answer. But then again, they'd had Cirrik tied up in the back of that trailer for days and the last conversation they'd had was heated and revealing, to say the least. He'd also somehow bounced her into the body of a witch who was part of the Coven of Thorns. Under ordinary circumstances, she'd have interpreted that as an attack; throwing her to the wolves. But Maria was no wolf and the experience had proven valuable. Almost like he'd been trying to give her a hint. Maybe it was worth a check-in.

"Okay, give me a minute," Nix said.

They walked up to the small aluminum trailer and Rachel unlocked the door, swinging it open. "Should I take his gag off?"

"Yeah. Whatever. Thanks."

The smell in the trailer wasn't much of an improvement over the rotting corpse garden Nix had recently vacated. It was dim inside, all the more so from the bright sunlight blinding her view. She lifted a hand to shield Elliot's good eye from the sun.

A raised iron bar encircled Cirrik in three rings. Nix knew from Danny's bragging during their boring road trip that the iron bars were hollow and packed with salt, then welded into the circular shape, one within the other. Rising up from these bars were more of the same mounted vertically and spaced five inches apart, forming a tight cell within the already small trailer. The whole contraption was welded to the floor and roof of the trailer so it wouldn't shift around while they drove or in case of an accident. Beneath the cell and strapped to the bars was the canvass cloth inlaid with crystals and painted with sigils—Rachel's doing. The same sigils were painted throughout the inside of the trailer, and bundles of herbs, including sage, dangled from the roof.

Within the tight cell, Cirrik sat on a metal chair looking miserable. He was trussed up with ropes and chains, for good measure. Danny was nothing if not thorough and paranoid.

The whole contraption meant Nix could speak to him from the door, but she couldn't enter. Even standing this close triggered her gag reflex. She didn't know how Cirrik was managing, but she supposed he didn't have a choice.

Rachel climbed up into the trailer and reached through the bars, pulling his gag off. "Behave," she cautioned. She jumped back down. "One minute." Rachel walked toward a brick wall to kick at some rocks, watching from the corner of her eye.

It wasn't exactly privacy. Nix moved a little closer, peeking into the darkness.

"A bird swoop down and peck the eye out?" came Cirrik's voice. He chuckled. "It suits you better like that."

Nix had all but forgotten Elliot's eye was missing and she no doubt looked like a pile of shit run over by a bus. Cirrik could probably see her more clearly from the darkness than she could see him from the light. "Went down exactly like that," she said. "Glad you approve."

"Planning on fixing it again this time? Come for my eye?"

Nix shuffled foot to foot. "Nah. Not this time."

"Why deign to be in my presence?"

"We need your blood."

She could hear the grin in his words as he said, "A cliché pickup line. I'd expect more creativity from you, after all this time."

"It's an off day for me."

He was quiet for a moment. "Is your host awake?"

She shook her head. "No. Been out since this whole self-enucleation incident last night. The other hunter's out of hearing distance, too. We can talk, just us."

"Just us," he repeated. "You did not tell your hunter friends about my host. I noticed that little fact, seeing as I am not yet forcibly wiped from the surface of the Earth."

Nix licked her lips, sighing. "Nope."

The dim light filtering into the trailer flashed off his white teeth as he smiled.

"Don't read into it," Nix said. "I can't keep that from them for long."

"Now you're trying to get me alone. Is this some sort of escape ploy?"

"Hardly."

"You could at least do me the courtesy of telling me what is going on out there. Cramped up in this disgusting trailer for miles of driving—I have overheard some peculiar things. Quite the loud argument over pizza and, as I understand it, cannibalism. Care to elucidate?"

Nix glanced at Rachel, leaning against the brick wall and examining her nails. "Uh...it's a long story."

"And now we are in some city," he said, shifting to crane his neck. "An industrial area. And you are asking me for my blood. Will you or your compatriots be drinking it?"

Nix laughed in spite of herself. "Of course not."

"Well, I can only assume."

"Fair enough. I've done weirder shit in the last two days, I guess. Why wouldn't I drink blood?"

"Sounds like you could use a good glass of vino and a friendly ear."

"Not on the menu today, unfortunately," Nix said. "I wanted to check on you...I guess." Her tongue flirted with all the questions she wanted to ask. Why send her to the witch? What was his play? Did he know where she'd land, or was it a random act of fate? Would he give her a straight answer if she asked, or would she be showing her hand? Nix pressed her lips tightly together, the words lodged in her throat. With a bitter taste in her mouth, she realized how much she missed talking with him. At one time, they'd shared everything. Now she ached for the lost familiarity, the comfort, the ease.

Cirrik didn't seem to notice her hesitation. "Trapped in this foul roaming cell as I have been these past days, I have had some time to think. About our last conversation. The Order's intentions. It...would not be the first time I have made a mistake. Chosen the wrong side. Believed I was making the right decisions when, perhaps, I was misled."

She met his eyes. "I can't let you out."

"I am aware. I only wanted you to know. The worst thing I ever did was abandon you. Or at least, that is what I thought the worst of it was—certainly, my only regret. You do not get to where we are by allowing regrets. But if you are right about the Order, I killed the only father I ever knew. My grandfather, he...well, it hardly matters now. And the plague. I lost four brothers to the sickness. A best friend. A fiancée. The man I might have been. The good king my grandfather wanted me to be. I never regretted any of that, until you put it all into question."

"Cirrik, I—"

But he continued, saying, "That they could have brought the plague. Manipulated me into... I don't know what to believe any longer. I'm angry, Nix. I do find that rage scratching like hungry rats again inside me. But it is not you I'm angry at. We are too old now to throw childish blame at messengers."

Nix swallowed. "So you believe me about the Order. You're mad at them?"

His voice dropped low. "I am saying: when you find your teeth on their throats, I want my chance to take an equal bite. Consider it the cost of shattering my delusion—you owe me a share of your prize. I want them to suffer like my grandfather suffered on his deathbed."

Rachel walked up behind her. "More than a minute. We good to move this along?" She looked at Cirrik. "We need a blood sample."

"It'll help us track down the Order," Nix added experimentally.

Cirrik held her gaze. "Take it all."

Chapter 28

Reconvened at the table with a bloody cloth in hand, Nix pulled out the gravity knife and pressed it to Elliot's palm. Violet held up her hand. "The scrying will be stronger if you combine your essence with the blood of the witch."

Nix glanced at Rachel. "Why?"

"Her blood magic is powerful." Violet took the knife, rolled the handle between her palms. "Blood of the host, though corrupted by the demon, is still half-host, half-demon. The token of the coven will lend direction to our search, but it is untouched by the Order itself." She plunked Maria's necklace into a silver bowl in the center of the table. Her fingers dropped to the broken blue glass inside with it. "Shattered glass touched by many spirits—the essence of the Order may be weak. So shattered, it will be unstable. Add a witch's blood to that of the demon spawned by the Order, and perhaps a chance is born to amplify the Order's essence among all others."

Nix dropped into a chair. "I think I get what you're laying down. Her blood makes mine stronger, and the combo might give us a better shot at pinning down the Order."

"Precisely."

Rachel swatted a passing cockroach. The garden shivered at her touch. "What about Elliot?"

Nix leaned back in the chair. "I guess this will be a chance to test if he can control his hunger. He hasn't eaten in a while."

Danny stood from the head of the table, adjusting his worn brown-leather jacket. "I'll cuff him and watch him. Ya'll handle the spell." He looked relieved to be excused from any spellcraft.

Nix made the switch and left Elliot half-conscious and groaning on the floor next to Danny. Danny was muttering, dragging Elliot to the other side of the room. Hushed conversation passed between them, Elliot's head lowered.

Nix's vision wavered through Rachel's eyes. She grabbed the table's edge to steady herself.

"Okay," Nix said in Rachel's voice. "Let's do this."

Violet dropped the bloodied cloth into the bowl.

Nix took the knife. The sharp edge of the blade bit into Rachel's palm, flesh splitting open. She squeezed the flow into the bowl, her essence mixing with Cirrik's.

Her heartbeat kicked up. If this worked, their next step would be into the fray.

Violet held one hand over the bowl and muttered something. She reached for the crystal pendulum on the black-velvet cloth, but it rolled across the table to Nix. Violet's purple hair veiled her eyes as her mouth twisted into a frown. She held out her thin hand, palm up.

Nix pulled Rachel's shirtsleeve down over her hand and picked the object up with a fabric barrier—her skin still tingled at the touch of it. She tried to pass Violet the pendulum, only for it to jump into the air and land at Rachel's feet.

Nix lifted it by the silver chain, hissing at the sting of phantom ant bites in her fingertips. It wasn't as bad as when she'd touched it earlier. It was allowing her to hold it.

"Guess it likes Rachel." Nix glanced up at Violet's scowling form, hunched over the large table.

"So it seems." Violet's fingernails scratched at the flaking skin on her neck. "Dip the pendulum into the blood and hold it over the map. Steady."

Nix rolled her eyes but followed the instructions—this was not her first rodeo and having the process idiot-splained annoyed her. A drop of blood dripped onto the map as she held it a couple inches above.

Rachel's fingers trembled with the psychic current pulsing through the pendulum. Nix focused, steadying her hand despite the discomfort. After a moment, the crystal began to circle.

Danny, Blaine, and Elliot—in a set of handcuffs—came to stand over them.

The pendulum landed on the map, pinning a location. Nix checked it. "US. California." She pursed her lips. "They stayed close after getting loose?"

Elliot shifted foot to foot. "Or the pendulum is locating us—Rachel's and Cirrik's blood, and the glass," Elliot said.

Violet tilted her chin up. "Another map."

Danny swapped out the world map with one of California. The pendulum swung again, this time landing on San Francisco.

"Not us," Nix said. "It's definitely locating something. Do we have a map of San Fran?"

"Hold on," Danny said. He ran out to the van and returned. The pendulum got them even closer, this time near the waterfront.

The location dropped them in the Rincon Hill area. "Huh," Nix mumbled, the scent of petrichor and iron suddenly sharp in her mind. The memory Cirrik shared with her had taken place on their way to the village Rincón de Soto, but of course that had been in Spain.

The others tittered excitedly. When they narrowed it down to a city block, the pendulum would go no further. It wasn't as good as they'd managed with Violet's archdemon, but it was better than the nothing they'd started out with. And Elliot hadn't tried to cannibalize anyone in the hour it had taken to perform the scrying. Things were looking up. The cut on Rachel's palm continued to drip blood on the table.

"Let's head out to San Fran," Elliot said.

Danny said, "We'll have to be more careful in the city." But he was smiling.

"We've got an archdemon on our side—I'm sure if we get pulled over by the cops, we can get out of it with some Jedi mind control," Elliot said.

"Well, now, that's an idea." Danny looked to Violet. "What do you think, will you come with us?"

Violet tilted her head, glancing away from the pendulum still in Nix's hand. "Certainly, Daniel Whipsaw. I always assist my friends."

Nix tucked the pendulum into Rachel's jacket for safekeeping, flexing her aching, stiff fingers. Rincon Hill. Could it be a coincidence? She'd thought Maria was a coincidence, and she'd been wrong. "I need to talk to Cirrik again first."

Danny didn't glance at her. He grabbed her bloody hand and splashed some alcohol on it. Nix gasped and hissed.

"We've got to get on the road." Danny shoved some gauze into her palm and before Nix knew what was happening, Rachel's hand was wrapped up.

"I'll be fast."

He grunted. "Things are really lookin' up."

"Hold on," Nix said as the gravity of the situation crashed down on her. "What are we going to do when we get there?"

Everyone stopped. The cockroach flowers chittered in the silence.

"Yeah." Nix pushed loose strands of Rachel's dark hair behind her ears. "That's what I thought."

Danny plopped down at the table. Elliot joined him, his handcuffs clanging against the polished, faux-wood tabletop.

"We can't go in without a plan of attack," Nix pointed out. They may have survived this archdemon, but there was no way they'd be that lucky again—and Nix wasn't so sure yet that they could call this luck.

"You're right," Danny said, possibly for the first time since Nix had known him.

Elliot leaned forward. "We have the exorcism."

Nix shook her head. "That's not a plan. They'll have you hunters choking on your own blood long before you can get the words out. They're probably expecting us, and the exorcism."

Danny scratched at his wiry beard. "We have to pin 'em down first. Too bad we've only got one bottle of that binding oil left—it won't go far in a fight like this."

"Do we even know if the exorcism would be strong enough to work on an archdemon?" Elliot asked. "We don't know how they got trapped in that roman glass in the first place. I'm not fully convinced it could have destroyed them outright the way it did lesser demons. We could trap them again, but we have nothing to trap them in."

Nix thought of the hunters' earlier attempts to trap her in random objects, including a crystal ball. None had been viable. The objects hadn't been able to sustain her energy. Even though the blue roman glass sphere had looked more like a delicate garden ornament, it must have been tremendously powerful to hold so many disembodied entities in stasis the way it had. One of a kind. To find something else like it may not be possible.

Nix steepled Rachel's fingers, leaning her elbows on the table. "It wasn't the exorcism that took out the archdemon you called Val. All the demons she trapped in the roman glass tore her apart on their way out. She wasn't as strong as the Order though. And who's to say if she's even really destroyed or wounded and in hiding somewhere."

"Well that doesn't help us right now," Elliot said. "So we know these archdemons can be trapped in roman glass, but ours is broken. Are there others out there?"

Nix shook her head. "Val said she'd searched for ages for this one. I doubt we could recover another before our time runs out. And once they're at their full strength, nothing is going to stop them. Certainly not some tiny glass prison."

Elliot huffed. "I've got some super glue."

"Inadequate." Violet tilted her chin up. "But the Nereid goddess Psamathe's sand would heal the glass."

Elliot's blond eyebrow rose over his one good eye. "Seriously? We could fix it? How do we get something like that?"

Violet drew patterns on the tabletop. "Very expensive. Very far."

"How far?" Danny asked. "Can we drive there?"

Violet smirked, her hand stilling. "No. But I can open a door to the other realm. The price for Psamathe's sand is high in the market. Have you anything to trade?"

"How high are we talking?" Danny rubbed the back of his neck. "Funds are...tight."

"We're already running from the cops, maybe we rob a bank on the way," Nix suggested.

"Human currency is of no value," Violet said. "I know a trader. Many valuable goods. But eccentric tastes. You will have to pique their interest."

"I've got some stuff from the house," Danny said. "Things we couldn't risk leaving behind, in case people stumbled on them. A box of cursed coins. Old. Worth a pretty penny—but, I wouldn't want them in the wrong hands."

Elliot sighed. "Not sure we have a lot of options here, Pops."

"Suppose you're right."

"What else to trade?" Violet asked.

"A few trinkets, I guess," Danny said.

Nix remembered her bag of stolen tricks from Blaine's office. "I have some objects that might be worth something, too. Maybe we go and check it out. Is sand all we'd need to fix this bauble?"

"Yes. You may also consider a binding agent to supplement your oil. Perhaps we might find something at the market."

Danny slapped his palms against the tabletop, rising. "Well, let's go then. Daylight's burnin'."

"Daylight is no concern where we are going." Violet met Nix's eyes. "Unfortunately, only immortals may pass through the barrier."

Danny's shoulders dropped. "Meaning?"

"Meaning me and her," Nix clarified. "You're staying behind."

Danny started to shake his head, but Elliot reached a cuffed hand out and placed it on his shoulder. "We have to do this."

Nix shoved her hands in Rachel's jacket pockets. The black jade was cold against her fingertips. To Rachel, Nix said, *"I know we're all getting rundown with these swaps, but I think it's best if I take Elliot with me and you stay here."*

She felt Rachel's spine stiffen. *"To another realm where you might never return? You're dreaming if you think I'll allow that."*

"I'll take care of him. But this could be our only shot at some private time with Blaine without Violet around." Nix glanced at Violet, but she was chatting with Danny, no indication that she was overhearing Nix's thoughts and Nix couldn't sense the oily, sticky feeling of the archdemon in her mind. The stone seemed to be helping so far. *"You need to hide that pendulum. She has her eye on it."*

Rachel took a moment to chew this over, her mindscape a still, barren field between them. *"Okay. I'll get some intel from Blaine and see if I can check in with Lizzie, too. But you better come back here in one piece. I thought you wanted to talk to Cirrik before we left."*

Another problem to deal with on the unending list. *"No time. Later."*

Nix walked up to Elliot. He'd been popping happy pills since she switched to Rachel, and he'd been having private conversations with Danny about the whole eye-gouging thing, but Nix hadn't been privy to most of it.

His skin was pale and gaunt, skeletal. The contrast of the black eye patch made it worse. With the amount he'd been eating in the last couple weeks, it was incredible that he hadn't packed on the weight. Instead, he seemed to be burning through anything that touched his lips. His hoodie and blue jeans looked like they were hanging off a wire.

Nix kicked Elliot's boot. "You look like shit."

Elliot frowned. "I feel okay. I mean..." He looked at the ground. "It hurts, obviously." Nix couldn't imagine it hurt that much with the quantity of narcotics she'd seen him consume, but it would make for a more pleasant ride on her end, at least. "Can you tell Rachel I'm sorry I freaked her out yesterday? I don't know what came over me. But I do feel better...that way."

"We can't be sure about that yet." Nix crossed her arms. "Rachel and I agreed we need to switch back. You and I will go with Violet to the market and Rachel will stay here."

His gray eye widened. "Oh. Really?"

Nix nodded.

"Sure, I guess. I mean, I'm a little tired."

"This is the way it needs to go down," Nix said. "We wouldn't want anything happening, would we?"

Elliot squinted his eye at her but acquiesced. They made the switch.

Nix shook Elliot off, settling into his sharp bones and flexing his taut muscles. Rachel stumbled into a wall when she tried to stand, a hand on her stomach.

"Not sure I can keep doing that." Rachel swallowed and slid to the floor.

"We won't be long," Nix said, having nothing whatsoever to base this on.

Danny handed her a heavy bag. She handed him back his handcuffs. His head tilted. "How'd you get those off?" He patted himself down. "I have the key still."

Nix winked. "This all you've got to trade? What's in here, your rock collection?"

Danny opened the bag and pointed. "The box of cursed coins. Do *not* open that. Leave them in the box. They're called cursed coins for a reason." He handed her a fancy-looking key on a chain and she slipped it over Elliot's neck. "Not that you need it. There are also Louisiana gator claws, an Aztec death whistle, and a monkey paw." He poked her in the chest in a manner that could almost be interpreted as affectionate. "What could you possibly have to trade?"

Nix shifted her bulging backpack off her shoulder and opened it for Danny to see. She shook it a little, revealing the objects inside. Squished between a box containing the fingerbone of St. Francis Borgia and a velvet-mounted jewel purported to be from the tomb of King Tutankhamun was the bagged remains of a crushed driver's side mirror from James Dean's Porsche 550 Spyder, 'Little Bastard.' A few amulets and ritual candles were interspersed. Nothing Nix had particular interest in, nor were they anything she could see a use for. But they were weird, rare, and in some cases, powerful. Could be what they needed to pique the interest of some eccentric shop owner.

"Looks like a bunch of fake junk," Danny said.

Wandering past, Blaine said, "Hey! Those are mine!"

Nix jerked the bag back, holding it close.

Violet shot Blaine a glare.

"Well," he muttered. "At least get a good price for them."

Nix wandered over to Violet. She stood next to a blank wall crawling with ivy. "Ready for departure?"

Violet picked up a piece of brick from the ground and used it to trace a false door on the wall. She whispered under her breath the way she had to her tea leaves, then pressed her palm flat against the wall. The concrete gave way with a groan, pushing inward. Dust puffed into the air like a sigh.

Rachel gripped her arm before she could step forward. "Be careful."

Nix glanced back at the others. Danny stood next to Max, who lay on the floor licking his paw. Blaine watched from a far corner of the room, suit still crumpled and torn, dirt caking the lines of his forehead—a different man entirely from the Doucheface she'd met not so long ago.

Rachel watched close by, leather jacket zipped tight, hair pulled back in a ponytail. They shared a look of understanding. Nix adjusted Elliot's eye patch and straightened the strap of the bag slung over her shoulder, gripping the other tightly in hand.

Violet stepped through the door, into the darkness beyond. Nix followed.

Chapter 29

When Nix stepped over the threshold into the other realm beyond, the door behind her disappeared. An expanse of glittering black sand stretched in every direction. Violet turned to her from six feet away, short purple locks bouncing. She raised an eyebrow expectantly.

She looked every bit a teenager in her scuffed Vans, punk-rocker jacket, artfully torn jeans, and piercings up the side of one ear. If not for the madness behind her eyes and the shimmer of scales emerging along the skin of her neck, the change in her might go undetected. And that occasional flash of a forked tongue, but Nix supposed teenagers were into that nowadays.

Nix stepped forward but found herself slowed by the soft sand. Too bad they couldn't use whatever this was on the glass. Nix didn't bother asking though—she knew the answer. It was always some special sand from some special vendor at some exorbitant price. Probably the same damn stuff in a different package.

They trudged along, Nix struggling far more in Elliot's heavier, lankier body than the archdemon seemed to be in Violet's much smaller one. They were circled by solid walls of dark-gray rock for miles in a perfect ring.

Above them, an orange glow lit the sky evenly across, but no sun or clouds were visible. It took Nix a while to figure out they must be walking inside a massive volcano. Hopefully a dormant one, and probably not on the Earth she was used to.

Strange, stout flora grew in bristly patches. Nix had traversed other realms when necessity called for it, most extremely unpleasant, but this one was unfamiliar to her.

Elliot observed their surroundings with awed intensity, comparing it to some video games Nix had never heard of. His hunger had halved, appropriately, seeing as he was down half his vision.

"Was it worth it?" she asked him idly as they trekked across the endless sand. *"Gouging your own eye out? Stupid stunt you pulled."*

"It was my only chance," he said. *"Not like I get a lot of alone time lately."*

"You didn't think to run something like that by me? I'm down an eye now, too."

"My eyes are not yours. You would have tried to talk me out of it."

"Not necessarily." Nix stepped over a rock, keeping Violet in sight. *"I can be swayed by a reasonable argument. Sometimes an unreasonable one. You know that."*

"You'd have told Rachel, and she would have. It was my choice, not either of yours. For once. I'm not letting my body be some insatiable killing machine that I can't control."

All the hunters seemed to have a complex about that sort of thing. *"Fair enough. You think you can control it now?"*

"Better than before. Better than doing nothing."

She couldn't argue, though his methods were a little extreme. The empty socket itched and burned. She could still feel the effects of the pills he'd downed in her absence—the acid burn of them as they fizzed in his stomach, how his liver and kidneys were working a little harder today to process them, and the marvelous dull haze at the edges of his reduced vision.

His depth perception was shot to hell and there was an aching headache wrapped in unspoken fear that lingered like a bitter candy lodged in the boy's throat, but she found a significant apathy there with it that had a distinct oxycontin aftertaste.

Rachel and Danny had been talking about infection and there was no way they were going to be able to take him to a hospital for real treatment, so the left-over meds from his previous injuries were the limit of their options for the time being.

Nix wiped a hand across her forehead. A little more fevered than usual. Well, that's what he got for gouging his eye out with a rusty gardening tool. Not like she could monitor him twenty-four-seven while they were trying to take down an Order of archdemons—what was she, his keeper?

It was bad enough, Rachel flipping out at her over her future-self allegedly committing some crime, which was complete bullshit. But the fact that Rachel was trusting her now with Elliot had to mean she'd gotten over it, right? Besides, it wasn't as though it were true. Nix had no intention of offing her teammates, strange as this new reality had become to her. They were stuck with each other.

"If the archdemon could magic a door into existence, why wouldn't it have brought us closer to the intended destination? Seems like this is a lot of walking," Elliot pointed out. *"You ever been here before?"*

Nix's stomach dropped, suddenly very aware that the portal had disappeared and she didn't know where they were. It *was* a lot of walking. *"No. Not here."*

Glancing around, Nix couldn't see how they were getting any closer to a market. Visibility was clear for miles, and there was nothing but sand.

"Hey," Nix said, waving to the archdemon ahead. "Where exactly is this market?"

Violet turned around, looked at her, and disappeared.

Chapter 30

Nix gasped as Violet disappeared in front of her. "Oh shit." A cold wind whipped around her, scooping sand up into small dust devils. Words swirled with it through her mind. *Trapped. Foolish. Stranded.*

She ran toward the point where Violet disappeared.

The air clapped around her.

Nix covered Elliot's ears, squinting and sucking in a breath of hot air. Something shoved passed her, knocking her over.

When she looked up, a bustling market exploded all around her.

Violet stood over her, reaching out a hand. "Bazaar, not market. Must pass the veil to enter."

Nix frowned, lifting herself up and dusting off. She glanced around at the crowd and stalls that hadn't been there a second earlier. *Veil?* Another glamor. No wonder Violet was familiar with this place, it was right up her alley—built on illusions.

Violet picked up Danny's bag and handed it to Nix. She took Nix's free hand before she could protest, dragging her along.

"Keep possessions close," she whispered. "Pickpockets. Much fun to be had in the bazaar. I will show you. This is your first time, yes?"

Nix narrowed her gaze. "Yeah. In this realm."

The black sand scratched at Elliot's eye and squished beneath his heavy boots as Nix tried to keep up.

"Ay, laddie. Nice eyepatch," an old pirate selling bootleg DVDs called to her as they passed, bony finger tapping his own patch. Closer inspection revealed half the DVDs to be snuff films and recordings of assassinations. *Which Time Traveler Killed JFK?* one title asked.

"This place isn't what I expected," Nix said. The skeleton of a parrot on the pirate's shoulder squawked at them and they moved on.

They passed a table selling replicas of Draupnir, a Norse ring forged by dwarves—they seemed to have no shortage of the self-replicating object. The next stall was crammed with junk, from toasters to llama fetuses—for good luck—and snake-skin shoes claiming to be made from the genuine hair of Medusa. Across the tight lane were rows of glowing green bottles containing a love potion made of Dryad essence.

Violet said, "You held expectations of a place you have never been?"

"Well, yeah," Nix said. "Most of this seems like junk. Half this stuff is modern human garbage."

Violet winked. "Ah, must know where to look at the grand bazaar."

They passed booth upon booth stacked almost on top of each other, each varying in size and shape, differentiated by swathes of colorful cloths and decorations, some with roughly-drawn signs chalked with sigils.

Shopkeepers called out to them as they passed. One offered an authentic Cintamani stone with the promise of immortality and knowledge, the green trapezohedron flashing in nonexistent sunlight. Considering everyone here was immortal, Nix could see why it wasn't selling.

Another hawked a shriveled, pickled Hand of Glory said to open any door. It twitched in the box as they walked by. Others had various creatures perched out front—gargoyles, black ravens, three-headed snakes, phoenixes. When the creatures weren't pets or for purchase, they were the proprietors.

They passed a stall with a giant blue slug manning the counter and Violet frowned, pulling Nix away, muttering about highway robbery.

They stopped at one stall thick with cobwebs. Violet dropped Nix's hand and waved. "Nell?"

A massive hairy leg emerged from the dark recesses of the shop. Another seven followed daintily as the spider carried itself to the front of the stall, knocking things over on her way.

The arachnid had a woman's naked upper torso and head, with a pretty, feminine face and spider legs for arms. Strapped to her large body with webbed ropes were all manner of televisions, radios, and computers—old-fashioned and new, human and otherwise. Some flashed with static while others buzzed and chattered in technicolor.

"Lovely to see you, my dear," she trilled. She reached out one long leg. "The outfit is darling. What are you looking for? New radio from the seventh circle? Perhaps a fake-newspaper, special edition straight from hell—only place you'll find it at these prices."

"Actually, friend Nell," Violet said, "I seek Rusty. His stall was gone. Has his place of business moved?"

"Oh yes, dear. He's moving up—bigger shop in the center avenue now. Gaudy neon signs and dancers. Couldn't miss it if you were blind," she said, staring at Nix with a predatory smile. She reached out with her spiny leg, brushing it against Nix's cheek from across the booth. "Aren't you a gorgeous specimen. A little ghoul, a little human, a little demon. Mm. I could eat you up." She smacked her lips. Nix felt Elliot's body shiver.

"Thank you, friend Nell," Violet said obligingly, pulling Nix away.

They pushed through throngs of shoppers, some of whom Nix recognized as her kind, but most were creatures of other sorts. She was so caught up in the electric bustle of the place that it took a second between being bumped into by a small bird-like man with a bandana and noticing the slight absence of weight in her back pocket.

"Son of a—" Nix spun around, searching the little man out in the crowd and patting at Elliot's pocket. His wallet was gone.

"Not my wallet," Elliot was saying, *"please, not that…"*

Violet's hand fell on her shoulder. "What troubles you?"

"Some little bastard stole my wallet!" Nix glimpsed him in the crowd and pointed. "Him!"

Violet moved even before Nix could. Nix ran to catch up, jumping and dodging through the throngs.

She tripped over a bucket of writhing mutant eels, threw an apology to the shopkeeper, and leaped ahead.

She'd lost them. Violet was nowhere in sight, nor was the thief.

Violet's voice carried over the crowd. Nix wove through and finally spotted her. The thief was limping back into the shadows. Violet held Elliot's wallet in her hand. She smiled, tossing it to Nix.

Nix caught it. It fell open in her hand. Elliot probably had twenty bucks inside, but his family photos stared back—he and Rachel fishing as kids, all three of them standing in front of their house. The only ones he had left. Internally, Elliot sighed.

"Thank you," Nix said. "That was…thanks." She felt herself redden, cheeks heating. Violet had, after all, explicitly warned her, yet she'd still been pickpocketed like some rube. It was a silly thing to go after, but of all the crap she was dragging around today, it was probably the most valuable to her host.

Violet grinned and shrugged. "Almost there." She pointed toward flashing neon lights, one of which was an actual arrow.

"So we are," Nix said.

When they finally reached the middle of the bazaar, a covered shop at the center of it advertised "Live Girls" on a large sign but the "Live" was crossed out and "Dead" was spray-painted above it.

Nix raised an eyebrow. "This another friend of yours?"

Violet scrunched up her face. "Certainly not."

"Ah. I get it. But he sells the fancy sand stuff in his weird strip club?"

"Yes. A proprietor of many unique items and eccentric tastes."

A hinoenma met them at the threshold. The slender woman wore a red silk robe, her long black hair cascading over her shoulder. Her captivating beauty belied an unquenchable lust for the life energy and destruction of men. She motioned for them to enter. Cirrik had dated one of these for a time. Typical. Nix scowled at her, but she only smirked.

As they passed through the threshold of flowing scarves and beads, pounding dance music rolled over them. The sand floor shivered with the beat. "A little loud," Nix said.

Along one wall of the large tent a rickety stage was constructed with wires hanging off and a microphone in the center. As advertised, several dead girls flung their rotting body parts around the stage in synchrony with the music as another wailed into the microphone.

The scent of putrefaction and decay didn't even bother Nix anymore—it was becoming akin to a bad cologne. Onlookers reclined in seats in front of the stage, smoking and howling. Someone lost an arm on stage and picked it back up, carrying on with their sexy dance unperturbed.

Violet led Nix to the back. A big man in a suit that looked nice enough to be buried in leaned against a pole. His polished dress shoes sank into the sand as he straightened.

"Long time no see, pal. Ya here for the show or a little somethin' special?" He gestured to Nix. "Who's your friend here? Ya ain't no snitch, eh?" He laughed, slapping Nix on the arm. "Kiddin', kiddin'! Who ya gonna snitch ta, am I right?"

Nix looked to Violet.

"We are in need of the *something special*," Violet said.

"I see, I see. I can do ya. For the right price, ya feel me?"

Violet asked about the blue roman glass, in case they could skip the repair altogether, but Rusty said he hadn't seen one in a dragon's age. Violet changed tracks, asking, "Are you in possession of Psamathe's sand?"

Rusty raised his finger to his lips and ushered them through another series of hanging scarves and beads into a smaller tent beyond. "I might be. Let me see here." He dug through a cabinet.

Something caressed Nix's elbow. She turned to see a white tablecloth hanging from a hook, the soft prehensile fabric reaching out to touch her. Nix stepped away.

Violet leaned in conspiratorially. "The Skatert Samobranka. Russian tablecloth. Magically produces food. Useful, but"—she shook her head—"too much upkeep. Gets lonely if left on its own."

Rusty closed the cabinet drawer and turned back to them. "Yup, there we go, Psamathe's sand." He held out a capped glass vial, but when Nix reached for it, he jerked it away. "Free to look, but it'll cost ya to touch, pal. Runnin' a business here. What've ya got to trade? This is some rare, high-grade shit, feel me?"

Nix took out the box of coins, unlocking it with the key around her neck. She set them on a table. "They're cursed," she offered.

The man plunked down at the table and slid on a pair of leather gloves while making smacking noises with his lips. "Mm-hm, oh yes." He pulled out a tiny magnifying glass and examined the coins, picking one up and biting it. "Cursed all right." He dropped the coin into the box with a clink and slid it back to her. "But what am I gonna do with a box of cursed coins? No market for 'em right now."

"They're worth a vial of your sand," Nix lied, having no idea what either item was worth and no interest in a conversation about market value. "You have people beating down your door to buy a vial of sand every day?"

He squinted at her. "Perhaps ya sweeten the pot and I find myself more inclined to relieve myself of this special, cherished item you wish to procure."

Nix squinted back, shaking her head. "What language are you speaking?"

He sighed. "What *else* ya got?"

Nix pulled out the Aztec death whistle from Danny's bag, bringing it to her lips to demonstrate. What sounded like a woman's shrieking death wail filled the space. Rusty frowned and shook his head. From her bag, she pulled out St. Francis Borgia's fingerbone and the cracked Porsche mirror. He grinned.

"All right, ya got yerself a dealio."

"There's something else we need," Nix said.

"And what would that be?"

"A binding agent. Something strong enough to keep an archdemon bound in place or trapped in a body for—well, as long as possible. You have something like that?"

Rusty rubbed his bristly chin. "Strange request." He laughed. "But hell, I'm a proprietor of strange requests, pal. I've got something. But…" He rubbed his fingers together.

Nix rolled her one good eye and dumped the remaining contents of both bags out on the table. "If you've got something that you can guarantee is strong enough for the job, you can take it all."

Rusty's grin stretched wide across his teeth. "I've got just the thing, pal. Nothin' in any realm is going to hold an archdemon for more than ten minutes if they don't wanna be held, but I've got enough you can get yerself in whatever trouble yer stirin' up with a whole nest of 'em. A get-in-get-out package."

"Let's see it."

He walked to a different cabinet, rummaging around in his pocket. He pulled out a small key and opened a drawer. From the drawer, he pulled out a large polymer case with a built-in handle, bringing it to the table.

When he popped it open, Nix could only stare. "Will it work?"

"Oh, pal. It'll work all right."

Chapter 31

The portal hissed as Nix and Violet returned through it with a vial of sand and a black case. Rachel and Danny greeted them at the vine-draped wall as soon as they entered, Blaine standing back and Max off in the garden.

Nix met Rachel's eyes, glancing to Blaine. Rachel pursed her lips, shaking her head almost imperceptibly. *No news,* Nix interpreted. At least, no news she could share for the time being. Rachel lifted her eyebrows and lowered her chin, eyes flicking to Violet. Nix raised one shoulder and nodded. *It went well.*

In fact, it had gone far better than Nix anticipated. They got what they went for. But more than that, Violet had ample opportunity to leave her behind or screw her over, but she didn't. She even got Elliot's wallet back from the pickpocket. She'd been nothing but helpful and supportive—a friend. The distrust Nix had felt toward her before started to feel misplaced...almost like prejudice. Violet could very well be the only individual here who really understood her.

"The sand?" Rachel said.

"Retrieved." Violet raised her hands in the air triumphantly.

"What's in the case?" Danny asked.

Nix broke into a grin. "You're not going to believe this." She handed the gift to Danny. "Happy birthday."

"Ain't my birthday," he said, but he was smiling. He set the case on the table where their supplies were laid out and popped it open. It seemed to sigh in anticipation as the lid eased up. His eyes widened. "A tranquilizer gun?"

The gun was dismantled into pieces, nestled in foam padding. Nix stood next to Danny and tapped the tranquilizer darts and the six vials next to them. "One shot of this solution will bind an archdemon temporarily in its host and immobilize the body, similar to the oil. Should give us ten minutes."

"Maybe it is my birthday." Danny chuckled.

"We have discussed," Violet said, appearing beside them, "and I am willing to 'guinea pig.'"

"We have enough to test it out first, make sure it works," Nix clarified. She'd wanted to test it before purchase, but Violet wouldn't insult Rusty's honor as a businessman.

Danny faced them both. "Thank you."

Nix shrugged, looking away. "I'll let you two experiment, then we can try fixing the roman glass."

Danny's fingertips brushed over his new gun. He was, after all, the best shot in the bunch. It wasn't long before they'd confirmed the tranquilizer solution was effective to the ten-minute mark. Violet wasn't struggling very hard against it, so they had to factor in an adrenaline response. They'd have to be ready to move fast. After using one as a test, they had five vials left as well as Danny's last bottle of oil. More than enough.

Shaking off the effects of the tranquilizer, Violet walked Rachel through the process of repairing the blue glass. Since it was so damaged, they hemmed and hawed about the instability of the object, but a spell and some alchemy later, they had a functional roman glass ball back in action.

"Two wins today," Rachel said next to Nix at the table. "Ready to try for a hat trick?"

Nix's borrowed stomach tightened. She swallowed. "What's our game plan, exactly?"

Rachel looked to Danny, who was playing with his new gun. "Got a location, roughly. Have to narrow it down." His gaze didn't shift from the un-birthday gift.

"Recon." Rachel pulled the elastic out of her long hair, ran her fingers through the thick locks, and refastened the ponytail higher. "We go to the area and scope the place out, see what we see. Maybe Violet can narrow it down once we get there, sense them out."

Sweat slicked Nix's palms. "And if we actually find them?"

Danny set the gun down. "We ain't in bad shape, but we need to make today count. Full moon is tonight. We strike once we know our location and how to infiltrate. Cutting it close, but no way around it."

"Will they be guarded?" Rachel asked Nix.

Above them, unseen birds fluttered in the vibrant green foliage.

"Not sure. Cirrik said he didn't know where they were, so maybe no one does. Not as if they need protection, but at the same time, they're building an army. And with what they're planning, they'll be making enemies of everyone once word gets out."

Rachel leaned forward, steepling her fingers. "So we prepare for an army."

"We don't exactly have the weapons to fight an army." Nix bit her lip, images of a brutal massacre unspooling through her thoughts and leaving her guts twisted.

"Not as entertaining when you're the one being massacred?" Elliot asked, watching the images playout in their shared mindscape.

"You are a weapon," Rachel said. "So is Violet. Max will help us fight. Danny and I can hold our own."

Danny squinted at Blaine. "Maybe we should leave Blaine behind."

"No." Blaine stood straighter at the end of the table. "I'm coming."

Violet's sharp gaze locked on him and her mouth opened as if mid-reprimand, but she closed it after a moment. No one argued with him.

"I'll handle the tranq gun." Danny's hand brushed over it as he spoke. "And Rachel can have Kevin's blessed gun, take out any demon army that get between us and the Order. Can't be wasting darts on any lower demons."

"So we do what we can to sneak wherever we need to sneak, but we fight our way in if we have to. Better not to alert the Order to our presence if we can help it, though. If our experience at Winterspoon's ranch taught us anything, it's that fighting a demon army means mass casualties of human hosts, not to mention anyone who gets caught in the crossfire—this is bay area San Francisco, it's going to be way more populated than we're used to."

"We find 'em, we get in, we tranq 'em, we exorcise 'em into the little ball." Danny smacked his fist against the tabletop.

Nix leaned her throbbing forehead into her splayed hands. "I feel like that plan is ignoring a lot of the important in-between parts. Like all of the logistics. Or the parts where they catch us and we all die horrifically."

"You got a better plan?" Danny asked.

Fuck everything. She didn't. Nix shook her head, taking a deep breath. "We're winging it, then?"

Rachel pursed her lips. "Yep."

Nix glanced around the table at what Cirrik would call her comrades. *Cirrik. Shit.* She needed to deal with him...and with dismantling the metaphorical bomb he'd left in her hands. They couldn't move forward with their plans if any of them were holding back, and certainly not if there was any hesitation about trusting each other. Nix spread her hands flat on the table. The others looked at her.

She cleared her throat. "About the casualties. There's something I haven't shared. When I spoke to Cirrik and he told me the Order was planning the whole human-factory thing to ensure they have a continual supply of hosts for their army, that's not only a future plan. Apparently, they've already started this, and somehow they've managed to collect host bodies that are…empty."

"What do you mean, empty?" Danny leaned forward. "Are they dead?"

"Not exactly. From what I understand, the bodies are alive and healthy but void of consciousness. The human souls inhabiting them must have either been absent to begin with or are departed. I have no idea how they pulled it off or if it's even true, but Cirrik says the new host bodies *last*. They don't seem to degrade like regular hosts. In fact, the more I've been thinking about it, the more I've been wondering if maybe the reason normal host bodies degrade so fast is because they're shared with a human soul. The bodies can't sustain both the presence of a human consciousness and a demon."

Rachel wrapped her arms around herself. "They collapse under the energy drain."

"Exactly. Normally, the bodies need a human consciousness to sustain life. Like when I escaped in the dead realtor Val had used up—the body was fresh and there was still enough of a spark of consciousness, of life, to sustain me in the body long enough that I could survive in it for the trip to Sonora, but barely. If it hadn't been fresh—if there hadn't still been a spark—I wouldn't have been able to. I don't know how they circumvented the need for a human consciousness, but I do know they aren't the first to try it. The archdemon you called Val had been attempting it long before you met her. She failed. Maybe they picked up where she left off."

"Cirrik knew about all this?" Rachel's face darkened.

"He mentioned the Order had achieved this feat of empty host bodies…and he indicated they had quite a few of them on tap to select from. The Order's army, and potentially the Order itself, could be made up of these new empty host bodies. Though the demons wouldn't be bound to them—they could still jump as much as they chose to. My point is, if you killed any demons while in these host bodies, you wouldn't be killing a host anymore."

Rachel asked, "Are you sure about this—these host bodies aren't people? How can we know which demons are wearing regular people and which are wearing these new host bodies?"

Nix shook her head. "I don't know. I can't be sure. This is only what I've been told."

Danny's brow furrowed. "Your boyfriend told you all this. And you didn't think it was relevant to share with us until now?"

Nix opened her mouth, closed it.

"Cirrik is wearing one of those empty host bodies, isn't he?" Rachel's arms fell to her sides. "You didn't want us to kill him."

Nix examined Elliot's blunt fingernails. "I should have said something. There's one more thing. When we attempted that mindreading spell and it went sideways, he showed me something."

"I thought you ended up at the old witch's house?" Rachel asked.

"I did. But before that, he showed me a memory. A, um…personal one. Something we shared. I didn't think anything of it, because it was something I remembered, too, from a long time ago. But now I think he picked it very specifically for me. And I think he meant to help by sharing it—and by bouncing me out to the witch's place."

"Help how?" Rachel narrowed her green eyes.

Nix licked her lips. Elliot was quiet inside her. She was on her own for this. "At the time, he seemed to think you two were going to kill him with your exorcism before we left Blaine's the next day. He also seemed to think there was still a possibility I'd try and escape with him. He couldn't have shared any information with me directly if it would have gotten back to you, but in his own way, I think he was trying to help me. Give me another chance or something. A puzzle piece I'd be able to put into place later if I needed it and he wasn't around. I don't know." Nix scrubbed a hand down Elliot's face and pointed to the map on the table. "But the memory he shared, it took place on our way to Rincón de Soto, Spain. And now we've tracked the Order to Rincon Hill, San Francisco. I know it's not an uncommon word, but there's no way it's a coincidence, not in combination with Maria being a member of the Coven of Thorns. That medallion helped us find the Order."

Danny's face reddened. "So he does know where the Order is. He has this whole time, the lying bastard."

Nix stiffened. Her heart raced. "I've spoken to him about the Order's lies and manipulations. I got through to him. I think he can help us. I think he *will* help us, now."

"He's less of a liability if he's out of the way. Can't believe I've been fretting over that poor fella he's been possessing this entire time—played for a fool."

"I can convince him to help us," Nix said.

Rachel touched Danny's shoulder. "Pops. Hear her out."

Danny's bushy eyebrows rose. "The demon? It's been withholding information from us this whole time and you look at me like I'm being unreasonable here?"

"We don't have the luxury of picking and choosing our alliances right now, Pops. We're all in this together. And if Nix says Cirrik can help us, we should take all the help we can get."

Danny huffed. "What could he do?"

"I'll talk to him," Nix said.

"Darlin', you too." Danny looked to Rachel. "Don't neither of you get pulled in by any tricks or silver-tongued words. Just as easily lead us into a trap."

Nix took what concession she could get from the old hunter and rose from the table.

Rachel accompanied her once more to the trailer and before they reached it, Nix asked, "Anything from Blaine when Violet and I were gone?"

Rachel blew out a stream of air, looking up at the clear blue sky. "He's terrified and kowtowed. That much we knew. He thinks she wants the pendulum, so I hid it like you suggested."

A hot breeze swept away the sweat at the nape of Elliot's neck. The tall industrial buildings bracketing this one remained quiet and still. "Did you find out why they were hiding out here?"

Rachel lifted a shoulder, dropped it. "Says he doesn't know. They were moving around for a while. Thinks she's searching for something. They landed here and stayed. Said her tea leaves told her someone would be dropping by—friends who could help her find what she was looking for. Might explain why she didn't kill us outright. He wasn't sure how long they'd been here, only that she meditates a lot and is unpredictably violent. He doesn't know how to get his niece free of her. He's desperate and depressed."

"You think he cares that much about Violet?"

Nix watched as the bright sun added a glow to Rachel's skin. Her lips curved downwards. "If you'd asked me that before all of this, I'd have said no."

"But now?"

Rachel pulled at the cuffs of her leather jacket. "Yeah. He cares. The way he looks at her...it's the same look in Pops' eyes. He won't lose her."

Nix kicked at a rolling tumbleweed with Elliot's heavy boots, missing it by inches. They closed in on the small aluminum trailer sitting out in the hot sun. Cirrik would be sweltering in there. Something that might have been guilt stirred in Nix's chest, a snake hidden beneath her ribcage. She shoved it down, mentally chastising her continual slide into banal human sentimentality. "No texts?"

Rachel patted her jacket pocket. "Nothing yet. How was Violet with you?"

A chuckle escaped Nix's pursed lips. "Surprisingly, great. Protective. A good ally. I wasn't sure about traveling to another realm with an archdemon, but it turned out better than I could have hoped." Above them, the broad, dark wings of circling vultures beat against the hot air. "Might be the weapon we need to win this."

"The roman glass?"

"No, Violet." Nix's eye tracked the birds, avoiding the trailer and the fleeting thought, *Can they sense him burning up in there?* "You were right. She might be the ally we need in this war."

As they stepped up to the trailer doors, Rachel placed her hand on Nix's arm. "Hey, listen. There's something else we need to talk about." She bit her lip, looking away. The concrete shimmered as she shuffled one foot to the other.

Nix pulled back. "What's so serious?"

"You were honest with us back there. I appreciate that. And I get why you didn't want to say anything earlier. I know it's been...a trial. All of us, carving out this trust. I don't want to mess that up now, so I'm going to share something with you. No more secrets, between any of us. But I'll be frank, Danny and I are concerned about how you'll take it."

Nix's borrowed stomach churned. Her heart rate spiked. "Say what you're gonna say, already."

Rachel pulled out her cell. "We saw it in the news before you got back. I'm sharing this with the understanding that you *aren't* going to freak out." She pressed the phone into Nix's hand and walked to the far fence.

Fingertips tingling, Nix flipped it over. A news article was pulled up in an RSS-feed reader. Callie's young face smiled back at her, long flaxen hair pulled back in braids, big blue eyes open wide. Nix gripped the phone, careful not to break it. The confusingly worded headline read: *"Formerly Missing Girl at Center of Murder Case Committed."*

Committed what? Did they think she killed that clown? There was no way they'd link her to that. Nix read on. *Oh. Committed.*

"Callie St. Germaine, missing ten-year-old California girl recovered after disappearance from local carnival where a beloved children's entertainer was found murdered, is reported to have been committed to San Francisco County's St. Mary's Psychiatric Facility for Youth. Reports from the girl's mother suggest a pattern of ongoing unstable behavior over the last year, including stark personality changes and disturbing obsessions. When questioned regarding the man's death, police characterized the girl as incoherent and delusional. Psychiatrists at the nationally renowned institute decline to comment on the girl's condition or diagnosis…"

Nix took a deep breath, lungs burning. The screen cracked in her grip and Rachel looked over at her. Nix thought she'd been doing right by the girl. Protecting her. Keeping her safe. And sending her back, hadn't that been the right choice? Now she was locked up somewhere. What if she was alone and scared? What if they were hurting her? She was too small—she couldn't defend herself. An image of Antheia, limp in Nix's trembling arms, materialized in front of her, so real she could have reached out and touched her sister's cold skin.

Rachel walked back over, taking her cracked phone without comment. Nix dropped down on the bumper of the trailer. Was it Callie's mother who committed her? Or was it Callie's own behavior that landed her in the psych facility? Either way, Nix's interference in their lives had resulted in this. She tried to fix it and somehow made it worse. She'd have laughed, if her throat wasn't so tight.

In their shared mind, Elliot was silent.

Rachel plopped down beside her. "Should we talk with Cirrik?"

Nix shook her head. She didn't want him to see her like this. "Maybe later."

"We have to head out then."

"Yeah."

"Maybe we can try to help Callie after all this."

Nix stood. She didn't meet Rachel's eyes as they headed back inside.

Chapter 32

They loaded up the van at the back of the factory and hitched the trailer. Max ambled up to the van with a pep in his step, released into the open air. Nix glanced around but didn't see any passersby who might be concerned over the sight of a massive bear strutting around in the middle of the city's factory district.

Danny side-eyed him, hitching up his belt. "I'm sorry, pal, but you know you won't fit."

Max mewled.

"Of course you can come. We need you. But…you'll have to shift to human. For a while." Danny held his hands up.

A snuffle followed, then a growl.

"I know, buddy. When we're through this, I'll take you back home."

Max stretched and keened, the sound a low wail through the deserted street. His neck and front paw jerked to the side. Rachel stepped away. His massive jaws ripped at the thick hide of his forearm. Blood and fur stained his teeth.

The others stepped back. Danny shuffled through his own bag, pulling out clothes—a pair of jeans, boots, a plaid shirt.

The bear huffed and panted, bones cracking, snapping, and reforming as a man began to emerge from beneath the coat of fur.

Jowls dripping, Max tore himself apart.

When it was over, Danny took him to the side of the building and hosed him down, cleaning up while the others pretended to go about their business of packing and arranging. Excess meat steamed on the sidewalk. Elliot's stomach growled. Nix dug out some pizza boy from the cooler before they loaded it and sated her host's shaky appetite.

Danny was slated to drive while Violet was granted the passenger seat privileges, with the other four left to cram into the back of the van. Technically, there were five seats in the back, but it was a tight fit and that meant some of their baggage and the big cooler had to be shoved into the trailer with their captive—not ideal. Danny didn't want Cirrik somehow getting into anything back there, unattended, so half the luggage ended up at their feet and on their laps. Blaine ended up with Rachel's bag of books in the very back with Rachel. The now human Max and Nix were to sit in the middle portion where there was more leg room.

The route to San Francisco was long and winding. Nix would be lying if she said she didn't want to be anywhere but here. Thoughts of Callie weighed heavy on her. Images of her own sister, Antheia, crept in unwelcome when she wasn't mindful.

Elliot lamented the dead pizza boy working through his digestive system, whose name may have been Gerald or Zane or Tony. Nix wasn't sure it mattered if you didn't know their name, if you didn't have a connection with someone. Elliot argued otherwise.

Cirrik was still stuck in the trailer. It was probably where he belonged. She knew that. Yet, she couldn't help but think this was a betrayal on her part. There was something about the memory he had shared with her—given to her, really—that made her think she owed him something in return.

As the road opened in front of them and wind swept through the stuffy van, Nix was lost in thoughts of what they used to have. A long time ago. Another century. This was no time for nostalgia. In all likelihood, they were driving to their deaths, and she more than any of them was acutely aware of this.

She needed to focus on the mission, or there would be nothing else to worry about in the future. Certainly no chance to right wrongs or redeem herself for how things had turned out with Callie.

Elliot's empty eye socket ached. The silence of the van was only emphasized by the rumbling of the pavement beneath them as the odometer *click-click-click*ed.

In the seat beside her, Max scratched at the locked door as if aching to open it and leap to freedom. Every time she glanced at him, Max was staring longingly at the passing scenery. Danny's clothes were a bit tight on his big frame. Max's face was cloaked by his long, shaggy hair, such a dark brown it was nearly black. A sprinkling of gray salted his beard.

She'd never seen anyone so uncomfortable in their skin before, and she'd seen some serious discomfort in her time. She had her own discomfort, tight skin that pulled and itched and stretched in all the wrong places. Max, she couldn't imagine. The pain of shifting into a form that fit him so poorly—shedding that skin every time. It would be unimaginable.

Nix wondered if she were capable of that kind of loyalty— to shatter every part of herself because someone she cared for asked. Sounded more like madness. Idiocy. But a part of her envied that closeness.

Behind her, Rachel and Blaine occasionally spoke in low voices, but mostly Nix only heard the quiet flipping of pages as Blaine read through Rachel's collection. Violet looked out the passenger window, eyes wide, mouth slightly agape. Her forked tongue occasionally slipped free, licking at her lips. She watched the scenery like a child watched a circus. Nix couldn't imagine this was new for her, if her claim was true that she'd spent so many decades in the body of Edgar Winterspoon. Nix could only assume it would have been tediously dull. Trapped in one hunter's body, in California, where the days all seemed to blur together and the scenery with it.

At one point, Max, Rachel, and Blaine all fell asleep. Only Violet and Nix, eternally awake. And Danny, behind the wheel. He was the best rested of them all, and of course insisted no one exceed the speed limit.

When the red-and-blue lights started flashing in the reflection of the rearview mirror, she saw his eyes go wide and could almost taste his heartbeat jump.

Rachel jolted awake. The others quickly followed. When the Highway Patrol Officer behind them didn't move on to another vehicle, Danny reluctantly pulled over to the side, cursing.

Nix thought about Cirrik in the trailer. The human meat stored in the cooler. The guns and weapons in the vehicle with them. In their shared mind, Elliot and Nix saw the bodies stacked up on paper next to these hunters' names.

They'd finally caught a break in the mission—a location, a game plan. The Order's ascension was tonight. This could all be over before it started.

"Stay calm, everyone. Don't say anything." Danny smoothed back his hair and beard in the mirror, straightened his blue plaid shirt. "I've got this, you hear?"

Elliot's heartbeat hammered in her ears. Danny unrolled his window as the officer came close. The officer's trooper hat was tilted over his eyes, shading them from the sun, and Nix couldn't make out their color. But she could see the way his hand hovered over his gun at his side.

"License and registration, please."

She could kill him. It would be easy.

"Sure thing, officer." Danny leaned over Violet and dug around in the glove box, handing him what he needed. "May I ask what the problem is?"

The officer sucked air between his teeth. "Seems you have a taillight out on that trailer back there."

If she killed him, the whole state would light up red and blue. They'd arrive at the Order's ascension with a long escort of cops in tow, sirens blazing, any semblance of cover blown—if they managed to arrive at all.

Sweat dripped off Danny's forehead as he handed the stolen registration over. "Sorry about that, officer. Checked the other day, and it was fine. Seems things don't last like they used to."

"No doubt about that." The officer walked back to his vehicle, as slowly as a stalking lion.

Nix's fists clenched on her lap.

"This is a stolen van," Danny muttered. "In about thirty seconds, he's gonna glance at that registration and run the plates. He'll know. What do we do?"

Nix wasn't sure she'd ever heard Danny question what to do next. He was always the one with the answers, or at the very least he'd never admit to not having them even though he rarely had good ones.

Elliot's palms were slick against his jeans. Even if it caused more problems than it solved, snapping his neck might be the only chance they had.

Nix heard the click of the passenger door sliding open. She glanced up.

Violet exited the vehicle.

"Excuse me, young lady," came the officer's voice through Danny's open window. "You really do need to stay in the vehicle."

"What is she doing?" Rachel hissed, gripping the back of Nix's seat. "Is she gonna kill him?"

No one moved to stop her.

"I don't know, darlin'." Danny's mouth hung open as he stared into the rearview mirror, fingers gripping the steering wheel like he could control the situation through sheer force of will. "I don't know what to do."

"If she kills him…"

The officer reappeared a moment later at Danny's window. "Well, this all looks fine, sir," he said, his voice low and even. "I'll let you go with a warning. Get that light repaired."

Now that Nix could see his blue eyes, they seem glazed and unfocused. The officer handed Danny the papers and his license. He went on his way back to his vehicle.

Violet slipped into the van, closing the door behind her. She buckled in.

"What happened?" Danny asked.

"Suggested to the gentleman the papers were in order," Violet said. She stared ahead. "Shall we continue?"

Beside them, the police vehicle drove off along the highway. They waited until they couldn't see it any longer and then pulled off the shoulder, continuing their journey. Danny seemed to watch more carefully for cops as they drove onward, seeing as they wouldn't be able to fix the trailer light. Nix figured if they did get pulled over again, Violet could put the whammy on another cop and they'd be fine. She only hoped that once they did reach their destination, Violet would prove as useful against their real enemies.

Chapter 33

They wormed their way into downtown San Fran after hours of highways and traffic. Danny circled the block twice to scope it out and still couldn't find parking. The pendulum had given them a one-block radius near the waterfront in a busy tourist spot, but in this area a block narrowed them down to a dozen clumped buildings. There was also the possibility that, like their little group of misfits, the Order could be mobile.

Blaine pointed out the window on their second pass. "Hold on, I've been there." Violet narrowed her eyes at him, but when she didn't get aggressive, he continued, saying, "The Queen's Veil Hotel." He indicated a building across the street from the block they were scoping out. "Haunted, allegedly. Featured on my webseries…which you clearly didn't watch in my absence."

"That ain't where the doodad pointed," Danny said.

Blaine's gaze shifted away from Violet. "No, but there's underground parking and they know me at the front desk. We can get a penthouse suite at the top and spy on the whole block from that vantage point. Even get roof access if we needed it, I'm sure."

The van was quiet. "Not the worst idea." Danny swallowed as if the words choked him. "Besides the penthouse suite. Can't afford that."

Blaine reached into his tattered jacket and pulled out his wallet. "My treat. Unless, of course, you've reported us missing to the authorities and all my cards are flagged."

Danny shook his head.

"Unbelievable," Blaine muttered.

They pulled their monstrosity up to the hotel and had Danny wait at the wheel. Max paced outside the van to get some fresh air, drawing concerned stares from the concierge. Nix followed Rachel, Violet and Blaine inside the posh turn-of-the-century hotel. The lobby was lined with floor-to-ceiling mirrors, and the polished black-marble floor sparkled. Despite the throngs of tourists on the streets, the lobby exuded calm, and hardly a living soul passed by.

A grand staircase peeled open like a metal womb, plush red carpeting ushering guests down from the second and third floors and beyond, though it was doubtful anyone took the stairs. A quadruple set of elevators dinged pleasantly nearby.

Blaine ran a hand through his disheveled hair and straightened his jacket as he walked up to the speckled-marble front counter spanning the left wall.

A young man in a tuxedo glanced up with a broad smile. "Oh, Mr. Cobaine, how nice to—oh my god, what happened to you, sir?" His expression tilted, dark-brown eyes wide. "Are you all right? Shall I call for a doctor?"

Blaine smiled like a man with a gun to his head. "No, no, James, it's quite fine. Costuming, for a video I'm shooting." He gestured to his tattered clothes, dried blood sticking his torn pant leg in place. "Very convincing, isn't it?"

The boy, James, stared for a moment. He laughed haltingly, fingers carding through his thick brown hair. "Oh, sir, you had me for a moment. You really did." He gestured to Nix. "And the eye patch—nice touch."

Blaine chuckled. "Indeed. We'll be needing the penthouse. Highest floor, if it's available, James. *Private* parking, too—two spots, to suit a trailer. You can charge my card for the additional expense. And we'd like to shoot a scene on the roof. Do you suppose we could get access like last time?"

The boy kept staring at the lot of them. "I'll have it all arranged, sir." He took Blaine's card and wagged his finger. "You sure got me. The concierge will help you with your luggage and camera equipment."

"Not necessary, James. We'll handle it this time—very delicate equipment, you understand."

"Of course, sir."

Blaine limped out, waving and joking as the others followed back to the van. Crowds shoved by them on the sidewalk. Rachel and Max loaded back into the van.

"Private parking," Nix said, "as in, we're leaving *the trailer* out there? And its contents?"

Blaine shrugged. "They have locked concrete stalls like miniature garages for the wealthy clients. People who don't appreciate their BMWs getting dented by soccer moms throwing their car doors open in regular parking stalls. They're roomy. And the double stalls are big enough for film crews that have to leave equipment on board—expensive equipment. It should be secure. Then again, I don't anticipate we'll really stay overnight, do you?"

Nix exhaled, thinking through options and finding none. Cirrik had been fine so far. She supposed he'd have to stay fine. "You're awfully chatty again, like you used to be."

"She's on her best behavior with all of you here. Before…" He looked away. "I want this over. I want my niece back." He glanced at the van, the others chatting animatedly inside, and turned back to Nix, leaning in close. "When you went through that door, Rachel let me read some of her grimoires. There was a spell in there to transfer a malevolent spirit…something like you. Would it work on that thing in my niece?"

"I'm not sure what you're talking about," Nix said.

"We didn't have much time to talk, since you were only gone thirty minutes or so. She said it could be used to force a demon out of one host and into the spellcaster."

Thirty minutes in regular time? That was news to Nix. Memory sparked in Nix's brain. "Oh, you mean that Kevin guy's spell? It's of limited use, since you can't direct the spirit anywhere but into the chanter. And once it's there, it would be disoriented for a few seconds, but it's not obligated to stay. It could jump right out and go back to whatever it was doing."

Blaine pursed his lips.

"Violet's really been helping us," Nix said. "If we finish this and reunite her with her real family, things will be fine and you'll get the real Violet back, too."

The sliding back door opened, and Rachel stuck her head out. "Are you two coming?"

Nix and Blaine climbed into the van, but Blaine's expression remained troubled.

Chapter 34

In the penthouse, everyone showered and patched up their wounds. Food was handed out—including special meat for Elliot—and even a grimy load of laundry was run in the en suite laundry machines, though Nix had to subtly ensure the stones were transferred into the right pockets. Blaine was handed some clean-enough clothes to borrow from Elliot's bag, the closest to him in size, and they all saw him in jeans and a t-shirt for the first time. He looked miserable.

Elliot, claiming to want some goddamn privacy for once, insisted on showering and cleaning up his eye by himself, with the explicit agreement that he wouldn't gouge out the other one. Nix swapped with Rachel yet again while the boy had some quiet alone time. All in all, the rank smell of the group dropped by a solid eighty percent. Only Max refused to bathe, and they were all the worse for it, but he was wearing clean clothes from Danny and he ate, so Danny flittered around happily like a mother hen.

Nix settled with Rachel in front of the massive floor-to-ceiling windows of the penthouse, granola bar in one hand and binoculars in the other. Somehow, in Rachel's mouth, the granola tasted delicious and sweet. She scanned the buildings across from them for the millionth time. She tilted Rachel's head, cracked her neck, and settled comfortably into her bones.

A far better fit than Elliot's. Hopefully, he wasn't cannibalizing anyone in their brief time apart, though in a weird way Nix was getting used to the idea.

Nix's gaze drifted over to Danny, who was cleaning a gun across the room and prepping their supplies. It took a moment for her to realize it was Rachel's attention that guided their shared eyes.

Inside, Rachel was quiet and still, like a sheet of ice stretching across a lake. There was something there, beneath the surface, but Rachel managed to learn some control during their time together, so Nix wasn't sure what she was thinking. Perhaps it was the stone in her jacket pocket that blocked her. Still, it was Rachel, so she hazarded a guess, asking, *"Worried about the old man?"*

"No," Rachel said.

As if Danny could sense their internal dialogue, he glanced up at her. A frown pulled at his lips. Gone was the warmth and care usually directed at Rachel. Nix was used to cold glares, found a certain comfort in them, but she wasn't used to this sense of distance between Danny and his daughter. Odd. When Nix regarded the two of them through Elliot's eyes, the warmth was obvious. Danny and Rachel fought constantly, sure, but there was never an absence of warmth or care. She could always see the pain behind Danny's gaze, the urge to protect and shield. The way they both tried to connect for the same reasons, tried to be understood, but kept missing each other. Through Rachel's eyes, she couldn't see it anymore, like the girl was blinded by her own convictions.

"He's not my father," Rachel said. *"He realizes that now."*

Nix scoffed. *"Well, obviously. Pretty sure that's not news to him."*

"He thought he could be. That if he were, I'd be different somehow— better. That's why he never spoke about my parents. He knew what was in me all along, but he thought he could stop it. Now he knows he can't. Doesn't trust me. Not anymore."

With headache-inducing clarity, Nix remembered exactly why she didn't want to be in Rachel's skin. Sighing, Nix turned them away. *"You're telling me this like I give a damn about your stupid family drama. At least Elliot wasn't such a downer."*

"You asked if I was worried," she pointed out.

"I was making conversation. Not asking for a soliloquy."

"You want conversation? Let's talk about Cirrik."

"Fuck off," Nix dismissed. *"You're wrong about Danny, you know."*

"Now you're changing the subject."

"I'm just saying. I had to be in his skin."

"For all of five minutes."

"Five excruciating minutes," Nix said. *"He's an asshole, and there's not a single cell in him that isn't 100% committed to being your father. It isn't you he doesn't trust, it's the magic. He thinks it's like a cancer, that it'll kill you like it killed your parents. He's terrified. Powerless. He knows he can't stop it—he can't save you. And you and Elliot are the only things he can't bear to lose. But what he said at our weird tea party? He really is trying, if you'd let him."*

Rachel was silent.

Danny met her eyes from across the room. "Darlin'? You okay?" His brow furrowed. "I mean, demon, what's wrong with my girl?"

Nix blinked, wiping at Rachel's cheek. "Nothing. She's fine. Eyes are getting tired of these binoculars, is all."

He harrumphed and stalked over, swiping the binoculars. "I'll do that." He settled beside her on a settee. "Hmm." He waved Max over. "Let's see if we can get a better look at the block from the roof. Get you a little air, too, pal."

"Many pigeons above. Good hunting."

Nix raised Rachel's eyebrow.

"May I accompany?" Violet said, standing. "I would like to see the city. Great scope of sky."

"Great idea," Danny said, handing her the binoculars. "Maybe if you're looking through these, you'll see something we don't." He turned to Nix. "You coming?"

Rachel lit up a little at the invitation, but the shower turned off in the bathroom and she told Nix, *"We shouldn't leave Elliot. Probably time to swap back."*

"Good point. Leave the boy too long and he'll stick a fork in the other eye. Then where will we be."

Nix shook her head. "We'll wait for Elliot."

"I'll stay, too," Blaine said. "Not a fan of heights." Nix noticed he took any opportunity he could get to gain distance from the archdemon inhabiting his niece.

Danny punched him on the arm. "Weren't invited." He laughed. Danny, Violet, and Max left for the roof, a few surveillance supplies in tow.

Elliot emerged from the bathroom in a cloud of steam and some clean clothes, fresh gauze under the eye patch and a glow to his pallid skin. The alarm console next to the door started beeping, a low intermittent sound like the batteries were going. They all stared at the thing.

A knock sounded on the door. Elliot, standing closest to the door, peeked through the peephole with his good eye. "We already got our room service, thanks," he said.

"Can I speak to Mr. Cobaine, please?"

Elliot looked to Blaine.

Blaine unlocked the deadbolt, leaving the chain in place. "Oh, James. We're a bit busy."

"That's a new look for you, Mr. Cobaine. Must be some film."

"It will be, yes."

"Listen, um, sir. We're getting complaints in the parkade. Noises coming from your stall. The security guard is saying it sounds like there is something or someone inside. I told him, of course, that's preposterous. But he insists. I'm sure you're aware you can't store animals or people in the parkade."

Blaine stared at Elliot and Nix for a long moment. "Oh. Well. There's a very good reason for that. It's, uh, performance art. Part of the film, you see. We'll take care of that right away."

"The security guard would very much like to have a word with the individual currently in the trailer, as it seems they can't get out. We want to confirm this is a…well, consensual arrangement, you understand."

"We'll take care of it." He glanced back at Nix, slipping her a key card from his back pocket. "I'll follow you to the lobby to chat with your security guard."

"Excellent, sir. I appreciate it. My apologies for the trouble. Corporate policies, you know, what with human trafficking in the news and all. I'm sure we can get this all sorted in a jiffy and take the parkade and hotel out of this silly lockdown."

"Lockdown?" Rachel said. *"Shit. We won't be able to sneak him out."*

Blaine smiled. "When you say lockdown…my niece and two older coworkers are doing some prep work on the roof, as we arranged. I'd like to bring them in to sort this out, if you wouldn't mind."

"I'm sorry, sir, that won't be possible."

"But my niece…she's only a teenager. I can't very well leave her on a rooftop during a lockdown. It isn't safe."

"I understand your concern, Mr. Cobaine, but it's out of my control. The lockdown can't be lifted until the threat is cleared. There could be a bomb in there or something, you see—as silly as that sounds, this is the policy, sir. But the roof has ample cover for shade and seating, and a security fence. She'll be perfectly fine up there for the five minutes it takes to clear up this little misunderstanding." James leaned into the sliver of the open doorway. "I'll make sure your room is comped a nice dinner for the trouble, too."

Blaine's voice rose as he said, "I really must see my niece right this moment."

James disappeared from the space of the doorway. "I see. Well, if we can't rely on your cooperation, perhaps it's best I get the police involved."

"No!" Blaine unlatched the door and stepped out, closing it behind him. His voice was muffled as he walked with James down the hall, past the locked-down elevators toward the main stairwell. Nix caught fragments of *misunderstanding* and *we appreciate your patience.*

Nix met Elliot's eye and they rushed for the door, clambering through the opposite hallway toward a set of service stairs, jumping them three and four at a time down thirteen flights, then two more into the second-level parkade. Nix could have sworn they've been on the fourteenth floor but distantly realized the sneaks had superstitiously renamed the thirteenth floor. Just as well—it saved her a flight of stairs. At the bottom, she and Elliot were both huffing and gasping. Elliot was worse off, though not as bad as she'd expect from a human.

Above them, the world's most tasteful alarm system yipped in the stairwell—flat enough not to provoke real panic but out of place enough to pique interest in the cause. A robotic woman's voice proclaimed cheerily, "Valued guests and clients of Queen's Veil, please stay in your rooms. There is no cause for concern at this time. A Queen's Veil Hotel Ambassador will assist you shortly. Thank you for choosing the Queen's Veil Hotel for your vacation and corporate needs."

They hit the door to the parkade. Locked. Nix slammed her weight into it, snapping the handle with a satisfying crack. They slipped into the parkade, ready to bolt toward the van, only to see a security guard ambling in front of their stall.

Nix and Elliot ducked behind a minivan. The alarm was louder down here as the woman's shrill voice echoed off the concrete, complemented by flashing overhead emergency lights.

"What do we do?" Elliot whispered.

"I'll take care of him."

Elliot grabbed her arm. "No. You can't kill anybody. That's not going to lessen suspicion."

Nix shoved him away. "Well, what's your bright idea then?"

He huffed. "I'll distract him. You get to the trailer."

"No, wait!" Nix grabbed him before he could dash away.

"What?"

"I can't get Cirrik out of there—the sigils and the salt-iron bars bullshit and…it's a fortress that *I* can't access. You're human, you have to do it."

Elliot hunched over beside her in the dim parkade. "Okay, you distract him, and I'll get your boyfriend out."

"Danny has the keys to the trailer," Rachel pipped up. *"They're always in his jacket, and he's on the roof."*

"Oh shit," Nix said. "Neither of us have the key to the trailer."

"Shit," Elliot echoed as the alarm yipped above them. He looked to Nix. "You could break it open."

"We both need to do this," Nix said. "I'm going to have to kill the guard."

"You're not killing him."

Nix peeked out at the security guard, then up at the flashing roof. Cameras. "Damn. Cameras in here. We're probably already on them. Stairwell, too, I bet."

"This hotel's a police state," Elliot said. "This was a terrible idea. Of course it was Blaine's idea."

The stodgy security guard stared down at his phone.

"I have an idea." Nix fingered the key card for the private parking stall in her back pocket before handing it to Elliot. "Follow when I flag you over. Stick to the shadows in case this crashes and burns."

Nix swelled in Rachel's throat and jumped.

Chapter 35

Consciousness swirled up to meet her as Nix adjusted to the new host body. She stared at the concrete ceiling for a long moment. White light flashed in the corners of her eyes and an electronic woman's voice chirped that there was nothing to be concerned about.

Nix blinked, dragging her heavy body off the ground and glancing into the darkness of a parking lot. A dozen wide, unblinking Audi eyes stared back at her like they were shocked she made it this far. The pieces started reassembling themselves in her brain—Marcel's brain, she noted, quickly ushering the man off to dreamland before he could pick up on her unwelcome presence.

She shook her head, Marcel's thick, dark hair falling over her eyes. On the ground, she noticed his beige security guard hat and scooped it up, brushing it off. As her eyes readjusted to the darkness, she saw a hand waving to her.

Nix glanced around the parking lot and waved back. She pulled the hat on, finding it a little snug, and brushed Marcel's matching beige uniform off. Elliot stumbled out from behind a minivan, Rachel's arm slung over his shoulder as he dragged her along, her head lolling into his neck.

Elliot handed her the key card, though it seemed Marcel had some of his own, and Nix slid it through the electronic lock.

She glanced up at the cameras overhead as the sliding door shuddered open. There were only about a dozen of these private car ports, as Marcel mentally labeled them. Nix was relieved to find Danny's hideous stolen van was, indeed, behind door number one when it eased open, though it had been a safe enough bet with the guard standing out front.

Rachel groaned and Elliot set her down against the tire.

"You're doing better than she is with all these switches," Nix said to Elliot, snapping the sliding lock off the back door of the van. "I think we need to hold off for a while."

"Agreed," he said with a sideways glance at Rachel. "She used to hold up better with this sort of thing. You think it's the…you know?"

Nix shrugged. The ghoul thing had been blessing and curse in equal parts so far. She jerked the door open, cracking another internal lock mechanism in the process.

A powerful odor rolled out of the van. Sweat and general human filth sealed in a tight space and heated for added fermentation. Nix and Elliot stepped back, both covering their noses. Elliot gagged. From inside, Cirrik looked up and met Nix's eyes.

Nix turned to Elliot. "Okay, can you get him out?"

Elliot lowered his head. "Danny has the keys to the cage and cuffs, too."

"Lockpicks are in your pocket again, right?"

Eyes widening, Elliot grinned, climbing inside. If he hadn't already known how to pick a lock, he'd been paling around with Nix, picking locks in Blaine's house long enough to know the basics. She could walk him through the rest.

He worked for a few tense minutes, long enough for her to see he didn't need coaching. His lithe back hunched over in the small trailer, the sharp knobs of his spine visible even through his jacket. The cage door swung open. He went to work on the cuffs.

Looking away, Nix said, "Take the gag off."

Elliot did.

Spitting on the floor of the trailer, Cirrik rasped, "What is going on? Why are you wearing a little fat man?"

Nix raised an eyebrow. Marcel was big boned, not fat, and he didn't reek of stale urine and body odor, so Cirrik had no room to talk. "By carrying on and making noises back here, you got us caught."

Rachel pulled herself up to stand, wiping sweat from her pallid forehead.

Elliot finished, the manacles dropping to the metal floor of the trailer with a clang. The ropes followed in short order.

Cirrik rubbed his wrists. Rachel moved to stand beside Nix.

Elliot took a screwdriver that had been tucked into the wall of the trailer and popped the hinges off the top and bottom of the cage, allowing an entire side of the cage to open completely with the lock now off—a failsafe, Nix realized. Elliot jumped out.

Cirrik emerged slowly, standing at the edge of the trailer in his rumpled and soiled suit, looking very much like a tortured human-trafficking victim.

A distant slam was followed by voices.

Nix looked up at Cirrik with Marcel's most sincere gaze. "If you meant what you said before, about wanting to take a bite out of the Order, you'll work with me now. Work with us. This is your only chance, Cirrik. But if you take it, you can be with us. Not in that trailer. Not as a hostage. We can work together."

Straightening his blood-stiffened suit jacket, he said, "And if I don't, love?"

Nix held his gaze. "Then I guess this is it." She looked to Elliot. "Take Rachel back upstairs. Stay in the room. I'll meet you back there when I can."

Elliot and Rachel ran.

Blaine rounded the corner, followed by James from the front desk and another two security guards.

"Honestly, it's like performance art," Blaine was saying. "Part of the process of this new film—it's going to be a big hit, an indie thing and—"

"Goddamn..." a security guard said when they stopped in front of the van, hand lifting to cover his nose, "the *smell*."

James gagged, stepping back.

"You got it open," the other said.

"Protocol is to w-wait—" James stuttered. His eyes grew large as they fell on Cirrik. "Was this man in there the whole time? Sir, sir, were you being held in this contraption against your will? Perhaps it's time to call the authorities."

"There's no need for that. It's all a misunderstanding," Blaine said. "The film, you see, it's horror, and we simply aim to, well, shock. Our actor here is very dedicated—"

James stepped up to Cirrik, who was still standing at the edge of the trailer. He held a hand over his nose. "I think we should hear it from him. You, sir. What is going on here?"

Cirrik looked over the small crowd from his perch on high with an unreadable expression, his bloody suit and bruised face stark accusations.

He met Nix's eyes, spread his hands wide, and said, "Show biz."

Chapter 36

A bark of startled laughter slipped from Blaine. "Well, agents, you heard him. All part of the routine."

"Truly?" James' brow knotted.

Cirrik jumped down and everyone else stepped back. He took an elaborate bow, suiting an eccentric actor. "I practice what is known as method acting."

The two security guards and James from the front desk nodded as if now in the throes of great understanding. James apologized for the inconvenience and comped them all dinner as promised. Above them, the flashing lights ceased and the chirpy voice finally silenced, leaving only a buzzing in Nix's borrowed ears.

A smile escaped Nix as she watched Cirrik out of the corner of her eye. "I'll escort these gentlemen back to their rooms."

The three men mumbled and walked through the dim parking lot the way they'd come. Cirrik, Blaine, and Nix headed to the emergency stairwell and located an elevator close by. They didn't speak on the elevator ride to the top floor.

When they reached the door of the penthouse and Nix turned away, Cirrik grabbed her arm.

"You're not coming?"

She allowed his warm hand to linger. "I have some cameras to wipe first."

Cirrik hesitated at the door. "I'll accompany you. The others will not be so welcoming to me."

"Security isn't going to let you in. Marcel knows all the protocol."

Blaine's hand landed on Cirrik's shoulder. The two men hadn't known each other, but they'd both spent the last couple weeks as prisoners. "Let's swing by the gym first and get you cleaned up." He motioned to Nix. "I'll say with him. Meet back here in ten minutes?"

Nix nodded. She took Marcel, rooted through his memories, and decided to wipe their last twenty-four hours of security footage for the hotel and disable the camera system entirely—it would likely take them the next day or so to get back online, and Marcel might be out of a job after, but he didn't love it here anyway.

Nix left Marcel to sleep it off in the security room chair and took the air vents back up to the penthouse where Elliot was dutifully awaiting her return. Nix caught him by surprise while eating and woke up choking.

"Jeez, could've warned a guy," he complained halfheartedly. *"I don't know how you pulled that off."*

"Wasn't me. Cirrik rolled with it. We'd be screwed otherwise. Or at least have a few bodies on our hands and be on the run—more so than we already are. Not conducive to maintaining the element of surprise while tracking down the Order."

Nix brought the others up to date on Blaine and Cirrik, growing concerned when she found out the two men weren't back yet.

"I'm not sure about this," Danny said. "Demon's probably in the wind now, running off to tattle on us to his demon buddies. So much for getting the drop on them."

"You weren't there, Pops," Rachel countered. "El and I watched from the stairwell. He could have completely screwed us over. We'd have been marched off in cuffs, separated, and locked up. Best-case scenario. But he didn't."

"And now he's out there, free." Danny crossed his arms over his chest.

"Not completely," Rachel said. "He still has those gold bands binding him to his host. He won't be able to get those off until they're taken off...or until he chops his host's arms off, I guess." She looked away.

Danny shook his head as if to say that was a pitiful argument. He turned to Nix. "Why didn't your boyfriend screw us over, then? What's he playing at?"

"He wants the Order. I explained my—our—position, what the Order's really about. They betrayed him, too. I have to believe he's come around. Maybe. Or at the very least, like Rachel said, he could have screwed us and didn't. I'll take my wins where I can get them at this point."

Danny grunted. "We'll see about that."

Nix was ninety-percent certain Cirrik had disappeared, either to save his own ass and get out of Dodge or to rejoin the Order and take this fine opportunity to really hurt them while they were sitting ducks in this hotel room.

The front door opened a minute later and a much cleaner Cirrik in a new suit walked in, followed by Blaine, also in a new suit.

"There's a Valentino's on the second level," Blaine enthused, standing up straight and confident again for the first time since she'd seen him. Violet didn't look impressed—her pet was testing its boundaries.

Nix rose to meet them. So did Danny.

Cirrik held his hands up. The gold bands glittered at his wrists where his white shirt cuffs didn't quite cover them. "Nix asked I return here. To...unite against our common enemy. But I'll not endure further mistreatment from the likes of you." He glared at Danny. "After all, the enemy of my enemy is my—"

"Yeah, yeah. I've heard enough of that. If I find out you're playing double agent or some shit"—Danny shook his finger at

Cirrik—"I won't hesitate this time to exorcise you. I know there ain't nobody in there but you now."

Cirrik shot Nix a look. Nix lowered her gaze.

"Then I suppose we'll be working together, hunter." Cirrik held out his hand.

Danny grumbled, but moved forward and shook it. The two regarded each other with narrowed eyes.

Rachel said, "Do you want to share what you found on the roof, Pops?"

Danny grumbled some more. He scooped up the binoculars and walked to the window. "While everything was going FUBAR down here, we were making real progress on the actual mission topside." He pointed to a skyscraper across the street. "After some surveillance, Violet here identified this building as a psychic void. Couldn't get a read on it."

"Highly protected," Violet said, small hands clasped in front of her. "Much effort required to make a building disappear from the energetic field—we find this suspicious."

"Not protected enough we couldn't find it with the pendulum, but that's extra strength," Danny said. "Regular pendulums couldn't find Blaine's house, either. We figure they're using the same high-level psychic protections to appear energetically off-the-grid to anyone who comes looking. Since seekers could be looking from anywhere in the world, it would usually be a good play. But from up close and personal like this, it's the absence of an energy signature that makes it stand out. So it looks like we have the building, but we couldn't tell more about it than that. I sent Max out to scope the place at ground level." Danny glanced at his watch. "Only a couple hours till sunset though."

"Max?" Nix asked. "Isn't that risky? What if someone notices him?"

"He has a way of blending in, believe it or not," Danny said. "He's a good hunter. I'm banking on none of them recognizing him like they might recognize us. We don't know how much they already have on us, but Max has played peripherally. And if there are any demons on the streets or in front of that building, he'll be able to sense them in a way most of us can't."

"What is this building, anyway?" Blaine asked, moving toward the large windows. Danny handed him the binoculars.

Cirrik stepped forward in tandem. "The Center for Disease Control, administrative office."

"So you did know," Rachel said, her tone flat. "This whole time."

"You tried to tell me," Nix said.

"I did not trust your hunter friends. I'm not saying I trust them now, but I thought if I told you where headquarters was outright that would be the end of us both. I would outlive my usefulness and, soon enough, so would you. At the time, I thought if I delivered the message covertly, you would be able to use it when you needed it—to return to the fold—without the risk of the hunters turning on you." He scowled in Danny's direction.

"They won't." Nix looked at Danny and Rachel. They'd all had some serious trust struggles during their time together, but they'd worked through them despite the odds. "We're in this together."

Cirrik pursed his split lips. "So it seems."

Blaine passed the binoculars to Rachel.

"What else do you know?" Danny asked.

"I have never been to headquarters, nor have I personally met with the Order. I knew only the general location."

Danny scoffed. "I thought you were some bigwig?"

"Prior to you stuffing me in the trunk of my own car and abducting me, then torturing me for weeks, plans were being made to attend the ascension over the full moon." Cirrik's chin tilted higher. "All the highest-level demons, myself included, would have been in attendance. I assume this will still be the case."

"How many are we talking?" Danny asked.

"Dozens, of which I am aware," Cirrik said. "They should already be there as the ascension is underway. However, the Order had plans to build out their ranks before I went AWOL. There could be many more."

Nix turned to Cirrik. "Is this where you got your host?"

"They sent it to me as a gift, along with photos of their lab. I did not see the lab myself, though it could be here."

"Hey, look!" Rachel pointed out the window, passing the binoculars around. "Is that who I think it is?"

Danny peered through the lenses. "I'll be damned. The one fella is that late-night televangelist."

"Huh? No, not him." Rachel bounced forward on her toes. "Her!"

Nix grabbed the binoculars.

A limo was parked in front of the building in question and two people were walking together toward the front doors. One was a man in an extravagant suit that would put Cirrik's Valentino to shame. His black hair was slicked back and caught the light. On his arm was a woman with long blonde hair who looked to be in her late twenties to early thirties. She was sporting a silver-sequined mini skirt, break-neck matching stiletto heels, and a black shirt with no back. A frilly red scarf flowed down her arms, sparkling with rhinestones. Nix couldn't make out her face past a pair of huge sunglasses.

A gaggle of young girls stopped on the sidewalk, pointing. They pulled out their phones and the woman waved with a wide poison-apple lipstick grin as the man urged her onward. At the front doors, a tall, austere man in a white lab coat and glasses stood flanked by four black-suited security guards.

Danny took the binoculars back.

"I don't recognize any of them," Nix admitted. Elliot similarly drew a blank.

"Are you kidding me?" Rachel lit up like the schoolgirls on the street below, suddenly looking her age. She started singing some lyrics until everyone stared at her. She flushed. "Seriously? Jesus, none of you have any taste in music."

Violet piped up, saying, "Your Violet knows of this singer of pop." She shook her head gravely. "She does not like her."

"Well," Rachel said, shoulders drooping, "point is, she's super famous and most people love her. So what the hell is she doing walking into the CDC building on the arm of some televangelist?" She dropped into the nearest white leather chair and pulled out her phone, fingers fluttering over the screen as Danny and the others peered out the window. "Says here she's been on personal leave for the past couple months. Some pictures of her in San Francisco, tabloid speculation that she's working on some secret album or a charity thing, but not much activity on social media."

"The televangelist is an important man," Danny said. "Big late-night program and a megachurch in Los Angeles, which I imagine he isn't running right now. A whole lot of money and influence in that."

"Looks like he's got an assistant running things right now," Rachel confirmed, staring at her screen. "Can't be an easy thing to walk away from for long though, for either of them. So what are we thinking?"

"Suspicious," Danny muttered. He turned to Cirrik. "You know what that's about?"

Rachel's pocket vibrated and she stood, walking out of the hotel room into the hall.

Cirrik shrugged. "It is possible they are possessed. But this would bring attention to the operation—for demons to bring high-status hosts whose absence from the world would be noticed, it would be a needless risk, especially when it is not necessary. The Order is providing host bodies to recruits. Unless…"

When Cirrik didn't continue, Nix prompted him, "Unless?"

He turned to her. "Unless they aren't disposable hosts for regular recruits. And we saw the Order walk into that building."

Rachel popped her head back in the hotel room. "Pops, can I see you for a minute?"

"A little busy right now, darlin'," he said.

"It'll only take a minute."

Danny grumbled and left the room. Violet's eyes tracked them.

"Why take a couple celebrities?" Nix wondered aloud.

Cirrik shrugged. "Power. Influence. They are playing the long game this time."

"It seems like a jump from their usual choices."

"Meaning?" Blaine asked.

Nix shrugged. "They use archetypes to manipulate their prey. Always the same basic archetypes...adjusted for the ages and society. A perversion of human symbology. The healer, the preacher, the shepherd. Many of their followers do the same." Nix thought of the traveling shepherd she'd met in her village, his silver tongue, and how disgustingly easy she'd been to manipulate. No doubt he'd been one of the Order's early converts, following in their footsteps.

"Well, the televangelist is your preacher," Blaine said.

"I saw what looked like a doctor standing at the front doors, too," Nix said. "If he's one of them, that's our healer." She glanced at Cirrik, wondering if he recognized him or if it had been one of the doctor's disciples who'd convinced him to murder his own grandfather. Cirrik's jaw was set. She wanted to believe it was anger she sensed in his gaze, in his stiff posture—anger at the Order. But she couldn't be sure anymore, couldn't read him the way she used to.

"The shepherd remains," Violet said.

"So the celebrity is the shepherd archetype?" Nix turned her gaze out the window. Her fists clenched at her sides.

"Who better to herd the sheep in the twenty-first century," Cirrik speculated.

Danny and Rachel walked back in. Rachel came to stand next to them. Her hand hovered lightly near her holstered gun—Kevin's gun, Nix noticed.

The air in the room shifted.

As Blaine and Cirrik spoke, Nix glanced at Danny. Shuffling nonchalantly through their supplies spread out on the island of the penthouse's half-kitchen, he was opening the case containing the tranquilizer gun and quietly assembling its parts.

Her muscles tightened. Rachel and Danny still had the psychic-muddling stones on them, but Nix didn't. She couldn't help it when her mind finally slid the pieces together and her thoughts betrayed her, slipping out to the forefront as she realized: *"It was Lizzie on the phone."*

Violet's gaze shot to hers, and Nix knew their luck had run dry.

Chapter 37

Every window in the thirteen-story Queen's Veil Hotel shattered.

The room had gasped around them and exhaled in an explosive blast. The sound of a million crashing cymbals hit Nix's ears with a bang that left her in a resounding chamber of tinny echoes.

Cirrik and Blaine were thrown by the explosion into the main bedroom. Nix dove to the ground next to the open window.

Rachel grabbed for her gun but didn't get the chance to use it, instead finding herself pinned high on the living room wall like a bug by the archdemon as wind lashed through the gaping windows.

Danny, having ducked behind the kitchen island during the blast, lifted the tranquilizer gun to fire. It whipped out of his grip, spinning into a far corner. He grabbed for a small vial of oil—the last of their old stash—but the glass bottle shattered in his hand, dripping to the floor, useless. In a breath, Danny, too, found himself pinned to a wall.

Violet had both hands raised to keep them in place. Her short purple hair whipped in the wind, her eyes flooded dark pools. The shimmering scales emerging along her neck turned an oily black.

Danny's lips were moving, but Nix couldn't hear a sound.

She swallowed hard, ears popping, but still the world was a vague, oscillating murmur of noise.

The sounds leaked through slowly, then all at once. Below and around them, screams erupted from the building. Above them, absurdly, the sprinkler system kicked in.

"Lizzie. You have spoken with her. What were her words?" Violet asked in a voice much smaller than her power warranted, walking close to Rachel as she struggled and kicked against the wall, leaving black scuff marks where her boots hit. "Can't hear you...why can't I hear you? You did something."

Her head titled and her gaze dropped down to Rachel's jacket pocket. Violet flicked one finger and the jacket unzipped, opening. The stone rose out of her inside pocket.

Violet stepped back, mouth opening as if she'd been slapped. Her eyes watered.

Cirrik slinked over and helped Nix to her feet. They moved away from the smashed windows. Blaine inched over to Danny near the island and the only real exit that didn't include a thirteen-story drop. Nix thought he'd make a break for it, wouldn't have blame him, but he didn't. He stopped at the island, seemed to change his mind, and moved back, closer to Violet.

"You tricked me," Violet said, her voice heavy with the betrayal as her lower lip trembled. "We were friends. I helped you."

"I'm sorry," Rachel choked, fingernails scratching at the drywall as water rained down the walls and dampened her long, dark hair.

Violet shook her head, lowering her gaze. Her purple hair fell over her eyes, wet now, dripping. "Lizzie. Her *words*. Say them."

Rachel looked to Nix.

"I'm sorry," Nix mouthed. *Shit.* Nix glanced over to Danny, then the fallen tranquilizer gun in the far corner.

"Don't look at her, look at me!" Violet shouted. The walls trembled and cracked. "What did Lizzie tell you?"

Rachel gasped in a breath. "She—she said she's…afraid of you."

Rachel and Danny dropped down the wall as Violet's hands covered her mouth. Nix dove for the tranquilizer gun and found herself pressed to the roof next to a spinning sprinkler along with the gun, several feet out of reach.

Danny lifted himself off the floor, gripping the island for support and easing over to Rachel until Violet's glare stopped him. Violet lifted Rachel back up the wall and Nix realized she could only control two of them at once with the telekinesis. She was vastly outnumbered here, but they were outgunned. Of course, if that fact started to frustrate the archdemon, she could surely eviscerate them one by one and level the playing field in her favor.

Danny held his hands up and stepped back. Cirrik eyed Nix warily.

"Why?" Violet demanded.

"She said you scared her and the girls. Probably because of shit like this," Rachel said.

"We have to get that gun," Elliot said.

"Shush!" The last thing Nix needed was to piss her off more with traitorous thoughts.

"I only want to be with my family." Violet's hands shook and Nix felt the tremor ripple through her own chest. "Lizzie was not coming back. Was she?"

"No," Rachel said, toeing a dangerous line. "But she wasn't in New York anymore. She was in San Clemente. That's why you were there, isn't it? You tracked her that far, but she'd protected herself, and you couldn't get any closer. That's why you wanted the pendulum."

Violet nodded, her wet purple hair swishing and dripping on the soaking white carpet. "I thought…could explain…"

Nix tried to reach for the gun, but there was no way. Cirrik was right below her now. And Blaine…where was Blaine?

"It doesn't have to be this way," Danny said.

Violet looked up at him, eyes wide.

"It doesn't," Rachel echoed. "You're with us now. We can—"

A low murmuring sound built and Nix finally realized it was coming from Blaine. She twisted her neck to see him standing behind her near the door, gripping something tight in his hand.

Violet shrieked, turning toward him. Her mouth opened with a flash of fangs, skin flushing red.

She screamed.

A burst of smoke poured out of her.

Her host body collapsed in a heap on the ground. That's when Nix recognized the words—Kevin's transference incantation.

Nix fell into Cirrik's waiting arms, and he quickly righted her, setting her on her feet. Rachel slid to the floor, rushing over to Violet's crumpled form.

The stream of smoke poured into Blaine's throat as he finished and plunged a tranquilizer dart into his own thigh. He dropped to his knees, coughing and gasping. Danny ran to Blaine's side.

Trembling fingers grasping at Danny's shirt as his limbs started to fail him, Blaine said, "Do it. Exorcise the demon. Now. Please!"

"It'll kill you both," Danny said.

"Do it! I know the price. I can't hold it back any longer. Protect her." Blaine looked to his niece, a limp ragdoll in Rachel's arms.

Danny gripped Blaine's hand, his face blank, and motioned to Cirrik and Nix to leave. There was no conversation, no argument, no last rites. The archdemon had proven itself an ally and a liability.

Haggard screams followed Nix and Cirrik into the hall. The wet carpet squelched beneath their feet, bringing Nix back to her early encounter with the archdemon at Winterspoon's ranch. The sprinklers continued to flicker in time with flashing emergency lights in the hall.

In minutes, the archdemon was gone. So, too, was Blaine.

Chapter 38

On the streets below the hotel, sirens and fire engines wailed. Cirrik and Nix returned to the room when the exorcism was finished. No one spoke. Most of the hotel employees and guests had been evacuated. They now crowded outside the building, minding the police tape marking off thirteen-stories worth of shattered glass. Ambulances took the injured away.

A knock on the door heralded the presence of a firefighter requesting their evacuation from the penthouse. They assured him they would cooperate, and he moved on to the next door. They packed what they could without speaking and left Blaine's exorcised body in the master bathroom to be discovered in the immediate aftermath. There seemed nothing else to do.

Danny helped a delirious and confused Violet down the thirteen flights of steps since the elevators were once again out of order during this emergency. When they reached the lobby, the girl stared up at him. "Where's my uncle?"

"He had to go, darlin'," Danny said. "But he wanted to make sure you got home safely. Your Ma is missing you. I want you to go to the front desk there and call her to come pick you up." He put some money in her hand and a blank card with his private number written on it. "You let us know that you get home safe, ya hear? Keep this number secret. Wish I could see ya off, but—"

"I get it," she said, her lips quirked up in a smile. "I had the weirdest dream."

"I bet, darlin'. You take care."

The purple-haired psychic walked into the lobby on unsteady feet. They watched her make a phone call before a police officer approached and escorted her out of the building. If her memory was hazy, it wouldn't stay that way for long. Nix got the impression she was plenty present for most of it. The only part she may have missed was the end, and if that were the case, it would be a blessing for the girl, but it would be the only one she got.

Rachel put her hand on Danny's arm. "She's tough. She'll get through this."

He exhaled in a gale, like he'd been holding his breath since all of this started. "Maybe we should have kept her with us." Danny didn't look convinced. He just needed convincing.

"She's been through enough," Rachel said. At this point, Nix was sure they all knew this was a suicide mission. Violet had been spared the draft to the front lines. "Hey, where's Max?"

Danny slapped his forehead. "Damnit. We'll have to circle the street, see if we can find him. This mess out front, no way that went unnoticed."

They walked two more flights to the parkade and loaded up the van. Cirrik shot a dirty look at the trailer, then Danny, before climbing into the back of the van with Nix. Down to four occupied seats. Danny argued their way out of the parkade when an officer questioned them, but James from the front desk spotted the commotion and waved them onward, seeming relieved to see them go. If he wondered where Mr. Cobaine was, he didn't ask. It wouldn't be long before someone checked the bathroom, found the well-dressed paranormal investigator crumpled up in the bathtub with inexplicable burns covering his soaked husk of a body.

Nix glanced at Cirrik beside her—so much for his spiffy-looking suit. He resembled a drowned rat now. They all did. The van immediately started to smell damp. Rachel unrolled a window as if reading Nix's mind. But that wouldn't be happening anymore, would it? She had gotten used to the archdemon. They were down two of their team now, and Nix couldn't help feeling gutted. It had happened so fast.

"Did it have to go that way?" Nix asked. "Were you lying when you told her we could still work things out, at the end?"

Rachel looked to Danny, then said, "I wasn't lying. I thought...but maybe that was always the way it was going to go. I think Blaine had been planning for a while. He knew more about the archdemon than we did. Even when you were away with it, he was afraid to share anything. But when you gave us those stones, he was different after that, like it gave him his mind back. I think that's when he started planning."

"He wanted to keep his niece safe," Danny said. "I can understand that. I can respect that in a man, keeping his family safe. He knew he put her in danger in the first place, blamed himself—told me as much, in a private moment. Wished the demon hadn't locked on to the girl like that, but she was powerful, and it was a natural choice that it took her. I think when he finally realized getting the demon out of Violet in a non-violent way wasn't going to be a possibility, he thought he might never get it to leave. Made a decision to get it out of her once and for all so it could never target her again. He was damn sure scared of the thing, but mad, too. It was his choice, to go out that way."

"I'm still not sure it was the right choice," Rachel said. "For either of them."

"Me neither, darlin'. Me neither. All happened so fast." Danny looked out the window, big hands flexing on the wheel.

"A choice we gotta live with now, right or wrong." He slapped the wheel and said, "There he is."

They pulled over at the end of the block in a no-parking zone and Nix slid the side door open. Max climbed in, carrying a plastic bag. He was wearing a 49ers ball cap that he hadn't left with. No one commented on it. He didn't say anything about the fact all four of them were soaking wet or that their hotel was surrounded by firetrucks, cops, and ambulances. He didn't ask about their missing comrades. They peeled away from the curb.

Feathers stuck out of the bag clutched to Max's chest. "Pigeons," Max said as Nix stared. "Good hunting. Exciting day."

Nix shook her head and scooted closer to Cirrik. "Ours, too."

Elliot's anxiety stirred within her. *"We have to keep them safe. Pops and Rachel. Max. We can't lose anyone else."*

Nix stared out the window, blood boiling in an abrupt flashpoint. He was such a stupid boy. A stupid, naïve boy. *"No. They're already dead. Don't you see? That's how you win. You've got to cut your own heart out before they can do it to you. Nobody makes it out of war alive. When you've got nothing to lose, then there's nothing they can take from you. So they're both dead. You're dead. We all are. That's a given. But when we go down, we're going to take every last one of our enemies with us. We probably won't win this. But maybe we can hurt them."*

"I don't accept that," Elliot challenged, cold. *"Any of it. You're wrong. We'll win. And we'll survive."*

Nix chuckled, throat dry. *"That's not how the world works, puppet. This isn't some fairytale where the heroes conquer. We aren't heroes, anyway."*

"Any conclusions on the CDC building, Max?" Danny asked over his shoulder, eyes focused on the gridlocked traffic ahead of them.

"Many dark ones posted on guard. Counted nine, ground level."

"So it's confirmed? This is our building?"

"It is confirmed."

"You find an entrance?"

"Several. Heavily guarded. One, less guarded. We could fight our way in. We will have to go on foot."

"I'm not sure about fighting our way in." Rachel squeezed the water from her thick hair. "We'd lose the element of surprise. They'd all be on us right away."

"I'm not so sure we have any element of surprise anymore, darlin'," Danny countered. "After that fiasco. Then again, maybe it will be a distraction. Them lookin' one way, while we go the other. If we go in now."

Nix's stomach dropped. And rumbled. She realized for the first time in a while, Elliot was hungry again. Maybe he needed to be. "Are we ready for this?"

"When else?" Danny said.

"Your hunter is right," Cirrik said, shocking the others to silence. "Tonight is the full moon. The Order's power will be cemented, if it isn't already. There's no other chance to do this." He pointed out the window. "It's almost dusk."

Nix swallowed. "I guess we're doing this."

Chapter 39

Max leaned forward in his seat. "Park near the Embarcadero. We walk."

Rachel shot him a look. "People are going to notice us. We're a mess."

Staring out Cirrik's window, Nix watched strangers walk by. Many were dripping wet, towels over their shoulders, crying. Some had blood or bandages covering them as they stared up at the Queen's Veil Hotel. "We may not stand out as much as you'd think. I'm half-dry already."

"All right," Rachel said. "Let's do it."

They parked, gathered their weapons, swapped out some drier clothes and shoes where possible and abandoned the van and trailer with only halfhearted intention of returning. Nix grabbed a couple packets of meat for Elliot, shoving them into Rachel's bag, but some confused traffic cop would be stumbling upon pizza-guy remains soon enough.

Reluctantly, Max left his bag of pigeons behind, and Rachel, her books. Like Nix, she had all the important spells memorized. They weren't coming back from this. Nix wasn't sure if that meant they'd improvise their plans for the future, or if they had none.

Rachel carried the delicate roman glass in a padded box in her bag. Danny carried the now disassembled tranquilizer gun in its case.

Max pointed to the set of bolt cutters Rachel had removed from her bag and said, "We will need these."

Rachel shrugged, stuffed them into a duffle, and handed it to Nix. They stalked down the boardwalk like a handful of sore thumbs, Danny and Rachel with their heads down as passersby eyed them. Cirrik strutted in his damp suit, winking at her, and Nix had to laugh. In the greatest twist of all, Max smelled the least offensive of any of them and looked the most normal in his jeans, plaid shirt, and 49ers cap.

Danny conferred with him as they led the pack, saying, "I appreciate your help with this, pal. I'm sorry I got you involved. This whole time, I thought you were out there in the forest, free, when you were locked up."

Max grunted, speaking Danny's language.

"When we get in there, you're done, you hear? We'll take it from there. I want you to head out and get back home. I'll come check on you once this is all over."

"I will hold your exit," Max said.

"No, no. Getting us in is enough. We'll be fine getting out. Promise me, you'll leave once we're in?"

Max grunted again.

Rachel turned to Nix. "Elliot's hungry?"

Nix pulled back. "How'd you know?"

She slapped Nix lightly on the stomach. "You're not exactly quiet. That rumbling stomach is going to give us away." Rachel handed her a now-warm packet of raw meat. "At least eat something. We don't know what we're getting into."

Nix opened the ziplock and took a bite of the flesh, swallowing it down and relieving the tension in Elliot's muscles. "We have a solid plan. Mostly."

Rachel's eyes flicked to Cirrik. Seagulls cawed overhead. "Mostly."

Nix looked at Cirrik, too. They hadn't shared much of their plan with him and he hadn't asked. If she were being honest, she had to admit she didn't completely trust him. How could she? But she didn't have a lot of options, either, and he was of more value on her side than against her—at least this way she could keep an eye on him. Of course, she might end up watching him betray her again. The possibility sat like lead alongside the meat in her belly.

They'd sneak in—in so much as it was possible to sneak into a high-security building, which was likely the reason the Order chose the place—and Danny would dart the Order, and Rachel and Danny would use the exorcism to channel the archdemons into the roman glass. They'd conclusively determined that the exorcism did work on archdemons after all, seeing the archdemon in Blaine wither into nothingness. So it could be possible to perform it even without the glass, but three archdemons together could be a challenge. And the archdemon that had been possessing Violet did seem weaker in some ways—perhaps weaker than the Order, but there was no way to tell for sure until they tested their arsenal. They'd have to try it with the glass and hope they didn't need to test it without, but it was nice to have the possibility in their back pocket. Binding them into a glass ball was good, but Nix would much rather see them destroyed forever this time.

They had limited ammo in the dart gun now—only four shots remaining—so they couldn't waste it on random demons, and there was no telling the size of the army they'd accumulated at this point. Rachel had Kevin's gun to temporarily expel demons from their host bodies, but using a gun would draw attention while trying to sneak in.

They stopped behind some garbage bins and Max peeked around them. He shook his head. "Entrance was not so heavily guarded before. Now, more security."

Nix looked past him. At the back of the building was a shipping and receiving dock connecting to the port. Three sliding garage doors marked entry points, along with two doors, one near the sliding doors and one on the side of the building. All were guarded by men and women in black suits. Some openly carried weapons.

"If we go in guns blazing, we announce ourselves. The Order will run, go into hiding maybe. We'll lose our shot at this," Nix said.

"Are there other access points?" Danny asked.

"Front of the building," Max said. "Roof—requires helicopter. And sewer."

"Sewer is a possibility," Rachel said.

"May I make a suggestion?" Cirrik straightened his suit jacket. "Before we go traipsing through sewage. Why not walk through the front doors and make a grand entrance?"

Danny eyed him. "I'm listening."

"As far as they know, I'm still on their side. Let's say I overpowered you, captured you, and brought you in."

Nix shrugged. "It would get us inside, maybe even get us an audience."

"I'm not so sure about this," Rachel said. "No way they buy that he brought us all in."

Nix looked at Cirrik, then the rest. Rachel was right. Cirrik had a demon's physical strength, but he couldn't best Nix, let alone a shapeshifting bear-man and two hunters. What was he going to do, walk them up to the door on leashes?

"Can't all go," Danny said after a minute. He handed his bag to Max. "Sewer entrance is under the boardwalk?"

Max nodded, slinging the bag over his shoulder.

Danny motioned for Rachel's bag, taking the small, delicate box out as well as a length of rope before handing the rest to Max as well. From her pocket she pulled out Maria's coven medallion and the pendulum, handing them to Max for safekeeping. Neither were necessary now. Nix handed her bag over, too, bolt cutters and all. Max held the luggage like it was weightless.

"This is where we part ways, my friend. Take our stuff," Danny said, "and leave it by the sewer entrance. Get it open. We'll use it as an exit or a rendezvous point when we're finished. You get it open, and you leave."

Max's hand landed on Danny's shoulder. "Whipsaw. It does not feel right to leave you now."

"You've more than paid your debt to me. If anything, I owe you now. Besides, if we don't make it out of there, the world's gonna need someone leading the charge when this shitstorm hits. You're my only backup plan."

Max lowered his head. "I will arrange it. May the spirits of the forest guide you to victory." He clapped Danny on the shoulder and walked away.

Danny knelt behind the dumpsters, opening his case and assembling the tranquilizer gun. He loaded it with the remaining four darts, then stood. Danny handed the gun to Nix. She raised an eyebrow.

"What am I supposed to do with this?"

"Ya'll are going to have to be our captors. Only way this is believable," Danny said.

"Me?" Nix laughed. "They won't buy that."

"They will if you sell it, so sell it hard."

Rachel tilted her head. "Two demons against two hunters. Way more believable than one demon against two hunters and another demon. Who'd believe he brought us all in on his own?"

Nix glanced at Cirrik. "Yeah, I guess."

Cirrik held out his wrists. "And these?"

The gold bands holding Cirrik in his current host glinted in the falling sunlight. Removing them would be the final test—he could jump and be rid of them. But letting him out of the trailer had already been a test as far as Nix was concerned. The bands were the next logical step, practically meaningless. The real test would be walking in there and following Cirrik's lead, pretending he'd betrayed them and brought the hunters in when in reality that could be exactly his play right now. He wanted Nix to return with him to the flock, to be his queen and go triumphantly back to the Order with the hunters in tow—to quell the hunters' threat of exorcism once and for all. Would she be doing exactly that?

Danny nodded to her.

Nix had placed the bands on him herself—she was the only one who could take them off. She reached out and touched Cirrik's wrists. The gold bands melted into her palms, reforming into harmless gold bracelets, the sigils carved inside barely visible. She handed them to Rachel, who slid them onto her own wrists where they hung like regular jewelry.

If the hunters were committing to this, if they believed this was their best bet, then Nix figured she would fall in line. That, or they'd hit their heads too hard when Violet tossed them against the wall, and they were all doomed. Nix swung the dart gun over her shoulder.

Danny fondled the box holding the roman glass. The thing wasn't exactly unobtrusive. "Don't know how we'll smuggle this in. Think they'll frisk us?"

"Most definitely," Cirrik said.

"Maybe we won't need it," Nix said. "The exorcism worked on the archdemon…" she trailed off as the others looked away. "Well, it worked without the stupid glass ball."

"Big risk to leave it behind," Danny said.

"Hang on, I have an idea." Rachel unclipped a carabiner from her belt and slid it through the small handle atop the box. She stepped forward and latched it to Elliot's belt.

"That's super obvious," Nix said.

"Not finished yet." Rachel chanted something under her breath, her eyes flashing, and the box disappeared. She smiled broadly. "A glamor. Like the archdemon could do, but small scale."

Nix reached down to touch it but her hand went right through the box. "It's gone."

"It's still there," Rachel said. "Shifted to a different plane. I can undo it when we need it back." Rachel reached around and pulled out the blessed gun. She held it out to Nix.

Nix held up her hands. "I don't want that."

"If you don't take it, they will." Rachel brushed her fingers over the weapon then looked back up at Nix. "It hurts to touch for you, right?"

Nix bit her lip. "Only stings a bit. I'll slide it into Elliot's boot—the sock should cushion it."

Rachel handed off the gun and Nix accepted, fingers tingling on the barrel as if it were electric. She quickly slid it into Elliot's boot, the sensation dying down to embers.

Danny frowned at her. He scooped up the length of rope and handed it to Nix. "Tie us up. Not too tight that we can't get back out, but make it look real. Gag, too, or they'll question it. Could exorcise you without a gag."

"Right."

"El knows the exorcism. And if you need to lift the glamor..." Rachel whispered the words *claritas visionis* in her ear.

Rachel pulled a couple handkerchiefs from her pocket and Nix wanted to ask where they'd been and how much eye juice they were soaked in, but they weren't going in her own mouth so she didn't. Nix followed Danny's instructions, ending up with two gagged hunters bound by their wrists at the end of her rope.

She glanced at Cirrik. All the power was in his court and she'd allowed it. If he screwed them over now, it would be a sweet revenge for him. And worse, utterly predictable. Her stomach churned. How else to play this? The sun touched the water of the bay, a spattering of dark orange and blood red painting the sky. They were out of time.

"Follow my lead," Cirrik said.

Nix held the rope, wrapping it twice around her hand. Cirrik walked out from behind the stand of industrial garbage bins, his stride confident as they converged on the back of the building. Nix followed, tugging the hunters along behind her. "I thought you wanted the front doors," she said.

"This is better. Don't you see anyone you recognize?" Cirrik whispered.

At the back of the tall building, heads turned their way, weapons lifting. Three men and two women in black suits with black ties strode their way. At first Nix couldn't make out any distinguishing features from these plain security guard hosts. Then she saw their eyes. All her kind. No surprise there. But two of them struck a chord of familiarity in her.

One of the male guards pushed open a sliding and possibly electric fence. "Boss? That you?" He laughed, waving another over as he lowered his weapon. "We're fine here, boys. We thought you were a goner. Couldn't get a read."

"Took a while, but we made it out," Cirrik said, grinning.

He came up to them, looking Nix in her good eye. "Nixy? Damn. And you're wearing…that."

She squinted. "Lindle?"

Lindle chuckled and swatted her on the arm. "We gotta stop meeting like this. I knew the rumors weren't true. Siding with hunters—I told them that was nonsense, you can ask. You always make the surprise play in the end."

A woman stalked forward. "Nix! I'll be." She shook her head. Nix recognized the twang in her voice as Mars. "Wow, always with the bold fashion choices. Well, that's all right, we'll get cha sorted, won't we?"

Lindle lit up. "Oh, that's right. Big changes in corporate. I'll give you the tour—" He stopped, turning to look at the two bound and gagged hunters as if noticing them for the first time. "You brought those hunters. Alive."

Mars stepped forward. "That the other one you're wearing?" She lifted her nose as if smelling a foul odor in the air.

"The Order requested their capture," Cirrik said.

"Old directives, my man." Lindle shook his head. "You've been away. Ascension's tonight." He motioned at the falling sun with his gun.

Cirrik glanced at the sky with a raised eyebrow. "My. I suppose it is."

"Order isn't gonna want them around tonight," Mars said.

Cirrik sighed. "What am I supposed to do with them? I had my directives and I went to great lengths to follow them through. Perhaps I can confer with the Order on the matter."

"I'll take you. And your prize." Mars grabbed the rope.

Nix held it. "I've got it, thanks. It's my prize, too."

Mars glanced at her, bottom to top. "You can't be presented to the Order looking like that, wearing one of them. Lindle will take care of you, and I'll take care of your wards here. Not worried I'll tarnish them, are ya?"

Nix let go of the rope.

Elliot protested, stomach clenching.

Nix looked to Cirrik. He blinked, unreadable, and followed Mars and the hunters into the building. Rachel met Nix's eyes as she and Danny were led away, stumbling.

Lindle wrapped his arm over Nix's shoulder. "You're gonna love this, Nixy."

Chapter 40

Lindle led Nix through a different door and into a small, empty lobby. He pulled a card from his suit jacket and slid it through a reader next to the elevator.

"You fall into the bay?" he asked, chuckling.

"Something like that."

"Wait." He turned to her. "That hotel across the street." He wagged a finger in her direction knowingly. "Oh, you were involved in that. Random disaster, people runnin' out screaming, cryin', all wet. Of course. That's got you written all over it."

"That actually wasn't my fault," Nix said.

"Uh-huh." He laughed. "Never is, is it? Crazy shit happens around you, and it's never your fault. That's what I love about you, Nixy." He knocked against her shoulder. "Chaos! Can't blame a tornado for bein' a tornado, can ya? It's all those idiots on the ground's fault for not being prepared."

Nix shifted foot to foot. "It really wasn't my fault that time," she muttered.

In her mind, though, she was tracking it back—all the way back. She saw herself sitting on a swing in a park, wearing a cute little kid now locked up in a psychiatric institute and being investigated in relation to a murder Nix had, in fact, committed in the girl's body. From that swing set, she'd seen some hunters across the street, poking around a quiet town on Nix's turf. She'd wondered what they were up to, if they were there for her. And she'd made a decision in that moment to follow them and find out. She could have let it go, but she didn't. It was her choice, and so was every choice she'd made since. Here she was now, at the end of a linked chain of choices and consequences. Only, most of her consequences had affected someone else. The archdemon in Violet had seemed to understand her, but look how that ended.

They rode the elevator to the fortieth floor and stepped out into a glass hallway.

"This is a private floor. Special access," Lindle said. "Did Cirrik tell you about the new host program?" He waved to a guard standing at the bank of elevators as they continued onward. The guard frowned but nodded.

Nix pursed her lips. "A bit."

"Well," he said, opening a frosted-glass door, "welcome to the ultimate walk-in closet."

They stepped into what, on first appearance, looked like a hospital ward. Dozens of beds spanned the room, stretching along the length of the corridor. Each bed held a patient hooked up to an IV and a machine reading their vitals. Lindle led her down the line.

"Isn't it beautiful?"

"They're alive?" Nix asked.

"The bodies are. Alive and healthy. Just comatose. Permanently."

"You collect coma patients?"

"At first," Lindle said. "But now the Order has its own process. Any healthy body can be emptied, the soul scooped out, and the body readied to act as a viable host. And they last like you wouldn't believe. We haven't had the time to run proper tests, you understand, but the Order's picking up after lengthy trials from previous defeated factions—well, you would know all about that. So we have reason to believe these host bodies could last years, perhaps even a human lifetime if kept in good repair."

They stopped in front of one bed. All the patients looked healthy. Though they varied in ages, most were in their twenties and thirties. Their skin glowed and their chests rose and fell with life.

"Where'd they come from?" Nix asked.

"Everywhere." He looked at her. "Oh, don't worry, no risk of awkward encounters with these ones. They won't be missed. They're volunteers. Corporate business practices have to be so ethically rigorous these days."

Nix frowned. "What do you mean volunteers?"

Lindle shrugged. "You know, demonolaters. The faithful. Worshippers. Whatever you want to call them. These ones offered themselves up in service of the Order."

An image flashed through Nix's mind of a young man named Rat summoning her many years ago back in England, begging to be made one of her kind. "This is what they signed up for?"

"Well, a certain percentage of our recruits pass muster for full recruitment to our ranks as immortals. But with the bodies perishing quickly after that process, we have a greater need for host bodies than we do for recruits. Plus, the experiments need to continue, requiring more host bodies. And you know how we run through these babies in the field, even with the best of intentions to maintain them for keeps. Supply and demand. This way, at least they're still able to serve their masters and the cause."

"I didn't realize there were so many…believers."

"Oh yeah, super popular. We're living in great times, Nixy. Of course, we'll run through them quickly. Corporate's trying to pivot now, preserve the demonolaters for our ranks and shift to normies for hosts once the take-over's initiated. It's all early stages, but we're moving fast. Hard to keep up with all the changes, to be honest."

"I'll bet." Nix stared at the lines of beds. In their shared mindscape, Elliot was both disturbed and amazed.

"The way things used to be done," Lindle said, "it was good but not great. Only so much wealth and power we could amass when limited in the length of time we could possess a single host before wearing it out. Imagine how this can change things. We'll rule over the Earth."

"You don't need to convince me," Nix said. Jumping bodies at will could be a convenience, but more often it was a pain in the ass. It was an existence primed for destruction. Creation, the building of empires and legacies, that took time.

"You like this one?"

"Huh?" Nix hadn't realized she'd been staring. The woman in the bed before them was probably mid-twenties, her black hair long and lush as it settled in waves against the stark white of the pillow. The olive tone of her skin reminded Nix of warm sand beaches.

Lindle flagged a passing nurse. "Take her," he said to Nix. "You can choose another later if you change your mind."

Nix shook her head. "I'm fine, thanks."

"Not really a suggestion, Nixy. You know you can't keep wearing…"—he waved his hand at her—"*that*. The Order's going to have to deal with all three of them. Unless you're planning to go down with that ship. You aren't…are you?"

She straightened. "Of course not."

The nurse stopped in front of them, glancing at Nix with a raised eyebrow. Her bright-red bob caught the florescent light with a shimmer, seeming all the brighter for her starched white uniform.

"Prep this one, will you?" Lindle said.

The nurse smoothly began removing IV needles and some complicated-looking procedure with the intubation covering the girl's mouth. Nix imagined this was how they kept the bodies breathing and maybe even fed. She turned away.

"Okay, let's do this," Lindle said. "There's a room across the hall full of clothing to dress them up. Anything you can imagine. You get set up here and I'll pick out something decent for you, since you clearly have no fashion sense. I'll sign this model out for you at the terminal."

Nix nodded. *"I have to jump,"* she told Elliot. *"They're going to take you away after that."*

"What do we do?"

"Wait for our moment. You'll still have the roman glass on your belt. Remember, say claritas visionis *to reverse the glamor."*

"What the hell? I'm not a witch, it isn't going to work."

"It'll work," Nix reassured him. *"You've performed exorcisms and transference spells before. You didn't have to be a witch for those, either. It's not rocket science, puppet. Be ready to do it. Try not to eat anyone. At least, not unintentionally. I'll have to take both guns—they won't let you keep them."*

"Will I be with Pops and Rachel?"

"I don't know. Listen…hang in there." She was terrible at goodbyes, and she knew it.

Nix hung the tranquilizer gun on a hook next to her new host, hoping it wouldn't be confiscated from her and surprised it hadn't been so far, though demons were uniquely unafraid of bullets in general. Nix slid the blessed gun out of Elliot's boot and set it on the side table. The nurse finished prepping the new host, walked to a cabinet, then returned to Nix. She handed her a set of handcuffs expectantly.

"You wearing one of those demon-killers I've heard about?" she said. "Doesn't look so scary. Serves the bastard right."

"You've heard about them?" Nix asked, standing a little straighter.

"Oh yes, ma'am. Heard a lot about you, too." She winked. "Notorious Nix." The nurse leaned in close enough that Nix could smell the soap on her skin, could sense the body's steady heartbeat beneath her flesh. "Order said you turned on us, but most of us, we didn't believe the rumors. Not if all the stories about you are true. You set the kings free, after all."

"The kings?"

She shrugged. "The Order. Changing their branding with the ascendancy. I guess royalty is more impressive to the new recruits than calling them the Order."

"Huh," Nix said, snapping the handcuffs in place on Elliot's wrists, but keeping his hands in front of him.

"Yeah," the nurse said. "Seems a little silly to me. I mean, archdemons are totally genderless, so why kings and not queens when one is in a woman? It's an obvious ploy to manipulate human social power dynamics for the newbies. But, hey,"—she touched Nix's shoulder—"I didn't say anything, yeah? It's an iron-fist rule around here." She sighed and pulled the host's sheet down.

It seemed to Nix that not all the Order's army was completely brainwashed. Maybe the new recruits would be, but the old hats like Nix seemed to have a stronger bullshit detector and just be going along with the ride in their own best interests. Lindle had welcomed her back like old times.

"All right," the nurse said. "You're golden, sweet thing."

"Good luck," Nix said to Elliot.

Nix took a breath and made the jump.

Chapter 41

Nix blinked, staring up at the industrial-white ceiling of the ward. She sat up, stretching. The sheet fell away, leaving a ghosting of goosebumps across her naked skin. The host body's muscles were soft and atrophied from the bed rest. She worked them out, using her own strength to revitalize them. Her bare feet hit the ground and she stumbled on weak legs over to the side of the bed to check on Elliot's crumpled body.

Lindle returned with a stack of clothes in his arms. His mouth was set in a firm line and his energy had changed from his earlier easygoing attitude.

The nurse helped her stand and sat her back on the bed. "Don't worry," she said. "Lindle will make sure your hostage doesn't run off. Oh my, we'd better cover this boy's mouth. Don't need any accidents around here." She reached for a roll of medical tape and wrapped it over Elliot's mouth and around his head. His head lolled on the ground as he came to.

Lindle said, "I'll watch him. Get dressed. We'll meet up with Mars in the boardroom." He looked at her, his eyes strained. "The Order isn't happy, Nixy."

Nix slipped quickly into the underclothes, black pants and green silk shirt Mars had handed her. None of the clothes were remotely suitable for a battle. He handed her a pair of heeled black boots. "Heels?" It came out like an accusation, her voice low and sharp. She had to admit she liked the soft timbre, the smoky cadence of it.

"Best to make an entrance."

She rolled her eyes and zipped the boots up her calves. The nurse handed her a glass of water. It was only then she realized how dry and gross her mouth was. She drank, then stopped. Nix flexed her jaw, swallowed, set the glass down and pressed her fingers to her ears, wincing.

"Strange, isn't it?" Lindle said. "I'm afraid you won't have time to adjust. We need to go."

A ringing filled her head.

Empty, she realized suddenly. She was alone.

Lindle pulled a groaning Elliot off the ground and toward the glass doors. The nurse touched her shoulder. "You all right?"

Alone. Nix searched for the presence within her, but there was nothing to search for, no one to find. No mindscape at all. She felt...hollow.

"Nixy, let's go."

Nix glanced up and stood. She grabbed the hanging tranquilizer gun from its perch and swung it over her shoulder, then tucked the blessed gun into her waist band, trying to ignore the tingling itch as it rubbed against her skin. She spared a glance for the nurse and nodded her thanks, then followed Lindle out on unsteady legs.

Empty, her mind kept repeating.

This was no time for an existential crisis. She was about to walk into the pit of vipers. She had three hunters to protect, three archdemons to destroy, and one shot to make it happen.

Chapter 42

Nix and Lindle took the elevator to the top floor. Nix's new stomach fell with every shift beneath her feet. Lindle wasn't looking at her now. His brow was furrowed, his jaw tensed. He'd gotten in trouble. Probably while he was getting her ridiculous clothes from some grand closet.

The tranquilizer gun hung heavy against her back. She felt the need to adjust it but didn't dare draw attention. It was more obvious than the blessed gun burning against her back. She was walking around armed, and that couldn't stand for long, no matter how unconcerned her kind were about getting shot.

Glancing at the other demons so far, it seemed they were all armed—against humans? Nix wondered what they were worried about. Probably hunters like the ones she'd brought right to their door. Who knew how many external threats they'd already put down; other demons, hunters, and supernatural creatures who had a stake in keeping the Order from ascending.

Elliot was more alert now, standing tall. His hands, cuffed loosely in front of him, fiddled at his belt where the box was hidden. He, too, made a point of not looking at her. Nix had done a lot to secure her place with the hunters, but she wondered if they were feeling the same trepidation about her that she felt toward Cirrik. The same sense of impending betrayal.

Everything was on the line here, and not only their lives. If they failed now, the Order won. No revenge for Antheia. Callie wouldn't be safe. The world Nix had somehow become responsible for and every human and non-human in it would be under the Order's control. Even the Order's own army were disposable in their quest for ultimate power.

They stopped at the final floor. When the elevator opened, four demons with guns were waiting for them. Lindle waved them away. "No problem here, boys. She's on our side. The hunter's under control."

Three of the demons lowered their weapons and the fourth grabbed Elliot and jerked him forward. "He has to go with the others." The demon shot Nix a dirty look, then turned to Lindle. "Can't let her keep that gun in here."

Lindle whipped around as if noticing for the first time that she had a massive dart gun hanging off her back. "Oh, yeah. Sorry, gotta take that."

Shit. She'd had a good run. Nix kept her new face blank and unreadable. She handed the gun over without protest. Lindle slung it over his shoulder.

The demon who'd brought it up stepped into her personal space and patted her down. It grabbed the gun tucked into her pants, hissing upon touching it. The gun dropped to the floor of the elevator with a clatter. He shot her a disapproving look before signaling another demon over. His friend carried a box of weapons. The demon slid on a glove and tossed the gun unceremoniously into the box. "All weapons are checked at the door before entry to the ballroom. You can get them back from the box on exit."

There wasn't exactly a log or a lock box. The plastic container the demon toted around carried all manner of guns and knives, even a machete. Nix said a silent goodbye to the hunters' cherished heirloom. They'd never see that sucker again.

They were waved out of the elevator as the other demon took Elliot away. Nix watched him go and wondered if she'd see him again. He met her eyes once, fleeting, and kept his head down.

The demon with the weapons container parked himself at a booth in front of a set of doors where others were mingling. Nix and Lindle turned left down the hall to the very last door.

They entered a boardroom. Cirrik was sitting at a long wooden table with Mars. As Nix walked in, they stood. Big mahogany doors closed behind them. A dim overhead chandelier cast wavering shadows through the room. With a jolt, Nix glanced out the floor-to-ceiling windows spanning two sides of the corner office.

Below, the city lights sparkled against the water of the San Francisco bay. The sun had set. Did this mean they were too late?

Cirrik and Mars sat. Lindle joined them, but Nix stayed standing.

"What are we doing here?" Nix finally asked.

Cirrik answered, "The Order has requested an audience."

Her brain sparked. To get them in one room was exactly what they needed.

"Of course," Cirrik said, "as preparations are underway for the celebration, only one member of the Order will be present and only for a brief appearance. It seems they may not be as happy to see us as we had expected."

Nix walked to the window and looked down at the boardwalk far below. From here, the people looked like ants. Had Max secured their exit? Was he still down there, or had he moved on as Danny insisted? Somewhere in this massive building, she'd allowed her hunters to get separated from her. Were they together or apart? Dead already? If they were alive, Rachel was surely considering this Nix's Judas moment.

This was a terrible plan. Nix's fists clenched at her sides. Her gaze lifted to the bay and for a startling moment she saw her reflection in the glass. Green eyes stared back at her. Her own eyes. She stepped back, gasping.

The doors opened. Nix turned to meet the gaze of a tall man in a white suit. His silver-rimmed glasses glinted in the light of the chandelier. An ID tag with his photo was clipped to his front pocket, the CDC logo emblazoned underneath. She recognized his face now as the man standing in front of the building earlier, though he'd been wearing a doctor's jacket then. His dark eyes told a different story. Bianakith, the healer. Bringer of plagues and pestilence.

The others lowered their gazes, including Cirrik. Nix dug her new fingernails into her palms. The coward. If he turned on her tonight, she'd kill him herself.

The doctor strode toward her, lips quirking into a twisted grin. "Well, now. I don't believe we've had the chance to meet in person."

She straightened, her shoulders back. She imagined his head on a pike to calm her churning guts. "Your reputation precedes you."

He laughed, short and choppy, stopping within a foot of her. "I should hope so. As does yours, surprisingly." Looking her up and down, he added in a rich, deep voice, "I'd shake your hand, but, you know. Germs."

This close to his face, she could see red boils peeking out from beneath the collar of his white shirt. He'd stolen this host as they'd thought; it wasn't one of their higher-caliber experiments. Perhaps after their ascension their borrowed hosts wouldn't wear out either.

"Sit. I see you've been welcomed into our highly secure facility with open arms and given the nickel tour." He eyed Mars and Lindle. "Seems security is a bit lax today, of all days."

"But, sir," Lindle said.

"What was that? For a moment there, I thought I heard you call me something as pedestrian and demeaning as *sir?*"

"Your Majesty," Lindle corrected, head lowering.

"Unbelievable," the doctor muttered. "You may leave. And by leave, I mean return to your posts and refrain from allowing any other intruders onto the premises. In the future, I expect I won't have to spell this out for you. Be grateful I'm in a good mood today."

"Yes, Your Majesty," Mars and Lindle said in tandem, turning to leave.

As the doors swished closed, Nix made out the forms of at least three other demons standing guard in the hall. Lindle had walked off with her tranquilizer gun. Still, maybe she could find an opportunity in this.

The big mahogany doors only opened inward. They were sturdy and so were the handles. She could block the door easily—though demons could break it down as easily. Blocking the door with a table of this size might buy time. To do what? She couldn't perform the exorcism, only the hunters could do that, and she'd gone and lost them. Practically given them up willingly.

She could run. Break this window and jump, abandon the whole thing.

Nix blinked. No, there was no running. Not anymore.

Nix sat across from Cirrik, though the table was so large they may as well have been on opposite sides of the city. The doctor took the head of the table, leaning forward. He steepled his fingers, looking at Cirrik and Nix in turn. The room was silent but for the humming of an air conditioner.

"Well. If it isn't our prodigal son and daughter waltzing on home. Last reports said *you'd* gotten yourself kidnapped by the enemy." He pointed at Cirrik. "And *you* were the enemy." He pointed at Nix. "Enlighten me as to this twist of events that returned you to the fold. And do be brief, I have an ascension to attend."

Cirrik said, "It was all part of the plan, Your Majesty. Nix needed the hunters to believe she was on their side in order to uncover information regarding the exorcism. When I showed up, she convinced them to kidnap me to prevent them from exorcising me, and we bided our time to escape. We convinced the hunters to attack tonight so we could lead them here to you. A gift for the ascension."

"And you?"

"Yeah. That's right. Playing the long game."

"Well, what was this all-important information you worked so hard to glean from these hunters?" Bianakith asked. Cirrik opened his mouth but the doctor raised a hand to silence him. "I'm asking Nix."

"Right. The information. Well, they're the only ones who have it...the exorcism. They didn't share it with any other hunters. It starts and ends with them."

The doctor's eyebrow arched. "You're certain of this?"

"Yes. I knew it was imperative for us to be sure. The hunter who discovered it was Kevin Rousoe. I killed him. He shared it with Daniel Whipsaw and his two children, but it never had a chance to spread beyond them. Their hunter circle turned on them before that could happen and the incantation isn't written down in case it gets into the wrong hands. It ends with them."

He squinted, then pushed his glasses up on his nose. "Excellent. That is valuable. And yet, you decided to bring these nuclear-weapon-toting hunters here, to our great ascension, instead of simply killing them. Seems like a severe lapse in judgment."

"Well," Nix said, "considering the damage they've done, I thought you'd want to deal with them yourselves. Cirrik said...*implied* that it wouldn't matter anyway, you would be immune to the exorcism."

He interlaced his fingers on the table. "Quite right."

When the silence stretched, Nix continued, "And the exorcism is powerful. Once they're gone, so is it. Power like that…I thought there may be a more worthy place for it than the grave."

"Hmm. You lodge an interesting argument. Perhaps there is a place for such knowledge. However, I think you'll find we aren't the same Order of old. We've endeavored to change with the times. Our arsenal is plenty advanced now without the use of some quaint human curses." He leaned back. "Still, it was ballsy to walk right in here." He grinned. "I have heard that about you. And what do you think of our facility?"

Nix opened her mouth, closed it. "Amazing."

"I see you've already found the closet?"

"Yes. Thank you."

"Not at all. We expect everyone to be well dressed for the event. We're starting soon."

"We're invited?"

"Naturally. You were the one who set us free of our prison. Don't think we aren't grateful for that." His eyes darkened as he stood, prompting Cirrik to stand. "However unintentional it may have been. But even as a blunder, it benefited us greatly as none of our other lambkin have." He stepped close to Cirrik and ran a long finger across his jawbone. "After so many cycles trapped in there, you can imagine our surprise upon release to discover that during all that time, none of our clan had been searching for us."

Cirrik shifted foot to foot.

"But," the doctor said cheerfully, "that's all water under the bridge, isn't it, my children? You're always welcome at our table. We'll need a full house tonight."

The doctor turned toward the door.

Nix took a breath. "And the hunters?"

He glanced back at her. "No longer your concern. In fact, perhaps we'll invite them to dinner."

The door swished closed behind him. Cirrik dropped back into his chair, his head in his hands. Nix stood and walked to his side. She leaned down and whispered into his ear, "They're the ones you're playing, right?"

He looked up at her, frowning. "Has it been so long?"

"Since you've betrayed me? Not long enough."

"I should never have compromised your trust. Not yours," he acknowledged in a hushed tone, which was...a shocking plot twist, in Nix's opinion. He tilted his head. "She looks nice on you."

"You didn't really answer my question."

The door opened and two demons Nix didn't recognize entered.

One placed a hand on Cirrik, bent down to sniff him and cringed. "You're supposed to get cleaned up before the event. Come on."

Cirrik stood, turned to Nix, and kissed her hard.

"There's your answer," he whispered against her lips.

Chapter 43

The demon pulled Cirrik from the room, leaving one guard in the boardroom. Nix licked her lips and muttered, "Still wasn't an answer."

"Answer to what?" the female guard asked.

Nix brushed her hands down the front of her soft silk blouse, noticing the air had gotten warmer. "Nothing. Never mind."

The guard nodded, short platinum-blonde locks bobbing with the movement. "Cool. Whatever. I'm Crystal, by the way. I'm new here." She held out a hand to Nix.

"Crystal?"

"OMG is your name Crystal, too? That would be so cray," the girl gushed, borrowed hazel eyes wide and rimmed in thick black lashes.

"No, no, I...my name's Nix."

The guard's red lips pouted. "What kind of a name is Nix? Oh, were your parents, like, new-age hippies?"

Nix's mouth dropped open. "Look, it doesn't matter. It's probably better we don't talk, what with you guarding me and all."

"Oh right." Crystal mimed zipping her lips. It only lasted a second before she continued her chatter. She led Nix out and down the hall where she could see others filing into a room, talking in excited tones.

"Hey," Nix said. "Do you know where they're keeping those hunters?"

"What hunters?" Crystal said.

Nix sighed. It had been a while since her reputation *hadn't* preceded her. "I really need to use the washroom."

Crystal shot her a confused look. "I'm really supposed to get you to the ascension on time. It's, like, my only job. So, try to hold it?"

Nix stopped in the hallway and stared at her. Time for a new approach. "Okay, you know that guy in the boardroom?"

"Your boyfriend?"

Nix huffed. "He's not—fine, yes, my boyfriend. I can't go in there without him. Can you take me to him first?"

Crystal looked down the hall. "I don't know."

"Please? It's important. You know what, I can run and grab him. I'll be right back. You wait here."

"Well..." Crystal seemed as if she were seriously considering this half-baked ploy, and for a second Nix could see some light at the end of the tunnel. Then she straightened and not-so-subtly adjusted her bust. "Oh, look! Wow, what a hottie. You go, girl." She nudged Nix with her elbow, pointing behind them toward the dock of elevators.

Nix frowned, turning to where Crystal was pointing. Lo and behold, there was Cirrik, inexplicably showered, dry, and in a clean suit. How in the hell could he have managed that in what could only have been fifteen minutes max? The unfairness of the situation flooded Nix with irritation. And to make matters worse, he did look like he'd stepped off a catwalk, damn him.

Cirrik strode up to them.

"Thanks a lot," Nix spat.

He lifted an eyebrow but didn't retort. Instead he held out his elbow expectantly.

"What the hell is this?" Nix asked.

With a long-suffering sigh, he plucked her hand up in his, wove it through his arm and released it, leaving them arm in arm. "Shall we, my dear?"

Nix rolled her eyes and pulled him onward.

Crystal shrugged, falling in step with Cirrik's guard and continuing her chatter.

They stepped through a double set of metal doors into an expansive black-and-white ballroom festooned in human decorations. The doors were closed and pointedly locked behind them.

In that moment, Nix had two pressing questions answered. Where had her hunters been ushered off to? The answer was presented in the form of a stockade placed on the corner of a stage, three familiar heads poking out of it as the bodies struggled behind the stocks and a collection of demons in front laughed and prodded them.

How screwed were they? The answer: completely. The ballroom was packed with easily a hundred demons. Long tables were lavished with roasted lamb, grapes, and wine. The revelers were dressed for the celebratory occasion, save a few guards positioned at the doors. Nix noted that Mars and Lindle had been selected for this duty though they were surely higher-ranking officers for their seniority—a punishment, no doubt, and their sour looks confirmed it.

Danny's tranquilizer gun was still slung over Lindle's shoulder. Cirrik's old friends, Trus and Jin, were at the door, too, showing the new management had little tolerance for negligence of duty like that shown today.

Nix would have expected a far harsher punishment than this—what amounted to a slap on the wrist. The more she thought about it, the less it sat well with her. The Order was notoriously unforgiving of even the smallest slights. She'd been certain beyond certainty that Cirrik would show his face to them only to have his face forcibly removed merely for associating with the hunters against his will. And her punishment should have been infinitely worse. Mars, Lindle, and the others had let them walk right in, and their punishment was door duty? None of this tracked.

Nix's gaze flittered across the room. If all the demons here had been newbies like Crystal, there may have been a slim chance she could have taken a hundred of them through sheer force of competence. But as she surveyed the crowd, she didn't see the new ranks she expected. Many here she recognized. A solid two-thirds at least, that she'd been acquainted with at some point in her non-life, like the band was back together. It seemed the Order had assembled primarily their senior ranks for this celebration and only a selection of newbies. How many others were now in existence, she couldn't predict.

Crystal ushered her and Cirrik toward the front of the room near the stage. Nix could finally get a good look at the hunters. Which was probably the purpose of the move—testing her loyalties. She kept her face impassive as Rachel met her eyes, twisting awkwardly in the stocks with her hair hanging in front of her. Elliot thrashed and growled, which seemed to entertain the demons standing around jeering at them. Gags still carefully covered their mouths, the original loose bandanas replaced with buckled leather contraptions to ensure no unfortunate slip-ups. Their hands were trapped in the wooden stocks far from their faces, defeating the purpose of Nix leaving their binds loose enough that they might be able to escape if the opportunity arose.

The only good thing Nix could see in this is that they were in the same clothes, if divested of anything that could be used as weapons, so Elliot should still have the roman glass.

Before they could take their seats at the table, everyone was standing and a rush of applause and cheers filled the air. Nix looked up to the stage as Bianakith, Belbel, and Autothith stepped out.

Bianakith, the healer, emanated confidence in his crisp white suit. Bebel, wearing his televangelist, stepped forward with his hands open wide, as if to embrace the room, and took one of the three mics on stage. The preacher, distorter of hearts and minds, stood tall above his flock in a jet-black suit that matched his slicked-back hair, a gold Rolex on his glinting wrist.

But it was Autothith, in her shimmering blonde popstar, who stopped Nix's heart.

The shepherd. Inciter of grudges and enmity.

Nix had believed she'd never met the Order in person. She'd been wrong.

This close to the stage now, she saw a familiar presence behind the eyes of the shepherd. The same she'd seen in her home village all those centuries ago. The same that had stood beside her as her sister died in her arms. Nix's fists clenched and unclenched. Her nostrils flared.

It hadn't been some anonymous lackey of the Order, after all. It was Autothith. And here she was, only feet away.

Chapter 44

The crowd hushed and took their seats. Cirrik tugged at Nix's arm, urging her into her chair until she complied.

"My lambkins," Belbel said, his voice worn and raspy. Something about his cadence pulled at her thoughts as if calling her mind to unravel and wrap itself around his will. "Your presence on this most auspicious of nights warms an old man's heart. You bring us great pride with your unwavering support and dedication to the cause." His teeth gleamed as he smiled, and it felt like a gift.

Nix blinked, realizing she recognized the insidious, slick sensation pushing its fingers into her brain. The archdemon in Violet had felt similar when reading her thoughts—only it was sticky and clinging like tree sap. This was a smoky, smooth bourbon, cloyingly sweet and addictive, but far more subtle.

When Autothith stepped up to the mic, any lulling sensation thickening Nix's veins instantly chilled. The shepherd looked down upon its flock with a predatory grin. Mascara-thickened lashes hid the piercing blue eyes of a wolf.

"Tonight will mark the turning point, not only for our great clan, but for the world itself," the shepherd said. "Tonight, we make history. We recreate the world in our image. Each and every one of you will play a pivotal role. These were the promises we made, and tonight you'll receive your just deserts.

Speaking of *desserts*?"—she motioned toward the hunters at the side of the stage—"we're saving a little treat for after the main course. But I think you'll find the entire meal most satisfying." Her tongue darted out to lick a sharp canine.

The healer stepped forward, motioning someone to join them from off stage. A moment later, six older ladies in floor-length red robes lined up along the right side of the stage. They began humming, low, then punctuated with higher notes. Coven of Thorns medallions hung at their necks. At first, Nix thought they were singing, then she assumed chanting. Now she leaned toward a mixture of both. A murmur spread through the crowd as the women harmonized.

"As some of you are aware," the healer said, "many of our current leaps of progress are thanks to our valued coven members, who, though not our kind, are nonetheless still our lambkin. Unfortunately, progress is not without its cost. Our Coven of Thorns suffered great losses and not all survived unscathed in our experiments these past weeks. To them, we offer our sincerest gratitude for their sacrifices." The doctor raised his hands to clap and a flutter of applause spread over the room, threading through the women's continued melody.

Only one of the women looked to be younger than sixty. Nix could easily envision Maria up there among them, were she in better condition. Whatever work she'd done for them destroyed her, and who knew how many others. The vague, glazed stares of the women on stage suggested they hadn't been as untouched as they appeared.

A tremble shook the room. Nix watched the thick red wine in her glass shiver. The applause shifted to confused mutters as the women's chorused voices on stage rose an octave.

The shepherd laughed, red-painted lips spread wide over white teeth. "I suppose that's our cue to start this party."

Quiet, uncertain laughter rolled over the crowd in response.

Someone across the room gasped and jerked back from their table. Nix looked to Cirrik. He shrugged, one hand reaching for a steak knife next to his dinner plate. Nix followed suit.

"Now, now, let's remain seated, children," the preacher intoned gently. "I still have quite a reviving speech for you."

The shepherd flicked a lock of blonde hair over a bony shoulder. "I think you'll need to speed it up."

Someone gasped across the table from Nix, eyes wide as they fell from their chair. The haunting chanting of the coven rose. Nix's heartrate ratcheted up.

The partygoers chattered worriedly. Someone ran for the door and it rattled, locked. Her palms prickled with a cold sweat.

Sighing, the preacher tossed a set of cue cards in the air and they fluttered to the stage. "Very well. The point is, my dear, dear children, so many sacrifices were made to get us to where we are today. Mostly ours. After many years of imprisonment, only the three of us, to re-emerge and find a flock waiting for us with open arms...do not think our cold hearts were not warmed by this."

Something touched Nix's leg under the table. She gasped and jerked back, standing and pulling Cirrik up with her. From beneath the long white tablecloth, a green vine slithered out.

Someone screamed. Nix's fingers trembled, her jaw clenched despite the quick, rasping breaths trying to draw more oxygen into her lungs. The chanting rose to a fever pitch.

The preacher opened his hands wide, palms cupped in supplication. "Do not consider what comes an act of retribution for your earlier abandonment. Instead, consider it your penance. You are *forgiven*, my children. And on this night of our great ascension, we thank *you,* most of all, for your sacrifice."

Thorny vines shot out from under the tables, tipping some over and latching on to ankles, wrists, and throats.

Cirrik tripped over a chair, falling to the ground. Nix stumbled away from the tables as chaos erupted through the room. The noise was a blur beyond the thrashing of her heartbeat filling her ears.

Beside her, Crystal's wide eyes met Nix's as a rose-dotted vine wrapped around her neck. Thorns pierced her flesh like razors as she gaped, choking and clawing at the vine. Blood gushed to the ballroom floor.

Nix gripped her steak knife and slashed at the vine.

The blade snapped. The vine was undamaged, as strong as a cable of steel.

Crystal's face turned purple and her mouth and eyes widened even further. The vine tightened around her throat, blood dripping down. With a sickening crack, her neck snapped sideways and her head popped off. Platinum-blonde hair rolled across the floor as her body fell in the opposite direction.

Nix scrambled away from the splatter, barely aware of the screams pulsating in the air, blending together as one above the haunting choral hymn of the coven.

Crystal's dark essence rose up from her dead host body but as soon as Nix saw the smoke, it was absorbed into the vines. A black line carved its way up the shaft of the vine like a poisoned vein and as Nix instinctively followed its path, her gaze lifted to the stage.

It was everything she'd feared, everything she'd known would come from this foolish mission. Nix's worst nightmares of archdemons were brought to vibrant life, in triplicate, in front of her new eyes. This was the scenario she'd been too afraid to hear confirmed by the tea leaves. This was how it ended.

The Order stood in a circle, hand in hand, as the vines gently encircled them, twisting up their bodies. They pulsed with energy, their faces tilted to the ceiling, expressions serene.

From the foreheads of their hosts erupted the curved horns of rams. Perched upon their heads, nestled between their horns, the vines had formed themselves into blossoming crowns of thorns.

The massive chandelier over the ballroom tables crashed, leaving them in darkness but for a few wall sconces and the stage lights illuminating the Order and the choir.

A demon tripped over Nix in the near-dark, then a vine grabbed his ankle and dragged him back the way he'd come, screaming. Every muscle in Nix's new body tensed, her eyes wide.

Hands landed on Nix's shoulders and she struggled against them until she heard Cirrik's voice shouting above the noise. "The door's barricaded somehow! We can't get out."

A glance confirmed it. The crowd had stormed the only exit, trampling any unfortunate bodies that got in the way. Some were moaning and crawling away as vines sought them out. The majority of the vines were concentrated in the center of the room where people were still scrambling. Nix saw Lindle on the ground, unmoving on his back. Mars crawled next to him.

"We need that gun," she told Cirrik. "We can still do this."

He darted off.

Chest tight as dizziness spun her vision of the dance floor, Nix looked up to the left side of the stage, the shadowy dessert corner. There, struggling in the stocks, her hunters still stood. Cirrik was back beside her before she could mount the stage. He handed her the tranquilizer gun, his hands shaking. She pulled the strap over her head.

"Lindle?" she asked.

"Alive. For now. Helped pull them out."

She turned toward the stage. Terror choked her. She pushed the panic down. There was still a chance. She wouldn't let this all be in vain. "Let's do this."

Behind her, Cirrik shouted, "Nix!"

Chapter 45

Something hard smacked into Nix from behind, slamming the air out of her. Nix was flat on her stomach before she knew what hit her, a warm body pressed close to her back as she gasped in quick breaths. She rolled to right herself, twisting into Cirrik's embrace.

Blood smeared her green silk shirt as she looked down, struggling to bring the scene around her into focus, to follow the abrupt shift.

No pain. She wasn't hit. But the blood…

She met Cirrik's wide, shocked eyes.

Nix pulled away, gripping his shoulders with shaking hands.

A thin vine slid back through the center of Cirrik's chest, thorns tearing him up on the way out. Red blossomed on his white dress shirt. *He just changed that,* she thought, absurdly. The room seemed to whirl beneath her, her vision a swirl of color, no air in her lungs. Alone in her head, chaos erupting around her, she felt unmoored.

Cirrik gripped her hand. Blood gurgled between his open lips. Black smoke drifted out with it. She watched his eyes drain of life. Her own chest ached, a sharp throb spreading all the way down to the tips of her fingers.

Instead of floating upward, the smoke drifted down as if pulled, spilling from his mouth in a cascade and absorbing into the ravenous vines.

Nix blinked, the sound of her heart a million thundering drums in her ears as she pieced it together. "You...you pushed me out of the way, didn't you? You stupid...you..." She squeezed his hand and with her free one pounded his shoulder. Her throat tightened, strangling her words. "I hate you," she choked, "I..."

A vine wrapped around his waist and jerked him backward.

"No!" Nix shouted, grabbing him, and holding tight.

The vines dragged Cirrik back, pulling them both several feet across the floor until it lifted them and released its grip. Nix crashed to the ground, gathering Cirrik to her with weak, tingling limbs.

A crushing pressure built inside her chest at the sight of him, caving in on itself as she tried and failed to breathe. She touched his face, stared into his eyes.

Hollow. Gutted. He was gone.

She slammed her fists against the hardwood floor of the ballroom and screamed.

Nix dragged him back to the stage, leaned him up against it and sat, panting, with her head on his shoulder. Pulling her knees to her chest, she waited for them to come for her. She'd rip them apart with her teeth.

Nix tilted her head back. Her hunters. They were still back there. She squeezed her eyes shut, inhaling hard and fast.

"I'll be back," she said, hand on Cirrik's limp arm. She grabbed the fallen tranquilizer gun and swung it over her shoulder, her chin raised.

Nix climbed up onto the stage and rushed to the stockade, noticing now that it was planted on a larger platform with rollers underneath. She glanced back at the Order. Too close for comfort. "Don't worry, I've got you."

She pushed the hunters as far back as the stage would allow, then carefully down a small access ramp at the side until she had them nestled in the corner of the room furthest from the heart of the action.

The tiny locks on the leather gags snapped under her trembling fingertips as she removed first Rachel's, then Elliot's, then Danny's.

"What's happening out there?" Rachel asked, her view severely limited from this perspective.

The screams were quieting compared to the chanting. The realization hit Nix like a current of electricity in her aching chest. She felt like she'd been shot. Nix glanced out at the ballroom. Writhing vines whipped in the darkness, consuming everything they touched.

"Pandemonium," Nix said, moving to work on the heavy padlock at the side of the stockade holding it all together. Her voice was flat. "This is the ascension. They're…consuming all the demons. That's how they're getting their power." Giving up on the lock, she finally jerked the whole mechanism right out of the wood it was nailed to. She lifted the heavy wood and the hunters slipped free.

Danny straightened, flexing his neck. Rachel rubbed her wrists. Elliot remained hunched over, hands on his knees. Saliva dripped from his mouth as he panted.

With a pang, Nix regretted removing his gag. The heavy, thick scent of blood hung on the air. She stepped between him and the other hunters. "Elliot?" She nudged him with one hand, prepared to hold him back.

"El? Are you okay?" Rachel started.

"Don't," Nix warned. "Elliot, if you're going to attack someone, make it the fucking choirgirls. If we don't take them all out fast, you aren't getting out of here."

Elliot glanced up at her, gasping, his one eye squinted. He shuddered and swallowed, stumbling toward the coven.

"What the hell did you do?" Danny said.

"Sentenced a bunch of witches to death by Elliot." Nix wiped a hand down her face. She passed Danny the tranquilizer gun. "It's your only chance. More than a hundred powerful demons tried to bust that door down in a frenzy and couldn't. Those witches are keeping it blocked, that's the only answer. I think they're controlling the vines, too. If we stop them, we stop the ascension. If we can get that door open, the vines are seeking out demons, they might ignore you. You can make a run for it."

Rachel grabbed her. "We're seeing this through. Together."

"Oh Jesus," Danny mumbled as a squelching sound interrupted the choir's harmony.

Nix turned in time to see Elliot's teeth sink into a woman's trachea before he leaped with wild force onto the next one.

The choir disintegrated into glass-shattering and perfectly tuned shrieks. In a second, they were silenced.

A shaft of light pierced the darkness from across the room as someone opened the tall door. Nix saw a few bodies slip through as the remaining demons made their escape.

"All right," Rachel said. "We're doing it live. I'll get the roman glass from El." She ran toward the cannibalism fest with unwarranted optimism and self-assuredness in her gait.

Nix shook her head. Danny took aim at the Order as their serene smiles fell in confusion, the room now silent and the writhing vines stilled.

Thwap thwap thwap. Three shots, perfect aim.

The preacher fell first.

The doctor and shepherd turned toward them and took two steps. The doctor stumbled, fell.

The celebrity-wearing shepherd in the smallest host body met Nix's eyes, still standing, seemingly through pure rage alone. The archdemon's lips curled as it growled.

"You," it accused, eyes locked on Nix as it took another halting step. The crown of thorns slid from its head, catching in long blonde hair before tumbling to the ground. "I created you. I'll destroy you."

"Yeah, yeah," Nix said.

Danny shot her again with the last tranquilizer dart. She fell to the ground in a sparkly heap.

Rachel dragged Elliot over, blue glass bauble cupped in her palm. Blood dripped down his satisfied face.

"Cover your ears," she said. "Just in case."

Nix complied, stepping back but staying close enough to watch the show. She wanted to see them burn. The hunters' mouths were moving in tandem. The roman glass glowed in Rachel's hand.

On the stage, the three archdemons lay paralyzed but twitching. Their skin bubbled.

It was working.

Until it wasn't.

Chapter 46

The glass sphere exploded in a frenzy of blue sparks. Nix lowered her hands from her ears. "What the hell happened?"

"I don't know," Rachel said. "It shattered."

"Keep going," Nix said. "Maybe we don't need it." She covered her ears again, but her heart pounded and her hands shook. The glass had been too unstable, patched together as it was. But this wasn't over yet.

She watched their mouths move as they chanted their exorcism. The archdemons twitched on the stage floor, skin sizzling. Smoke drifted in fine curls from the scorched flesh. Minutes passed. Too many minutes.

"It's not working," Nix said, ears tightly covered. If they answered her, she didn't hear.

The preacher wasn't only twitching now, he was starting to shift and move. The tranquilizer was wearing off. Nix's stomach plummeted.

They were too late. The ascension had made them invincible. Nothing could touch them now.

Nix looked to the door across the room. Still cracked open. They'd have to run for it. Where?

The preacher started to pull himself up.

"Stop," Nix shouted. "We have to go." They looked to her, to each other, nodded.

They ran.

The hunters didn't glance back when they reached the door, but curses, threats, and growls followed them out and footfalls were close on their heels. Nix did look back, eyes seeking out Cirrik's body, finding him slumped where she abandoned him by the stage. She hesitated, losing a second's momentum before survival instinct kicked back in and urged her forward.

As she reached the hall, heart pounding, her eyes landed on a plastic container outside the door, its contents scattered on the ground. The hunters' blessed gun still lay inside, overlooked by the escaping demons who couldn't waste time trying to touch the burning metal. Nix swooped down and grabbed it, ignoring the sting, and shoved it in her waistband.

She slammed the door to the ballroom behind them, seeing no way to block it from this side. The hunters were halfway down the hall ahead of her before she could call out to direct them the other way. "Wait," she shouted. They didn't hear.

She spared a glance left toward the stairwell and the bank of elevators before running right in their direction, back toward the boardroom she'd been in earlier. Maybe there was another stairwell this way. Even as the thought flashed through her mind, she knew there wasn't another stairwell. They were running toward a dead end. The hallway was vacant, no one in sight.

By the time she caught up to the hunters, the archdemons were stumbling through the ballroom doors and any other exit was blocked. The Order's gait was still sluggish and drugged. It was all they had in their favor.

Rachel and Elliot tested doors down the hall and Nix hopelessly looked for another set of stairs. Danny found an open door at the end, the boardroom. "Here," he called. They flocked.

Nix sped in behind them, slamming the heavy door, panting at the exertion. No exit but a deadly drop through shatter-proof windows, though Nix was confident she had the incentive to shatter them. The hunters wouldn't make the fall. Nor would this shiny new Caddy of a host body.

No. No exit.

Nix shoved the huge table against the door, angling into the alcove of the threshold for added resistance. It could buy them five minutes. Danny clutched a steak knife in his hand, something he must have scooped up off the ballroom floor on their way out. Nix's guts twisted. She could think of nothing more useless.

Remembering she had the gun, she slid it out from her waistband and handed it to Rachel. It was useless too, against archdemons, but Rachel clutched it as tightly as Danny did the steak knife. It was all they had. Rachel aimed toward the door, but her arm dropped after a second. She tucked the gun into her jacket instead.

"What are you doing?" Nix asked.

"We aren't going to make it out." Rachel grabbed Nix's arm and looked her in the eye. "Go."

Nix shook her head. "What?"

"You can jump. Get out of here. Go!"

Nix stepped back. "No. I'm not leaving. I won't do that."

"Then you're an idiot."

"I am."

"You'll die here with us. Leave!"

"No."

Rachel's hand fell to Nix's and squeezed.

"What do we do?" Elliot asked, wiping a hand over his bloody chin.

"The gun won't hurt them," Rachel said.

"Exorcism doesn't work," Danny said, his voice dazed. "We have nothing."

Rachel tugged her hand. "That's not true. We have the transference spell, like Blaine used. We could…pull them out of their host bodies. Into us. Three of them, three of us. We could do that, right?"

Nix gaped at her. "What good will it do to have them possessing you instead? They'll jump right back out. You can't force them to…" Nix's eyes widened.

"That binding spell the archdemon in Violet was talking about—how Edgar bound it to his bones. You know it, right? It taught you?"

A chill crept down Nix's spine. "Yeah." Nix shared the short spell. The door shook. "Are you sure about this? It wouldn't be like with Edgar's archdemon—it was weaker and willing. They had some sort of arrangement. The Order is far more powerful. There's no way you could stay in the driver's seat for long. You'd only be trapping them in your bodies."

Danny stepped forward, tucking the knife into his boot. "If we died, they'd stay trapped in our bones though, ain't that right? We could still end this."

Nix sputtered. It was insane. But the pieces fell together in her mind. The archdemon in Violet had told them that, unlike Nix's experiences in mostly-dead host bodies as a lesser demon, when Edgar died, his body could no longer sustain its powerful energy. Rather than being able to control the corpse, it had been trapped in the bones as the flesh rotted, unable to speak, see, or move. Able only to hear. It was a huge risk, and the corpses would have to be disposed of carefully. But it could work.

"Sacrificing yourselves," Nix said on a harsh exhale. "Hell of a play."

"Seems to me we die here anyway. A man has to make his stand," Danny said. Beside him, Elliot nodded solemnly. Danny reached up and removed his anti-possession amulet, tossing it to the floor. "It'll be up to you to see this through, if it works." Danny reached out his hand to Nix. Nix looked down at it as the banging on the door turned to the cracking and splintering of wood.

She took his hand and shook it.

Rachel slid her golden bracelets off, the jewelry having gone unnoticed. She handed them to Nix. "Put them on yourself, so you're safe. You'll be able to take them off yourself that way." Nix slid the hateful things in place.

They dodged out of the way as the door smashed open and the table flipped over, crashing across the room and denting the far wall.

The shepherd stepped over a mound of splintered wood into the boardroom, the preacher and healer close behind. All three looked worse for wear after the failed exorcism.

"Was that all you had?" The shepherd's chin tilted downward as it tracked its prey.

Clucking his tongue, the doctor said, "How quaint."

"My children," the preacher intoned, arms spreading wide, "we will allow you to kneel in deference." His tone turned icy. "Get on your knees."

All four of them fell to their knees, unable to move as an unseen force held them in place. Cold crept through Nix's body, settling in her chest.

Danny started his transference spell, Rachel and Elliot quickly behind.

"What is this chatter?" the doctor asked. His eyes widened.

The Order's mouths opened as wide as their eyes as thick plumes of smoke sucked out of them and into the hunters.

Chapter 47

The golden bands on Nix's wrists tingled as the rest of her body trembled with adrenaline. Cold sweat trickled down her back. The celebrity, doctor, and televangelist dropped like heavy sacks to the floor, unconscious. The hunters crumpled.

The telekinetic hold pinning Nix on her knees lifted abruptly and she tilted over onto the industrial carpeting before righting herself. Nix stood, backing away from the hunters, wondering if they were still hers or if they were her enemies. Had this, too, been in vain?

Rachel moaned, lifting herself up. She blinked at Nix.

"Rachel?" Nix asked. They should have had a safe word.

She nodded and covered her mouth. From behind her fingers, she said, "I don't feel so well. This isn't right." A shiver wracked her body. Nix moved forward, helping her to stand.

"Hold on. You can do this."

Rachel swallowed, tilting her head back and taking a deep breath. "You were right. They're too strong. I said the spell to bind it as soon as I felt it in me. It's weakened, but it's so mad." Her head fell forward. When she lifted her eyes to Nix's, Rachel's gaze was murderous. She licked her lips, snarling. "It wants to hurt you."

Nix shivered, stepping back. She could guess where the shepherd had landed.

The smelled of smoke reached her nostrils. A massive flaw in their patchwork plan finally occurred to Nix. They'd given a rageful archdemon control over a powerful firebug witch. Looked like this building would be the next in a long line of burned architectural husks, curtesy of Rachel.

"You have to control it, Rachel."

Rachel took another breath and blinked, returning to herself. The smoke faded. "I will. I can."

Danny lifted himself up off the floor, groaning. He spread his arms wide and stared up at the ceiling, wobbling.

"Pops?" Rachel touched his shoulder.

"My child…" Danny blinked, then contorted in on himself, grunting. "Darlin'?"

Rachel choked, grabbing on to him and guiding him to a chair. "It's okay, Pops. I've got you."

Elliot was breathing hard, writhing on the floor. Nix checked on him. His eyes were rolled back in his head.

"I can't hold out for long, darlin'. Need you to do it now. Fast." Danny jerked forward, crumpling in on himself again as if in pain, then righted like it never happened.

"I know, Pops."

"Can you hold on long enough?" he asked her.

"You know I can."

"Yeah. I suppose I do. If anybody's got experience reining in monsters, it's my girl. Proud of ya, darlin'." Danny broke off into a groan, coughing up something that looked like coffee grounds. He wiped his chin with the back of his hand. "It's all right. Over now. You get it finished, ya hear?"

She swallowed, squeezed his shoulder, and held her chin high. Rachel pulled Kevin's gun out of her jacket and stepped back, aiming. "Goodbye, Pops."

Danny lowered his head. She pulled the trigger. His heavy body fell off the chair with a thud. It was finished. Nix held her breath.

Rachel shivered and kept shivering. The gun, held out like an extension of her arm, shook violently. Nix wondered if her arm would fly right off her body, but after a minute Rachel pressed her arm tight against her side, looked straight up at the ceiling and inhaled long and hard.

"One," she said. Her head lowered and her eyes met Nix's. Nix regarded her curiously. Rachel tucked the gun away behind the folds of her jacket. She knelt next to Danny's body and pulled the steak knife out from his boot.

Elliot's muscles looked so tense that parts of him could no longer unfurl. He hobbled forward, jaw clicking open, one hand twisted nearly backward against his chest, the opposite shoulder held fully a foot higher than the other. His skin had broken out in hives. "Christ, Rach, I can't—" His upper lip curled in a snarl, revealing a bit of bloody flesh still lodged between his bicuspids.

In a single twisted motion, Elliot simultaneously lunged toward Rachel and flung himself back against a nearby wall—Jekyll and Hyde at perpetual war.

He wailed, scratching ribbons down his own neck. "So hungry...and *he likes it*, Rach. The hunger. He wants my hunger. Oh god, I can't control it—"

"Shhh..." Rachel glided toward him on a breath and cupped his cheek in her palm. "El, it's okay. Everything is going to be okay."

He took a deep, shuddering breath, blinking tears from his eyes. Elliot melted against her as though he believed her claims. "Remember when we used to go fishing when we were little at the dam near La Grange? We were so happy then," he said. "I wish we could go back there." He rested his forehead against hers.

"We will. We'll go there now. That's where I'll meet you." She kissed him.

He gasped against her mouth, eyes wide, then slumped forward.

Rachel guided his weight down the wall.

When she pulled back her hand, Nix saw the bloody knife in her grip. She wasn't sure where she'd plunged it precisely, but it had gotten the job done quickly. As the archdemon in Violet had prophesized, Elliot's great love was the death of him after all. Rachel closed Elliot's remaining silver-gray eye and stood. The knife clattered to the ground beside her.

Rachel swayed where she stood.

Nix released the breath she'd been holding.

Danny and Elliot could finally rest, and as far as Nix could tell, the archdemons bound to their bones were still unwilling passengers trapped in the skeletal remains of their hosts. Once carefully interred like Winterspoon's remains had been, they would be trapped within those bones eternally.

Rachel wiped at her eyes and strode toward Nix. "That's two. One to go, right?" Standing in front of Nix, eye to eye, she laughed jarringly. "So weird seeing you like this. Like looking into a mirror, only now you're...I don't know what you are. A real person? A dead person? Is she dead, or what?"

Nix's new eyes squinted and they felt like her own. Shock. That's what this was, but Nix didn't mind it. To be honest, she'd always found shock entertaining, like the fun drunk cousin of terror. Maybe they were both in shock. Nix went with it.

"Body's alive, brain's empty. Only me in here. Not sure how they did it." Nix shrugged. "It's as weird on this side of the funhouse mirror, trust me."

Rachel frowned. "You must hate the quiet."

"Better than the alternative," Nix quipped, recalling Rachel's whining and moaning and her oh-poor-me rants. But she wasn't wrong, either. It was deafeningly quiet in here. Nix wasn't sure if she could stand it forever, but something told her she needed to give it a fair shake.

She looked Rachel up and down, only now noticing the similarities between her and the model she'd grabbed off the rack. It had been the familiarity, she'd told herself at the time, the draw of the devil you know. A vague remembrance of a body long since returned to dust, the only body she'd been born to, that she hadn't needed to borrow or steal to get by. And maybe that's why her eyes had fallen on Rachel in the first place, too. The niggling hint of memory, the call of the past. Maybe that's why she'd hated her on instinct. She wasn't sure why she'd warmed to her now. Some sort of change had occurred in her, in both of them.

Now Rachel had killed the only family she'd ever known, without Nix behind the wheel, without Nix's prompting, and Nix couldn't tell if Rachel was completely unhinged or actually handling it all pretty well. Something else for them to have in common.

"It was always going to come down to this," Rachel said, her gaze unfocused. "You and me, in the end." She pulled the gun out again, cocked it. Unspooling a bandana from her belt, she wrapped the butt of the gun in the cloth and handed it to Nix.

Nix's arms felt heavy as she took it. She held the gun loosely in her new hands, the blessed metal barely a tingle through the cloth. Her green blouse clung to her skin, sticky with Cirrik's blood. She stared at her hands—they were delicate and soft, not gun-calloused or scarred like Rachel's, not large and strong like Elliot's or Danny's. *These are not yet the hands of a killer,* she realized, *but they are about to be.* An inevitability.

She didn't notice Rachel had stepped away until the rattle of an office chair on rollers slid in front of her and Rachel plopped down into it, mounting the thing backward with her arms over the backrest. Nix's lips twitched upwards. She'd rubbed off on the girl. And now here she was, getting sentimental.

"—burial will be key," Rachel was saying when Nix wasn't listening. Rachel rubbed her temples. "You will handle it all, right? I'm serious, I'm relying on you to follow through here on body disposal and I feel like you're not even listening. Am I an idiot to be trusting you with something this important? Do I need to lay out how it benefits you directly in order to ensure you get this done?" She motioned to Danny's now cooling corpse. "Promises were made. Just do it, okay?"

Nix rolled her eyes and sighed. "Fine."

"I'll seriously haunt your demonic ass if you screw this up. I'm not sacrificing everything for you to mess it up." Rachel smirked but it didn't reach her eyes.

"I'll see if I can fit it in my schedule."

"That's all I'm asking." Rachel motioned toward the gun in Nix's hand. She raised her eyebrow.

Nix wasn't sure why she was stalling. Her heart throbbed in her throat.

Rachel frowned, wiping her cheeks. "Don't get soft on me now."

"I promised I wouldn't kill you. I swore it." Nix's voice sounded weak even to her. She was a demon. Her word didn't exactly hold weight.

Rachel placed her hand against Nix's. "Make this the last promise you ever break. From now on, your word is gold. You have my permission. And my forgiveness. I'm asking you to do this for me. This is how it was always going to be. I see that now." She shook herself out, tilted her head back, and shut her eyes. "I've got places to be."

Nix stepped forward and tucked the barrel of the gun under Rachel's chin.

Leaning down, she pressed her new lips against Rachel's—a Judas' kiss, fate sealed and delivered. She felt Rachel smirk.

Nix pulled the trigger.

Chapter 48

When it was done, Nix laid the hunters out in a row. Danny, Rachel, and Elliot, side by side. She took Danny's lighter and Elliot's wallet from his back pocket and tucked them into her own, glancing at the photos inside the wallet as she did so. She'd already made sure the hunters' friends and family were all dead when they first met, so she supposed there weren't many people left to remember them. And now, for the first time in her non-life, she might actually be able to hold on to something.

Nix sat in a chair, leaning into the seat rest as she watched the bodies cool. A blanket of stillness fell over her mind despite the heaviness in her chest.

Footsteps echoed in the hallway. Shit. She'd forgotten some of the demons escaped the massacre. Maybe there had been others in the building, waiting for the Order to finish their ascension. And here she was, lingering.

She'd messed a lot of things up in both her life and her non-life. She could see that now, admit to it. It didn't sting the way she thought it would to acknowledge, didn't consume her. Some secret part of her expected her past to rear up out of the shadows with sword in hand and slice her open, guts spilling out slick on the floor. But it didn't happen.

She was a fuckup. There. She'd admitted it, and there was no one else in her mind with her to hear it now. No one to tell, now that she'd had this great revelation. Nix started to laugh as the footsteps grew louder.

She wouldn't fuck up one more thing. Not one. She'd finish this. She'd given her word and she intended to keep it.

When bodies pressed through the busted door, Nix stood. Her grip on the gun tightened even as it burned in her hand. She'd fight her way out of this if she had to, and put the gun's true purpose to the test on her own kind.

Promises were made.

"Where are they?" a voice said.

"What happened in here—oh."

Nix turned, head held high. Mars and Lindle stood to her right, Trus and Jin to her left. The nurse from earlier and several demons she didn't know filled the corridor behind them. More bullets than she had left in this gun. Still, considering the odds she'd just faced…

"Are they…dead?" Trus said. "How can that be possible?" He stared down at the unfortunate bodies of the celebrity, the televangelist, and the doctor.

No one moved to apprehend her.

"Nixy. You did this?" Lindle asked.

Grinding her teeth, she nodded. She'd take them all out if she had to. Even those she thought of as old friends. The bodies were hers to guard.

She considered the window—it wasn't ideal, but she could toss a few out and see what happened.

A demon stepped forward, but Lindle raised his hand and no one moved. Nix narrowed her eyes.

Lindle took his own weapon and laid it on the ground in front of her.

She held her breath.

He remained kneeling, one arm across his chest as he said to the others, "We're free. The old kings are dead."

One by one, the other demons laid down their weapons and knelt before her. A tingling sensation spread through her. She stepped back, frowning, knocking into the chair on her exhale.

"The old kings are dead," another repeated. "Long live the Queen."

Epilogue

The moon was waxing but still bright as three hearses drove up to a dam near La Grange. Stars spattered the night sky like bullet holes through the fabric of the cosmos. Lindle turned to Nix when they parked.

"I still don't see why you want to do this here. Not like the big bad hunters are going to come back and haunt us."

"I'd like to be sure," Nix said.

Lindle shrugged. "All right, boss."

The chirp of cicadas filled the air as they exited the vehicles. Lindle had arranged a couple lackeys to accompany them on the trip and as the boys pulled the first casket out of a hearse, they nearly fell to the ground with the weight of it.

Lindle chuckled beside her. "Well, they sure as hell won't be coming back as zombies."

Nix pursed her lips. "Good. I hate zombies. For sure the cement had time to set?"

"Guaranteed. Those suckers weigh a shit ton."

Two demons lugged Danny's casket to the edge of the dam. Inside, the big man rested in a bed of concrete, handcuffs, and sigils. His blessed gun and necklace accompanied him. The casket itself was marble and welded closed, wrapped in chains. The ass ends of the hearses had sparked against the asphalt as they drove up the steeper hills to get here.

"Why here?" Lindle asked.

"They won't be disturbed here. And I have a friend in these woods I've asked to make sure of that. He'll guard them."

Lindle and the others didn't get it, she knew. But they made assumptions that she knew more than they did and that she was protecting them. She heard their whispers—about the exorcism and how these hunters were deadly, how they could never risk rumbling with them again. As far as they were concerned, the hunters had taken down the Order with that exorcism and she'd taken down the hunters.

Others questioned why the televangelist, celebrity, and CDC doctor had survived the exorcism if that had been the case, theorizing the Order had tried possessing the hunters only to get exorcised in the process—and who knows whose side Nix was on in that scenario. Nix wasn't about to enlighten them otherwise. At the end of the day, they didn't seem to care who killed whom; they liked the new management and the freedom it conveyed.

The televangelist, celebrity, and CDC doctor recovered from their possession encounter and Nix arranged their release back into the wild to avoid drawing unnecessary attention to their operations. They left all three in a disreputable drug den with some psychedelics in their systems and sent the reporters in. Problem solved.

Through none of the clean-up process did any of Nix's new devoted brethren consider the possibility that their Order could be trapped in the bones of the three dead hunters. Max, ever the loyalist, had still been waiting by the sewer exit when Nix finally got down there. She'd sent him on his way with the hunters' things, and he'd agreed to keep watch over the bones of his fallen friends in this forest now that the world was no longer in need of saving. Glancing into the thick trees now, she saw animal eyes watching them from afar.

She'd returned Maria's borrowed necklace to her, stayed for tea, and pet some cats. With the coven and the Order now gone, she seemed to be on the mend, and so was her grandson. His attitude had improved considerably.

"You want us to push it over the side, ma'am?" a demon lackey asked from the edge of the dam.

Nix walked over to them and stared into the water below. Dark, deep, and writhing. Further down, the water was peaceful and still. Nix still held Elliot's memory of fishing here with Rachel and Danny. She smiled, placing her hand atop the casket.

"Yes. Let them go."

Danny's casket fell over the side, plummeting for ages before hitting the water with an incredible splash. The sound echoed through the dam. Sleeping birds startled awake and fluttered free of the treetops.

The next two caskets followed, lined up at the edge. Elliot, no longer insatiable and hungry. Rachel, no longer searching for her place. One at a time, they tumbled over the side and Nix said goodbye to her hunters.

Her lackeys rolled out the final coffin, this one lighter, but she felt heavier to see it go. Cirrik's last host was nestled inside. Although Cirrik was gone and this husk of a host body wasn't a real replacement, she'd still said she'd come back for him. She kept her word now. He hadn't let her down in the end, and she intended to return the favor in some small way. She touched her fingertips to her lips then pressed them against the cold marble surface and watched him go over the edge.

She'd fulfilled her promises to them. But more than that, she had finally done right by Antheia, her sister, after all these years. Though Cirrik wasn't here to see it, there was justice here for him, too, in all this loss. She'd keep making things right. Nix looked up at the stars.

"Where next, boss?" Lindle asked.

"One more stop."

***

It was 4 a.m. when they pulled up behind San Francisco County's St. Mary's Psychiatric Facility for Youth. Situated at the outskirts of the city, the modern concrete building resembled a prison. Nix signaled the others. "You know what to do."

Lindle and Mars flanked her. Trus, Jin and three others spread out onto the grounds.

"I got security footage," Mars said. Her host crumpled in place on the green grass as she vacated.

"I'll get the door," Lindle said, following suit.

Nix grinned, bouncing on her tiptoes before walking up to the font doors. She skipped up the concrete steps. As her hand touched the barred entrance, the door pushed open from the other side.

"*Entrez, madam,*" a small, portly woman in a security uniform said in a French accent. Lindle winked from behind blue eyes.

Nix stepped inside the dimly lit vestibule.

"Still only the one, or have you changed your mind?" Lindle fiddled with an access card clipped to a lanyard around his host's neck, tilted his head, flipped it, then tried the thing again. It clicked, flashed green, and the next door opened for them.

"We'll take her with us," Nix said, "but hell, let's spring 'em all."

Lindle laughed. "That's what I thought. Pour a little chaos on the fire."

The security cameras lining the hall above them flashed from green to red. A door opened a moment later and Mars stepped out, wearing another security guard.

"Whole grid is out. Took down a couple nurses and orderlies while I was in there. Haloperidol. Should stay quiet."

"Shall we open some doors?" Lindle said.

Nix nodded and set them loose. They howled, running down the halls, drawing out the occasional night-shift orderly and knocking them out. Doors popped open and heads started poking out. Several teens made a run for the exit, pushing through the now wide-open doors. Nix read the names printed next to the rooms as she made her way to the children's ward.

Finally, she found what she was looking for. *Callie St. Germaine.*

A patient chart sat in a locked plastic box next to the door. She cracked it open, glancing through in the dark and missing Elliot's night vision. The words *Dissociative Identity Disorder* stood out. They thought she was crazy. Or, worse, Callie thought she was crazy. No, Nix couldn't leave her in this place. She didn't belong here in a gray jumpsuit like the kids running through the halls. She belonged in pink princess dresses.

Nix opened Callie's door.

In the darkness, sitting at the edge of her bed, Callie sat as if waiting for her.

"Nix!" Instant recognition. A wide grin spread over the girl's face and onto Nix's own.

Callie jumped up and ran to the doorway, blonde braids bouncing. She wrapped her arms around Nix's waist. Nix hugged her back. Alone in her mind, she could have sworn she heard her sister's giggling laughter.

Nix's new heart, her own heart, swelled as she held the girl tightly.

Callie looked up at her and smiled softly. "I knew you'd find me."

The End

About the Author

J.J. lives in Alberta, Canada with two affectionate hellhounds and bookcases full of nightmares.

To give feedback to the author, please leave a review on **Amazon** or **GoodReads**. To keep up with future releases from J.J. Reichenbach, follow the author on any of the following social media platforms:

Twitter @jjreichenbach
www.facebook.com/jjreichenbachNIX
www.jjreichenbach.weebly.com
Instagram @j.j.reichenbachNIX

Acknowledgments

Anyone who has written a book will tell you, it's a lot of work. And a series? I had no idea what I was getting myself into. But like any great adventure, it's probably better that I went into it without reservations. Writing can be a very solitary endeavor, but nothing happens in a vacuum. Having a tremendous support system of fellow writers and avid readers is what made it possible to pull through with this project. To that end, I'd like to extend my heartfelt and eternal thanks to the following individuals who helped this final book of the Nix Trilogy make it into the world.

My thoughtful and brilliant beta readers (and treasured friends): Rebecca Piazza, Vicky Reed, and Julie Hiner. Thank you for the time, the support, and the boundless enthusiasm.

To my Aunt Patricia and Uncle Rick Richardson. Two of my biggest fans and supporters. Uncle Rick, I wish you could have read this one. I know you waited a long time for it, cheering me on the whole way. This one's for you.

Haisel, Gustavo, Santiago, and Fabiola. I wrote most of this in a beautiful house in Costa Rica, rented through AirBnB. I never anticipated getting stranded there for ten months during a pandemic, but I can honestly say it was one of the best experiences of my life thanks to the incredible people I met during my stay. Thank you for your unparalleled hospitality, care, and friendship.

My family, my friends. Thank you all, for your love and support.

The Calgary Crime Writers—who embrace me and my horror writing. You've made me a better writer and I cherish the friendships I've made with each of you.

When Words Collide – WWC, Chapters/Indigo, Sarah Johnson (Owl's Nest Books), and Jim Jackson (Prairie Soul Press), thank you all for supporting indie authors and creating spaces for us to thrive together.

So many wonderful people—too many to name, but each so important.

And to all my readers and supporters. You stood by me through this series, embracing and celebrating some pretty disturbed characters with the enthusiasm one could only expect to see from fellow horror fans. I've been humbled by the positive response to these books. I'm honored to have a place on your shelves. Thank you!

More from This Author

Nix Trilogy
Book One: *Nix*

Nix has one goal: escape. Hunted by the demonic hierarchy for a murderous joyride that she *may* have committed but definitely wasn't responsible for, Nix has been jumping from one unwilling host to the next in order to stay hidden—and it was working, for a while. But Nix soon finds that there are other hunters closing in.

Desperate, she borrows the body of a young paranormal hunter named Rachel. All Nix needs to do is lead the hunters away, and then disappear. Hiding among the hunters seems brilliant at first, but of course nothing's ever that easy.

Trapped inside the uncooperative hunter, Nix is damned if she leaves and damned if she stays. Even worse, Nix discovers that her idiot hunters are involved in a nasty plot to destroy the world—and sure, Nix loves chaos and destruction as much as the next demon, but she still has to live in that world. Nix has objections to that sort of nonsense.

Nix isn't the hero the world deserves, but she's the hero it's damn well going to get.

Find it on Amazon, Kobo, iBooks, and Barnes & Noble

Nix Trilogy
Book Two: *Notorious Nix*

A pleasant night at the carnival takes a weird turn when a few of Nix's old foes crash the party to ask for her help. For hunters, "asking for help" and "kidnapping, with a side of extortion" are synonymous. Nix has been around a long time. She's seen a lot of stupid people do a lot of stupid things, but never like this. And now she's stuck with the fools.

Hunted by their own, stalked by vengeful demons, and generally bursting apart at the seams, these hunters already have a foot in the grave. Nix can't imagine why they willingly summoned her back into their lives. Their reasons end up being much darker than she could have anticipated—and there's nothing Nix loves more than darkness.

Find it on Amazon, Kobo, iBooks, and Barnes & Noble

***

If you've enjoyed this author's work, please take a moment to leave a review and recommend it to your friends.